CHARMING AS PUCK

PIPPA GRANT

ONE

Nick Murphy (aka a hockey god on the verge of being demoted back to mortal status)

KAMI STAYED OVER. That's weird. I must've drunk too much last night. Or she did.

Actually, is she still drunk?

She doesn't usually lick my ear. Or sleep in my bed. We don't do breakfast together unless it's some god-awful early morning meeting demanded by my sister, in which case we pretend we're just the same old friends who don't bump uglies, because Felicity would fucking kill me.

However, risk of death aside, if Kami's up for something this morning, I could get on board.

My dick's already showing off.

My eyes are gritty. I definitely had too much to drink last night. I barely remember Kami showing up at all after the game. It was our season opener, at home, our first regular season game after winning the cup last year, and it was fucking brutal.

We won. Of course. But it was still brutal.

"Lower," I tell Kami, my voice ragged in my throat, angling my head, because being licked is nice, but if she's going to lick me, she could go for somewhere better than my ear.

"*Mmmooooooooo*," she answers.

She licks my ear again, reaching the tip of her tongue right into my ear canal, and I lift a heavy arm to guide her face.

And then I freeze.

She's...furry.

Like a smooth kind of furry, but still furry.

And I'm king of morning breath, but she smells worse than my sister after one of those vegan wheatgrass garlic avocado smoothies she likes to drink.

"Kami?" I rasp out.

"*Mmmoooooooo.*"

I touch her lips, which are wet and sticky and thick.

My eyes fly open.

Kami has brown eyes.

The eyes staring back at me are brown.

Except these brown eyes are huge.

And set behind a thick fuzzy brown snout, beneath a rigid brow line, with ears sticking up where I expected to see morning bed head.

"*Fuck!*"

I trip over the tangled sheets while I leap up, my head swimming. The cow watches me with those calm brown orbs. "*Mmmmooooooooo,*" it says again in its baby cow voice.

Shit shit *shit*. "*Ssshhhh,*" I hiss at it.

I can't decide what to think first. My head's pounding. I'm going to fucking kill my brother-in-law, who is absolutely behind this, unless Kami's a shapeshifting cow, which isn't possible, even when I'm hung over.

Also, after the duck incident, if I get caught with another unapproved animal in my condo, I'll get kicked out of the building.

I don't have time to move. The season's just starting. My parents would move me, but I'm thirty-one fucking years old. *My parents aren't going to move me.*

Especially since if they did, they'd probably move me into their house, and that's not happening.

I might be playing in my home city, but I will *not* move in with my parents.

I fumble in the dim light, looking for my phone. "Don't shit in my bed," I tell the cow. "I'll get you out of here, just please don't shit in my bed."

My phone's not where it belongs. It's not by my bed. It's not on my dresser. It's not in the bathroom.

My pants.

Maybe it's still in my pants.

Where are my—*fuck*.

My pants are under the cow. Which is still lying on my bed.

It moos at me again. I fist my hair and stare at it. "Get up," I tell it.

It stares back.

It also doesn't move.

Or *moooooooo*ve, I can hear my teammates saying.

This would be hilarious if it was anyone else's apartment.

I grab one pant leg and pull. The cow sniffs at my dangling dick. I shift out of the way, because I'm *not* into getting my family jewels licked by a freaking baby farm animal.

I'd wonder where the fuck Ares found a baby cow, except I, too, know a thing or two about delivering unexpected livestock to apartment buildings.

And the fucker just one-upped me.

For a quiet dude, he's fucking *evil*. He better never put a baby cow in Felicity's bed or he'll wake up strapped to the underside of an elephant halfway around the world.

I tug and pull on my pants, the cow gives an indignant baby *moo*, and *finally*, my jeans come free.

Without the phone in the pocket.

I press my palms into my eye sockets and think.

There was the game.

Vegas scored on me twice. We still won, because Ares and Frey and Lavoie were on fire, but I shouldn't have let Vegas score. Not that second one anyway. The first—nobody could've stopped that biscuit. But the second was an easy shot to block, and I flubbed it.

I skipped Chester Green's with the team afterward. Haven't been in a mood to hang with the bunnies at the bar since charm school last season. Opened a bottle of Jack at home instead. Texted Kami because I shouldn't drink alone.

She showed up with that wide, borderline innocent smile. I was buzzed. She teased me about it. Said she wouldn't take advantage of me in my compromised state.

Turned on *The Mighty Ducks*.

I fucking love that movie.

I talked her out of her pants before the Ducks won their first game, and—and that's where my phone is.

Next to the bottle of Jack I finished in the living room after Kami left.

The baby cow stares at me, those eyes bright and friendly and asking for love.

I trip into my jeans and head for the living room. The sun's telling me I need to get my ass in gear and over to the rink for morning skate before long. I snag my phone off the end table by my leather sofa, and I don't think twice as I dial a video call.

Kami's soft brown eyes come into focus, along with that wide smile. Way smaller than the cow's eyes. Sweeter too. She's always sweet. "Morning, sunshine. You feeling okay today?"

"How do I get a cow out of my bed?"

She wrinkles her brows at me. She's walking somewhere—the buildings behind her make me think she's heading to her clinic—and her brown hair's tied back in a ponytail that's whipping in the wind. "A cow out of your bed?" she repeats.

I flip the camera on my phone so she can see forward and march into my bedroom, watching the screen while I center my bed and the cow for her. "Yeah. A fucking baby cow in my fucking bed."

She nods thoughtfully. "Huh. That does appear to be a calf. Happy birthday to you too."

"It's not my fucking birthday. It's a fucking prank. Can you take care of it?"

Her expression goes still. "Can I...what?"

"Get it out of my condo. It's an animal. You're an animal doctor."

Silence.

Even her expression is silent, which is odd, because Kami's expressions are always big and loud and...and *expressive*. Not because she's loud. She just *likes* things.

She's an optimist.

Yeah.

She's an optimist. Cheery. She makes loud, happy faces.

Fuck, I need to quit drinking.

"I said, *happy birthday to you too*," she says.

I squint at the phone. Since when does Kami talk in code? In the months we've been banging behind my sister's back, the only code we've ever used is *I'm calling it an early night*.

Plus, this is hardly the first time she's gotten a call to take care of an animal at my place. Hell, half the team has her on speed dial.

Which might be my fault.

"I get it," I say. "I deserve this after the donkey thing, but I have to get to morning skate, and we're hopping a plane to New York after the game tonight, and I don't want to come home to a dead baby cow. I'll pay whatever it takes. But it—"

"Fine. Whatever. I'll take care of it."

I freeze.

I know that tone.

That's *pissed off woman* tone. And yeah, it's probably rude of me to call her first thing in the morning like this, but we're friends. I'd help her get a cow out of her place if I had time, but during the season, it's hockey first. Always.

"Thanks, Kami. I owe you one."

"No, Nick. You owe me *nothing*. In fact, you can consider this a goodbye present. Because this little arrangement we have? It's over. I'm *done*."

She disconnects, and I'm left staring at my official Copper Valley Thrusters photo on the background of my phone.

I don't know what just happened, but I have a feeling it's worse than waking up with a baby cow.

TWO

Kami Oakley, aka a birthday girl on the edge

ANGER and I aren't friends. I hate anger. It's ugly and it's vicious and it makes me do awful things.

Things like stalking into Nick Murphy's apartment with specially formulated calf grains and hay when I'm supposed to be giving Mrs. Okeson's new kittens their first exam and checking on Mr. Wilder's elderly boxer-lab with the failing kidneys.

I know, I know. Anger wouldn't inspire most people to haul calf grains.

But anger has inspired the stalking. With extra-heavy pounding of my feet against the fancy carpet. And some flaring of my nostrils. And that thick wad of crumpled, frozen dreams clogging my chest.

I like to think I usually stride happily. With a bounce. And a smile.

Today, it's all foot-slaps and scowls and *what the hell have I been thinking*?

And as I shove my key into his lock, I'm listening to my phone ring a number that anger has *also* inspired me to call.

Because I'm *done*.

Just *so* damn *done*.

"Muff Matchers, how can we match your muff today?" my cousin says cheerfully while I push into Nick's condo.

"Muffy, it's Kami. I need you to find me a husband."

There's silence, both on the phone and in the apartment, where a brown calf is blending in with the leather sofa across from the hockey-man-size television hanging on the wall over the gas fireplace.

And she is utterly, perfectly *adorable*.

"Kami as in Kami Oakley? My cousin Kami? The Kami who already told everyone to save the date for her wedding to Nick Murphy this Christmas?" Muffy asks.

"Quit holding last year's drunken Thanksgiving ramblings against me. And yes. That Kami."

"Wow," she says at the same time the calf moos at me.

Despite probably not being more than three or four months old, the calf is already working those big cow eyes to her advantage, using them to ask for someone to love her. As if I couldn't with those twitching brown cow ears that she hasn't grown into yet and her soft muzzle and that cute little baby *moo* on top of everything.

Fresh anger surges through. She should be on a farm. With her mommy.

And she probably would be if Nick hadn't started the farm-animals-in-the-apartment game when Felicity fell in love with one of his teammates a year ago.

"Don't you worry, Sugarbear," I tell her. "I'm going to find you the *best* new home *ever*. After I figure out where you came from. And you are *not* going to be ground beef. But until I can find a place, you need to stay here for a few more hours. I recommend pooping on the bed if you need to do it again."

I wince, because I've spent a lot of time in that bed with Nick driving into me until I shattered like spun glass on marble.

Though last night it was on the couch.

Where the cow is now.

I blink back the angry tears stinging my eyes.

Nick Murphy might be an ass, but he knows how to use his equipment.

And I was an idiot to think he could've ever seen me as something more than an easy lay.

But not anymore.

"Ground beef?" Muffy says, and I realize she'd actually gone silent. "Pooping on the bed? What—who's Sugarbear?"

"The calf that I agreed to get out of Nick's condo this morning."

"Oh. This is all starting to make sense. I can give you the friend and family discount, but I have to add the over-thirty surcharge."

"The *what*?"

"Sad fact of being a woman. You'll be harder to match now that you're the big three-oh."

Of course *she* remembers my birthday. "Fine. But I want a rush job. And don't cheat me, or I'll charge you the old-cat surcharge the next time you bring Rufus in for his shots."

"He's three!"

"That's like seventy-six in cat years." Okay, it's not. But I'm mad. At everything. Except the cow.

"Ooooh, I get it." I can *hear* Muffy nodding. She inherited the loud nodding gene from Aunt Hilda. "He forgot your birthday, didn't he?"

"Can you do the rush job or not?"

"I'm gonna match your muff so hard and fast, you won't know what hit it."

"Oh, gee, add a muff punch while you're at it. That'll go great with the knife twisting my heart," I mutter.

"Okay. Let's do this. New file, Kami Oakley…"

While keyboard keys click on the other end of the phone and Muffy breathes in my ear, I give the calf a quick once over. I don't work with large animals, even if I'd love to live in the country and have a small farm of my own, but she seems reasonably healthy. Especially with that mess she left on Nick's rug. Both messes, actually. Kidneys, intestines, and colon are all apparently in perfect working order. And she's clearly interested in the grains, so that's good.

I was worried she wouldn't be weaned yet.

"You're such a good girl," I tell her.

"I know," Muffy says.

The cow moos at me and nuzzles my hip.

I glance around the living room. Since I'm here, I should clean out anything I might've accidentally left here, but with our arrangement, I don't even have a toothbrush.

Still, after I set out food and fill Nick's biggest pot with water in the kitchen, I wander through the empty apartment, Sugarbear on my heels while Muffy talks to herself about all of my basic details.

Yes, I've named the cow. And she is definitely a Sugarbear.

I actually name all the animals I get called in to re-home when the Thrusters are done with them.

And there's another surge of fury.

Animals are *not* pranks.

But the only thing yelling at hockey players will do is encourage them to turn the pranks to me.

Unless…

Ideas are taking shape.

Ideas that rational, kind-hearted, animal-loving, *sweet* Kami—if I had a nickel for every time someone called me *sweet*, I'd be richer than all the Thrusters players combined—would never entertain.

But ideas that just might be necessary.

When in war, do what the most hardened warriors do.

"Okay, got the basics," Muffy announces. "Just a few questions."

"Just a few? Don't you have an entire questionnaire or something?"

"I do, but I know you well enough. I can do it for you. Now. Men or women?"

"You don't know me well enough to answer that question for me?"

"Sometimes family hides things. *Both* is also an acceptable answer."

I give half a thought to if I have any interest in women, and I decide I'm lacking that gene, which is probably too bad. "Men, please. But no hockey players. Or baseball players. Or football players. Or—"

"No sportsers. Got it. How many kids do you want? Keep in mind zero is a valid answer."

"Three," I reply without hesitation as I walk into Nick's bedroom with the cow on my heels.

The dark blue sheets on his king-size bed are disheveled and twisted and the thick navy comforter is tossed to the ground. I take my time straightening the covers and making the bed while I answer Muffy's questions about my favorite color, which planet I'd be from if I weren't an earthling, and how many times a week I masturbate.

And while I write Nick a note.

Dear Nick,

Bite me.

Kami

I have no idea what he'll think I did to his bed, if anything, but as a friend once said, sometimes making them *think* you did something terrible is just as effective as actually *doing* something terrible. And making his bed neatly—which he'll notice, since he never makes it himself—is a pretty good sign that I've been in his bedroom.

I smirk.

And then I leave a tube of my lipstick next to Nick's toothbrush in the bathroom.

When I realize he might think it's from a bunny he banged—no, I *don't* want to talk about not demanding that we be exclusive in our arrangement, and about never asking him if he was hooking up with anyone else on the side—I get mad all over again, so I also pull the toilet paper off the roll and hide it under the counter, knowing he won't notice until he needs it.

"Kami?" Muffy says.

"What? Oh. Um—wait. Did you just ask me what brand of dildo I prefer?"

"First, yes. Second, nice to see you're paying attention. That last answer had me worried."

"What answer?" What did she ask? Oh, crapola. What did I say?

"Would you consider moving for love?"

That wasn't the question, but I'm not sure I care. "Yes."

"Yes?"

"Yes. I always wanted to live on a farm. With goats and chickens *and cows*, but instead, all I do is get emergency phone calls from hockey players who need all my dream animals vacated out of their living spaces. You know what? Bonus points if you can find me a guy who doesn't know anything *at all* about sports and owns a baby giraffe."

It's possible I shouldn't make dating decisions while I'm mad.

But it's also completely undeniable that being mad is the only thing that could lead to me signing up for a dating service at all.

Especially Muffy's dating service.

"Age preference?" Muffy asks.

"Legal?"

She snorts. "Oh, you're in a mood. This is fun. I highly recommend being in a mood more often. It's good for cleansing your aura."

"My aura? What do you know about auras?"

"Nothing, really, but I was reading the article that came in my toy of the month subscription box…"

I tune her out, both because I already read that article and didn't quite get it, and because Sugarbear's nuzzling my arm. "Mooo?"

"He's an ass, Sugarbear." The words are sour and foreign, because I've always thought Nick Murphy was more than the world gave him credit for, but he called me first thing in the morning, *on my birthday*, to cuss about a cow and *completely* ignored my hints about what today is.

I can't deny it any longer.

He's a self-centered ass. He's always been an ass, and he'll always be an ass.

Just not *my* ass.

Sugarbear's sweet eyes watch me while I look around at the marble sink and the porcelain and glass tile lining the built-in shower with the rain spout and the wall nozzles.

Nick Murphy might be an ass, but he's an ass who knows how to give good shower sex.

I shiver.

"Are you done talking to the cow?" Muffy asks.

"Probably not. Do you have stats on penis size? I want a big penis."

"Wow, you're *really* pissed. Note to self: don't write off the men with weird fetishes. Okay, last question. If you were going to get caught doing something illegal, would it be smoking pot, stealing underwear, or grand theft auto?"

"That is *not* a real question."

"Maybe it is. Maybe I'm not just looking for a new partner in crime on a Saturday night. But you still have to answer if you want me to match your muff."

"You seriously need a new tagline."

"This one makes me money, baby."

I was pretty sure that was a lie, but I let her have it. "Stealing underwear."

"Great, and now I've got everything I need," she says. "I'm gonna run you through the muff matcher and I'll have you a date for Friday before you can say *my vibrator ran out of batteries*."

This is where I'm probably supposed to say thank you.

"You're right to move on, Kami," she adds quietly. "You deserve to be more than somebody's secret piece on the side. And you deserve a guy who'll remember—"

The line goes dead. I pull my phone back, a lump ballooning in my throat, and now I'm growling at the brick in my hand.

I freaking charged it last night, but the battery couldn't even get me to the office. I have *got* to get a new phone.

And I also realize I probably shouldn't have asked for a guy with a big penis before my battery gave way.

But that shower—and the way he liked to shove me against the wall and fill me and—

"Sex isn't everything," I tell Sugarbear, more because I need to hear it and I need to *not* give myself a reason to offer Nick another chance. "He never *once* ordered pizza with mushrooms only on half. Every single time, I had to pick them off."

And every single time, I told myself it didn't matter. Or that he liked sharing food with me, and he knew I'd pick them off, so he could eat my leftovers. Or that I only ate a quarter of the pizza anyway, so why bother with leaving mushrooms off an entire half?

Except I also know Felicity brings her own pizza to his place because he never thinks to get a veggie pizza with vegan cheese even though she's been vegan for *years*.

And it's not that we expect him to take care of us. It's that all the rest of us remember that he can't stand green peppers and that mangos make him break out in a rash.

"It's the little things that count, Sugarbear. Don't ever settle for a bull who doesn't pay attention to which patch of grass is your favorite. Because you deserve to be taken care of too."

She nods.

Probably because she likes me scratching her head like this, but I tell myself she's listening carefully and taking notes about dating.

I pull my phone back out of my pocket to text Muffy that my date can't like mushrooms, but I can't, because my phone is dead.

"*Argh!*" I scream.

And then I want to apologize to the neighbors for making noise, because that's me.

Sweet, compassionate, optimistic, *everyone loves her* Kami.

I'm so tired of being *sweet*.

And of putting everyone else's feelings first.

I leave Nick's closet alone, mostly because he's already done a good enough job of making sure he can't find anything in it, and rearrange the pictures on his wall so that the photo of himself laughing and pointing that's usually hanging over the toilet in his powder room is hanging over his bed instead, and the shadow box his parents made him with his championship ring from last season is hanging in the powder room where the pointing picture went.

His prized possession is now hanging in the shitter.

In the kitchen, I take back the massive pizza cutter I got him when I realized his was broken, and I put all of his microwave popcorn bags in the refrigerator.

He'll think he moved it while he was drunk and cut back on his drinking for a few weeks.

Especially since I also move a half-used stick of butter to where the microwave popcorn is supposed to live in his cabinet.

It's not that he'd be lost without me.

It's that he never wanted me as much as I wanted him, and he never even noticed half the things I did for him.

I sag against the counter. "It's not his fault, Sugarbear," I tell the cow. "He doesn't know anything other than being the center of the universe, and he's never even had to work hard for most of it because he's hot and naturally talented. But he can't be the center of *my* universe anymore. I need to matter too."

She nuzzles her face against my belly. I rub her soft ears. "But this is going to be the best thing to ever happen to *you*. I promise."

I bend and kiss her on the head, and though I don't want to leave her, I have to go.

I need to get out of Nick's space.

And I need to find somewhere to take her, and a vehicle I can transport her in.

And then I need to make sure he and his teammates never abuse a poor animal again in their quest to annoy each other in the name of camaraderie.

And once I've solved all *that*, maybe I can salvage what's left of my birthday.

Preferably with a new potential man of my dreams.

THREE

Nick

IT'S NOT USUALLY a wise idea to pick a fight with a guy who could crush you with his pinky, but Ares Berger is not only my teammate, he's also my brother-in-law.

Also, no one's ever accused me of being wise.

Plus, it's *his* fault Kami's pissed at me for the cow thing. I don't like when my friends are pissed at me.

And Kami doesn't get pissed at anyone. Not at the guy who spilled beer on her last week at Chester Green's. Not at whoever left that ding in the side of her car door. Not at her dogs when they poop in her house.

It happens, she always says with that bright smile. Sometimes a resigned bright smile, but always a smile.

But she's mad at *me*.

It's sitting wrong in my gut.

And in my nuts.

"Morning, jackass." I shoulder into Ares and push past him on my way into the dressing room to get ready for practice.

"Hey. Quit calling my brother names."

Zeus Berger, Ares's identical twin, is already inside, strapping on his skates in front of his locker. He's the new guy on the team this year, and despite making no secret of his intentions to retire—for real this time—at the end of the season, he's been working his ass off on the ice to prove himself. The two Berger twins together—known as the Brute and the Force—are seven hundred pounds and almost fourteen feet of pure hockey talent.

Ares gives me a shoulder brush back, and I almost lose my balance.

Zeus smirks.

Ares stays straight-faced while he heads to his locker and inspects his skate laces.

Duncan Lavoie shakes his head at me when I stop at my locker and start pulling out my gear. "You still haven't learned not to pick a fight with one of them unless you have six of us behind you yet?"

"He's hardly the intelligent Murphy sibling," Manning Frey points out in his fancy accent. Dude's a real fucking prince of a small country across the Atlantic, but he's so far down the royal line to inherit that he left home to play pro hockey here instead of taking some ceremonial job in the kingdom.

"He knocked my sister up," I tell Zeus. "I'll call the fucker whatever I want to."

I don't mention the cow to any of them, because it's part of the game. The next part of the game involves me getting Ares back, and I'm already plotting sweet, sweet revenge.

Probably something with a snake. Or maybe a litter of bunnies.

But it has to be somewhere that Felicity won't have to deal with it.

"Ares outranks you in the family hierarchy now," Zeus argues. "I'm fucking proud of him. Always wanted to be an uncle."

"You're already an uncle," Frey observes, since his baby daughter is technically Zeus's niece too because their wives are sisters.

"Only by marriage, and not on the Berger side of the family, dude. *This* baby's gonna be fucking *awesome*. It's already practically half me."

"Felicity still puking every day?" Lavoie asks Ares.

He shakes his head and strips off his shirt, grabbing his pads.

"Saw her last night. She's eating like a cow now," Zeus offers with a sly grin.

Mother*fucker*.

The cow's *his* fault.

Of course it is. Ares is too busy keeping Felicity happy when he's not on the ice to put much effort into pranks.

But Zeus—his wife owns her own flight adventure company in Alabama, and she didn't move here with him. *He* has time on his hands when he's not having phone sex or playing hockey. And what you do to one Berger twin, you do to both.

Should've seen that coming.

"Get dressed," Ares orders.

Dude doesn't say a lot, so when he does, we all listen.

I yank on my practice gear, lace up my skates, and send Kami a quick text before I head to the rink.

Thanks for your help. What's the name of that animal shelter you like again? Got ten grand sitting in my bank account with their name on it.

I wait, but she doesn't reply. The text doesn't change from *delivered* to *read* either.

She's probably doing some vet shit.

Or pulling a cow out of my place.

"You still pissed about the game last night?" Lavoie asks as we step onto the ice and start warm-up laps. Last year's championship banner hangs from the scoreboard over the ice, a reminder of what we have to live up to this year.

Of what *I* have to live up to this year. As goaltender, it's ultimately my responsibility to not let anyone score on us. The better I do my job, the easier the rest of the team has it.

And last night didn't give me a lot of confidence that I'll be able to take on the tougher teams in the league.

Indianapolis—last year's expansion team—nearly wiped us out in the first round of the playoffs last season.

Those two biscuits that got by me last night?

It would've been six if we'd been playing the Indies. I have a month to get back in my groove before we face them for the first time this year. The playoffs might be a long way away, but every game counts.

Especially the hard ones.

"Murphy?" Lavoie says.

"What? Oh. Yeah. The game fucking sucked. Thanks for those extra goals."

He looks at me like he knows I'm just blowing smoke. The guy's been with the Thrusters most of his career. Playing team captain this year, and he's not an idiot.

"What's her name?" he asks.

Kami's easy smile flashes in my brain. Then the feel of her pussy squeezing my dick while she comes.

The way her cheeks flush when she shouts my name.

I ignore him, because it's not like Kami and I are in a relationship.

We're friends. Friends who like to fuck. And I'm not gonna whine to Lavoie that Kami's mad at me about the cow, because I'm not acknowledging the cow.

The Berger twins are racing Frey, all three of them grinning like kids who just learned to skate.

Lavoie follows my gaze, and he shakes his head. "What it's supposed to look like," he mutters.

I don't know if he's talking about hockey or relationships, but I know the three of them all have something I don't.

Until two hours ago, I would've called them all suckers. Tied down with one woman. Domesticated.

But until two hours ago—*we're done, Nick*—can't say I'd been any different the last six or eight months.

Shit.

When *was* that night Kami and I hooked up? January? Or was it March? Was it really this year? I don't remember a lot about that night, but it seems like there was something about a cattle prod and my dick.

What the *fuck* is up with the cow thing?

Coach blows the whistle, and we all line up for drills.

After practice, showers, and lunch with the team, I head back to my condo for a pre-game nap.

I swear I smell Kami's shampoo in the elevator. She still hasn't read my text. Probably has her hands full with the cow. Wonder if she had to rent a truck or something. Probably should've offered to pay for that, but she knows I'm good for it.

The hallway smells like shit, and the smell gets stronger when I open my door. I don't know how she works with animals all day, getting blood and shit and piss all over her, but it apparently doesn't bother her.

Or maybe it does.

Because if it did bother her, wouldn't she have picked up the pile of shit on my living room rug?

And is that—oh, *fuck*.

That's cow piss all over my rug too.

My rug that used to be my grandmother's rug.

I shoot a look at the ceiling and inwardly cringe, because I'm in total agreement with my sister. My grandmother could carry a grudge for eternity, and being in the afterlife won't stop her. "Sorry, Gammy," I mutter.

"*Mooooo!*" she answers from my bedroom.

Except that's not my grandmother's ghost.

That's the fucking *cow*.

I dart to my bedroom and bolt through the door.

The cow's standing on my bed.

She looks at me, grins, and switches her tail up.

And while I stand there watching, she drops a load.

Right there.

In the middle of my very nicely-made bed.

With a picture of me pointing at it and snickering hanging on the wall over my headboard where my championship ring goes, and with a note on the floor in Kami's handwriting.

Kami's *angry* handwriting.

Can handwriting be angry? Because that handwriting looks pissed as fuck.

The message sure as hell is.

In that moment, three things become crystal clear.

One, Zeus Berger is dead.

Two, Kami did *not* take care of the cow.

And three, she was serious when she said we were done.

I had a shit game last night.

I woke up with a cow this morning.

And it's nothing compared to that hollow feeling sucking in my chest at knowing that I fucked up a good thing.

I thought Kami and I had something simple and easy and good.

Apparently, I was wrong.

So. Fucking. Wrong.

FOUR

Kami

I SHOULD'VE KNOWN something was up when Alina arrived at my house to drive me downtown for drinks with my best friends before the Thrusters' home game tonight. But I took her *It's your birthday, so you get a sober driver* to heart, and now, after pretending everything's fine the whole way into the heart of the city, I'm wishing I hadn't.

Because now, Felicity's hustling Alina, Maren, and me—all of us die-hard hockey fans—through the staff entrance at Mink Arena after Alina drove us here to game central instead of to the bar.

"I just forgot something in the office," Felicity lies, and it's clearly a lie, because she has that little lip quiver going on. It's a Murphy thing. "We'll head out for drinks after I grab it. Come on up."

She works for the Thrusters in their headquarters. She's one of those certified geniuses who can do anything and has something like eighteen degrees ranging from bowling management to marketing to physical therapy assistance.

Plus, she's a ventriloquist.

There's literally nothing she can't do. Except paint. She's a terrible painter.

She also can't magically make her brother not be an ass.

So there's two things Felicity can't do.

Oh, she also can't read my mind to know that I'm utterly terrified we're going to run into her brother and so far past suspicious right now that my knees are turning to concrete.

"Are you sure it's okay for us to be here?" I whisper, because I can't find a better excuse to get out of *whatever* is waiting for me inside the arena.

"Um, yes."

"I stop by here all the time," Alina assures me equally suspiciously, because I might've gotten a little squirrely when we pulled into the parking garage where she magically produced a staff parking pass. "It's totally legit. They just don't want us to touch the Cup."

"I don't want to touch it. I want to lick it," Maren announces while we step onto the elevator. She's decked out in jeans and a maroon Thrusters jersey with Zeus Berger's number on the back, because she says it'll be a collector's item one day with this being his real final season.

Alina's in a black sweater and full make-up, which means she probably spent all day working on her next YouTube video. She's a rock cellist with a huge following, and she's also halfway through a twenty-city tour, which means we only see her a few times a month when she's home.

And Felicity's in a custom Thrusters T-shirt with the rocket bratwurst logo—yes, rocket bratwurst, and yes, there's a story there —and the phrase "I'm carrying Ares Berger's Baby" printed across her chest and arrows pointing to her small but growing baby bump.

It's been remarkably effective in discouraging the number of men who hit on her when we're out in public.

I stifle a sigh. Felicity's not only smart, she's also gorgeous with her red hair and green eyes and gets hit on all the time even with the massive rock Ares put on her finger. *And* she's having a baby with the man she loves. Maren's an environmental engineer and one of the biggest Thrusters bloggers online. Alina's job is so cool, and she's famous in her own right.

And then there's me.

The third-generation veterinarian who sometimes cross-stitches profanity-laced wall hangings when my siblings—also quite brilliant —annoy me.

No wonder Nick only wants the benefits. I'm really fucking boring.

"How's thirty?" Felicity asks while the elevator rises.

"She's only been thirty for a few hours," Alina points out.

"But hopefully a few *really amazing* hours," Felicity replies.

"Thirty's happening," I tell them, and I'm so far off the happy boat that I just belly-flopped into Cynicism Pond.

All three of my friends instantly go on high alert and crowd closer. Maren pulls me into a hug. Alina pats my back. Felicity can't reach, so she settles for herding us out of the elevator on the sixth floor.

"Did that one difficult client bring in her biting hedgehog again?" Maren asks.

"Did your family forget?" Maren asks.

"Did someone drop a load of dick cookies on your front lawn?" Felicity asks, which would normally make all of us snicker, but not today.

"I took the day off," I tell them.

"Whoa," Alina whispers.

Felicity's brows go high enough to arm-wrestle her hairline. Instead of turning toward the guarded door marked *Thrusters Personnel Only*, she steers us toward the hallway outside the private viewing suites for the rink. "Is everything okay? Not that you shouldn't take your birthday off, you just seem...not happy about it."

"Did Ares put a baby cow in Nick's condo last night?"

"Oh," Maren murmurs.

Alina rolls her eyes. "Are you kidding?"

Only Felicity struggles to keep a straight face. "No, we went straight home after the game. But I can guess who else might've been responsible. Want me to text Ares? He'll find out where it came from."

"Farm animals belong *on farms*," I snap. "Not in the city."

Her brows lift again. Alina's eyes go wide. Maren squeezes my shoulders tighter, and I realize I feel like I'm being kidnapped. "Let's get you a drink, and then we'll come up with a plan."

"I already have a plan. Well, one half of a plan." *Thank you, anger.* "I'm working on the rest. There aren't as many no-kill cow shelters as you'd expect, and I've run out of my normal zoos and sanctuaries to call. Felicity, where are we? I *know* this isn't your office. It's—"

She swings a door open, and my entire family shouts, "*Surprise!*"

Except that's way more people than just my mom and dad in person, with my dad holding out a tablet to feature my brother and sister on a video call. That's also—

Oh, shit.

While they burst into a round of *Happy Birthday*, I realize Muffy's here. She's grinning widely under her Thrusters bandana while she sings, her twin brown braids falling low on her impressive chest. Aunt Hilda's here too. Some of the vet techs and office assistants from the clinic I run with my mom.

Felicity's parents.

Some of the Thrusters' girlfriends and wives.

Including Gracie, Manning Frey's wife, with their four-month-old baby.

Oh, such a cute baby.

I want a baby. With green eyes and brown hair and that ridiculously charming grin.

But the one person who's clearly missing is Nick.

He wasn't playing dumb because he was coming to a surprise party, no matter what that little pitter of hope in my heart wanted to believe when Felicity flung open the door.

He forgot.

Because I don't matter enough for him to remember.

My eyes water while I force a giant smile. The song ends, and my parents smother me in a hug. My brother and sister pile on the birthday greetings through the tablet, along with not-so-subtle reminders that I should treat myself to a phone of my own with a battery that will last longer than three hours. Everyone's talking at once. Birthday balloons float overhead, including several shaped like 30's, and a giant *Happy Birthday* sign is hanging over the glass that looks down on the rink where the Thruster Girls are doing their pre-game show.

"Isn't this amazing?" my mom gushes. She and dad have had season passes in a private box for years, but they've never been in the Thrusters' corporate suite. I've only been here once before, and only because Felicity needed to grab something. "What a wonderful birthday present. Did you have fun on your day off? I'm so glad you took some time for yourself today."

"It was good," I lie, and because Aunt Hilda is elbowing in, Mom doesn't question my lackluster answer.

"There's the birthday girl! I'm so proud of you, finally calling Muffy for help."

The entire box falls silent, because even the Thrusters' girlfriends and wives that I don't know very well know who Muffy is, and they probably also know that I've been nursing a ridiculous crush on Nick for *ages*.

My friends know.

My family knows, and they're all gaping at me, even my siblings on the video screen.

My coworkers know.

Muffy bumps Aunt Hilda out of the way. "I want another hug." She squeezes me tightly and adds in a whisper, "Ignore her. Are you sure this is what you want?"

"New decade, new crush," I whisper back.

"Look at her glowing," Aunt Hilda says. "That's what deciding to go after love will do for a woman."

Alina scoots closer and squeezes my hand while Muffy leaves me to muffle her mother. "Muffy?" she whispers. "Kami. Even Mister-GoodEnough.com's dating service would be seventeen steps over Muff Matchers."

She has a very valid point. "I'm trying them all, okay?" I whisper in a voice soft enough that no one else can overhear.

Also, I'm totally not trying them all. Even if she does have a valid point. I tried to make a profile for myself on Date to Mate and almost hyperventilated.

Asking Muffy to match me is basically like asking to not be matched at all.

And then I can slowly get used to the idea of dating.

For real.

"Are you trying just the ones for random hook-ups, or the ones for finding your soulmate?" Alina asks.

Before I can answer, Felicity's phone blows up with a series of texts.

I freeze, and I probably look guilty as hell, because I have a feeling I know what that's all about.

And that's another reason I shouldn't get mad.

Really mad.

I do some crazy stupid things when I get mad.

Everyone turns to stare while Felicity's phone keeps dinging.

"Maybe you should check that," Maren says.

"Or not," I mutter to myself.

Is it possible to sink through the floor?

Because I'm coming down off the angry high, and now it's possible I'm having regrets about *all* of my temper tantrum this morning after I got my phone plugged in at home.

My friends share another look, and Felicity whips out her phone.

Which is still dinging.

My birthday guests crowd around her screen.

I slink toward the bar and take a cautious glance at my own phone, which is—no surprise—already registering in the red on the battery line.

Maybe I shouldn't get a new phone. Maybe I should totally disconnect and let the world happen.

The bartender has this gorgeous, curly black hair and sweet brown eyes and a dimpled grin that gets bigger as he watches me approach. "Fancy a drink, love?" he asks me in a British accent, and I want to kick myself, because *why can't I be swooning over that*?

I tell myself that my problem isn't that Nick's the only attractive person in the world.

My problem is that guilt is preventing the swoonage over the bartender.

I'm a truly terrible person.

"Something strong," I tell the bartender. "*Really* strong."

My friends will probably all never talk to me again. Especially Felicity. Because she has this look like she's starting to put things together.

At least I'll forever have alcohol.

And pizza without mushrooms.

Everyone rushes to the window overlooking the ice.

"Oh my god," Alina whispers reverently.

Maren tips her head back and laughs.

And laughs.

And laughs some more.

"Holy *shit*, I knew having Zeus on the team would bring more antics, but this—this—I have to go."

Felicity spins, looking for me, and I drop my head to avoid her gaze and pretend I'm digging in my purse for money. It apparently works, because she's suddenly giving me a quick shoulder hug. "Put that away. The drinks are free in here. I'm having a birthday do-over with you tomorrow. Or the next day. You tell me when you're free, and I'm there. But this—I have to go get Thrusty. And a camera team. This is *gold*."

I don't ask, because I know.

It really is gold. And since Felicity—and her bratwurst-on-a-rocket puppet, Thrusty—are basically the Thrusters mascot, she needs to get down to the ice and use what she can for the Thrusters' next promotional video.

I should feel proud, but I don't.

"What the devil's going on over there?" the bartender asks me.

I give him a bland *I have no idea* look and venture closer to the windows. Maren grabs me and pulls me up front. "Look! Kami! The Thrusters got you a birthday present!"

An entire flock of penguins has taken over the ice at Mink Arena an hour before game time.

They're waddling all over between the nets. Someone's tossed pucks out, and a few penguins are using them like soccer balls. Security swarms the ice. The thin but growing pre-game crowd is all gathered at the edge of the rink, pointing and taking pictures.

"Fifty bucks says that was Zeus Berger," one of the girlfriends says.

"Probably Philadelphia sent a present!" My dad chortles.

"My money's on Nick Murphy," one of the wives says. "He's the worst prankster."

They're all wrong.

Those penguins?

That was all me. Me and a zookeeper friend downtown.

Because yelling at hockey players?

Not effective.

Pissing off their coach and general management over their use of animals in pranks on the ice an hour before a game?

That cow will be the *last* farm animal I pull out of any of the guys' homes this season.

FIVE

Nick

APPARENTLY TODAY *CAN* GET WORSE.

The game's delayed because we have to wait for a penguin specialist to get the penguins off the ice, then for the Zamboni to do its magic and clean up penguin shit. During the delay, Coach feeds us our asses, then puts me on notice that I'm headed back to charm school—or worse—if he gets one more whiff of any pranks involving animals on *or* off the ice.

I know what *worse* means.

I picked a fight with a reporter who touched Felicity wrong after a game last season. I'm the reason the whole team had to go to charm school for remedial lessons in not being Neanderthals.

Clean it up or you're done, Coach told me then.

He didn't mean I'd be traded.

He meant I'd be hanging up my skates. Benched for the rest of the season, and then *done*.

My agent insisted any other team in the league would want me, but I don't want another team.

I was born in Copper Valley.

My dad retired from hockey and always said he wished he'd played one more season, so he could've played here.

My mom covered the Thrusters in the paper for years after that.

Felicity works in the front office, and she's so freaking smart, she'll be running the entire organization in another five years.

It took me six years into my career to get traded here. I want to play for the Thrusters until the day my body doesn't work anymore.

Some guys don't care. Like the Bergers. Give them a hockey stick, they'll play for any team that wants them.

Me?

This is it. When I retire, I want to go out on my home turf. Hopefully not for another five or ten years—which would be a long fucking career for a goaltender—but *here*.

So when Coach sat me down for my come to Jesus moment last season, I took him at face value. I quit pucking around with the bunnies. I pulled back on the pranks.

Mostly.

I let Berger take care of the shitheads who bugged Felicity even though every fiber of my being demanded I protect my little sister the same way I always have since the first moment some shithead dared to call her *weird* in my presence.

I started hanging with Kami.

Who still hasn't texted me back when we leave the dressing room —again—to take the ice for the game twenty minutes behind schedule.

Zeus Berger holds out a gloved fist, and because he's my teammate, and because, yeah, a cow in the bed is actually a pretty fucking fantastic prank, which calls for an equally epic payback, I bump him.

"I got your back, Murphy." He smirks. "And your front. Ain't nobody getting past the Zeusinator tonight."

Like he knows I'm nervous.

His ego doesn't bother me, because he backs it up. The guy doesn't rely on just his size. He works hard to be one of the best D-men in the league.

Lavoie leads the rest of the guys past me, all of them rubbing my helmet for luck, like we do every game when we take the ice. "Head in the game," he tells me.

"Nowhere else exists," I reply.

It's the same routine we go through every night. Same order. Same script.

Except tonight, I catch sight of Felicity at the end of the tunnel, watching me with a frown.

I know she got called down to cover the penguins with her Thrusters mascot puppet—she's a ventriloquist, and she's so fucking hilarious it makes up for the freakiness that comes with her being able to talk without moving her lips—but I didn't know she was still down here. Heard she had plans in the team's suite.

We lock eyes.

She has a damn good poker face, but I know my sister.

And that expression says she suspects something.

Which might mean I'm a dead man.

Ares is last in line. He rubs my helmet and slides a gaze back toward Felicity, whose face transforms and lights up as she blows him a kiss, then waves with the puppet.

They're both weird.

And awesome.

My brother-in-law looks down on me. "Later," he says.

That's all he needs to say, and I get it. Whatever's up with my family and friends, we're saving it for later.

"My head's in the game, big guy," I answer.

He grunts and shoots a look at my crotch.

"Not *that* head."

He smirks and pushes past me.

I roll onto the ice last, pulling my face shield into place, stick in hand.

And with one last glance around the arena—Kami's here somewhere, I'm sure, because she almost always is—I put everything else from today behind me.

It's time to play hockey.

SIX

Kami

THE NICE THING about working for my mom in the veterinary clinic that's been in the family for over fifty years is that when I tell her that I need Thursday morning off to move a cow out of a hockey player's apartment, she doesn't bat an eyelash.

Nope, she just says she'll call a retired friend to cover my shift for me, so long as I get him an autographed stick, which I can *easily* do, because Nick Murphy owes me, even if I'll probably try one of the other guys on the team first, since they basically *all* owe me.

The next phone call isn't as easy.

"Kami! I was just about to call you," Felicity says.

"Do you have keys to Nick's Jeep?" I ask.

She makes a strangled noise that might be a laugh. "Yes."

"Great. Can you meet me at his place and help me move a cow?"

"We have the best conversations."

An hour later, Sugarbear's on a leash and we're pulling her into the elevator. I'm trying to pretend like everything's normal, except it's not.

"So how long have you and Nick been sleeping together?" she asks as soon as the door closes.

I gasp. "We're—I—you—"

Her lips twitch up into an amused smile. Her greatest talent is talking. Talking as herself, talking as one of her dozen different ventriloquist voices, talking like she's Ares or their pet monkey or, more recently, the baby, who's no bigger than an orange but still gets a voice. But since she fell in love with Ares—the king of one-word sentences and master of text by gif—she's gotten freaky good with silence too.

And she's using it *very* effectively right now, arms folded on the other side of the cow, not blinking while she smiles that innocent smile that makes her look like some kind of Irish goddess of love, because she's so damn pretty.

No wonder men don't notice me.

I'm the frumpy brown-haired, brown-eyed, plain, boring one next to all of my friends.

My phone dings, which is an awesome distraction.

Until I read it.

It's my zookeeper friend. *Visits to the penguin enclosure are up so much today, we had to enforce fire code rules limiting the number of people in the building at once. Donations are WAY up too. Thanks! Let us know if you get the scoop on any more opportunities with the Thrusters.*

I sigh.

Once again, Nick Murphy is going to come out of this looking like a hero, since everyone's already speculating it was *him* who got the penguins on the ice.

And now I'm mad all over again, and I want my friend to be just as mad as I am.

Also, it feels so good to finally get this off my chest. "It's my birthday week so you have to forgive me. And don't forget who gives you free consultations with your pet monkey and who gets the donkeys and camels and fish tanks out of your apartment when your brother's an ass. And he is. He's an *ass*. A total and complete ass. The ass to end all asses. He's the Assinator."

She tries to hide her grin behind her hand, but her eyes are grinning, and she can't hide that.

And she's *still* doing that silent thing.

"I broke up with him yesterday because he forgot my birthday," I tell her. "I cut him off from the Kami milk. I'm having a hypnosis session tomorrow to cut him out of my brain, and Muffy has me scheduled for a date tomorrow night, and I blocked his phone number so he can't call me anymore."

Okay, that last one's a lie. Actually, almost all of it is a lie, except the part where I'm done with Nick. *What is wrong with me*? I never lie.

Not like this. And I don't get mad, and I'm getting mad all over again twenty-four hours after I got mad the first time.

"I'm sorry he forgot your birthday," she says softly. "He seemed like he was getting better this last year."

I don't tell her that he remembered all of his family's birthdays because *I* reminded him, because then I'll start to reconsider breaking off our arrangement since clearly, he's horrible at remembering everyone's birthdays.

Except *he should remember*.

How much effort does it take to put a reminder into a smartphone? *None.* None at all. Even if he'd ask someone else to do it for him, even if he only put in Felicity's birthday, it would show that he sometimes thought about someone other than himself.

And he gets himself a new phone every time a new model comes out, so *he* never has dead battery issues, and all of his information is in the cloud, so switching phones wouldn't even affect notifications from his calendar.

I tug on Sugarbear's leash and lead her into the parking garage when the doors open, and apparently, now that Felicity knows, I can't stop talking.

"He needed remedial training when the whole team had charm school early this year and we ran into each other after that game he was benched for telling off that reporter who asked if he'd learned his lesson about punching people off the ice, and I told him if I could train a dog, I could train him too, and we had dinner one night at his place and we were joking about putting a shock collar on him so whenever he felt like punching someone for looking at you wrong, he'd get a jolt and that somehow led to talking about shocking his junk, and then somehow we ended up sleeping together, and it was —never mind, you don't want to know that—but we agreed we didn't want anything serious and that we could be friends with benefits except I thought he'd eventually want more, but he didn't even remember my birthday. So I'm done. And I'm sorry. And you have to forgive me. Please. Please? I promise I won't call him an ass in front of you anymore if you don't want me to, because he *is* still your brother, but I deserve better than a long-term friends-with-benefits arrangement. I want a man who looks at me the way Ares looks at you. I want forever. I want a family. And I'm not going to get that with Nick."

"Wait, *this spring*? You've been boinking my brother since—oh my god. My wedding. We thought you were hooking up with that cute caretaker on the island, but you were—and Nick—and—oh, Kami."

My face goes bright pink and glows so bright I can see the color shimmering in front of me. "The important part is, I am officially moving on. No more ridiculous, unrequited crushes."

She lifts his key fob, and the lights flash on his red Cherokee. "It wasn't totally ridiculous. Liking someone shouldn't be *wrong*."

"So...I should still care?"

"About Nick? No. He's an idiot. A lovable idiot who does have some good qualities too, but still not good enough for someone with a heart as big as yours."

"I'm sorry," I whisper again while I nudge Sugarbear into the back of Nick's car.

"It's his fault. He's such an egomaniac. And sometimes an ass. And sometimes he surprises you and does something really thoughtful and sweet, but overall, I really don't think he deserves you."

"I just thought..." I trail off, because I don't know how to tell Felicity that I thought her brother just needed someone to understand him, because that would imply that she and their parents didn't understand him.

But she's so smart, she graduated college almost before he was out of high school, and she's three years younger than he is. I always thought he worked so hard at hockey when he was younger to prove he was good at something too, because how do you compete with Felicity, especially when you add in how charming and funny and talented she is, and that he was always overlooked.

Like me.

My brother's an astrophysicist who regularly gets interviewed on the national news and who writes books that hit bestseller lists, and my sister's a biomedical engineer at a research lab with an entire staff.

I get it. I know what it's like to be the not as successful one.

Except unlike me, Nick has no ego problems whatsoever.

He's a professional hockey player. He's won the national Chester Green Award for goaltenders two years straight. He makes a crap-ton of money on endorsement deals on top of his healthy hockey salary. He's funny and talented in his own way, and I don't know why the Thrusters thought he needed *charm school*, because he shoots charm out his nostrils just by breathing.

He's not *just the vet* in his family.

He's equally as successful in his own right as Felicity is brilliant in hers, and he's every bit as successful as his dad was before him.

"So where's Sugarbear's new home?" Felicity asks as she climbs into the driver's seat.

I suck in a deep breath through my nose before I answer.

Because the hard questions are still rolling, and I'm pretty sure she's not going to like my idea.

SEVEN

Nick

THIS TIME LAST YEAR, I was heading home on a high after a blow-out win. Tonight—or more like this morning, as it's officially Sunday now—I'm straggling through the door to my building with the weight of disappointment making me sick to my stomach.

Lavoie's with me, since he lives two floors above me, and he keeps giving me one of those looks like he's thinking we need to talk about something.

The doorman scowls at me.

Join the club, buddy. Yeah, I'm the asshole who let New York score three fucking goals in the last period. That's right.

It's my fault the Thrusters have lost two games in a row, both our home game Thursday night and our away game last night. We're one and two.

Terrible start for defending champions.

Whereas Indianapolis is undefeated.

And they're down their enforcer, who's suspended for what he did to Jaeger in the playoffs at the end of the season.

He won't be when our game against the Indies rolls around next month though.

I skip the elevator and trudge up the stairs.

"The stairs?" Lavoie says. "Are the stairs going to make it better?"

"Losers don't get to take the easy way out. Losers have to work their asses off to become winners again."

My phone's sitting heavy in my pocket. Is it weird that I want to text Kami? I've texted her after every road trip the last eight months.

Not six. Not nine.

Eight.

She came over right before Valentine's Day. I remember because she made a joke about not having to explain where the hockey puck chocolates came from, since I wasn't the kind of guy to send Valentine's Day chocolates and we were just friends.

It's October. Eight months later. We were good friends for eight months.

Friends text back though.

Kami still hasn't texted me back, and my messages to her are still showing as unread.

Maybe I should've sent her hockey puck chocolates for Valentine's Day.

Or maybe she's disgusted at how awful I'm playing this season.

I hit my floor and punch the door open. Lavoie should keep going up to his own floor, but he doesn't.

He follows me.

The hallway still smells like hay and cow shit, but not as bad as when I left town Thursday night.

October.

It's October.

Fuck.

"Fuck fuck *FUCK*," I exclaim. "I missed Kami's birthday. Shit on a—"

"Kami? *Felicity's* friend Kami?" Lavoie turns sideways and blocks me. "Fuck, Murphy."

Embarrassment isn't something I do, but my face is getting hot and my nuts feel like they're dangling out in the open like a piñata waiting to take a hit, I'm that exposed.

"It was just a friends with benefits thing," I mutter.

I try to elbow past him, but he blocks me again.

"Was?"

Was. Have I ever lost a friend? I don't think so. I've lived with women a time or two, but never anything serious. Most of my hook-ups are just that—hook-ups. We all know the score.

I don't get tied down. It's just not for me.

But losing a friend—this fucking sucks. I can't look Lavoie in the eye. "She hasn't talked to me since Berger left that cow in my condo."

"Thought I knew that look."

"What look?"

"The heartbroken look."

I snort. "I am *not* heartbroken."

"No? You're acting just like I did when I got my divorce papers."

Dude's crazy. I shoulder past him. "I'm not you."

"Can't stop thinking about her. Game's shit. Blaming everything but the possibility that *you fucking care*. Sounds *exactly* like heartbreak."

I'd tell him to shut the fuck up, except there's a white paper hanging on my door, and I don't have to read it to know what it says.

Cold sweat snakes down my spine. I snatch the letter and scan it quickly to confirm my assumption, then bang my head against the wood a few times for good measure.

I don't have time to deal with an eviction notice.

"Fuck, Murphy," Lavoie mutters.

"My agent will handle it. Or he'll find me a lawyer to handle it." My key still works, so I let myself in, and—

And I quit.

The place is trashed. There's hay everywhere. Cow shit on my recliner. Did that thing—*fuck.*

"Holy fuck," Lavoie says. "You have a livestock orgy in here or something? Is that elephant jizz on your TV?"

"Better fucking be snot."

Christ.

I'm living in a world where *I hope that's cow snot* on my television.

My phone vibrates, and I yank it out of my pocket, hope welling in my chest.

Maybe Kami—but no.

It's Felicity.

"Dude. You have it *bad*," Lavoie says.

I ignore him, and I consider ignoring my sister too. I'd wonder how she knew I was home, but Ares should be getting home right about now too.

I swipe to answer. "Hey."

"I've spent the last few days trying to decide what I want to say to you," she announces.

She's not using any of her puppet voices, which is what she usually does when she picks a fight with me, because she always fucking wins when she has three different puppets on her side. She outnumbers me with her multiple personalities.

Fucking ventriloquist.

The fact that she's attacking me *without* her puppet voices isn't good.

"Can this wait another day? I'm tired, I had a shit game, a shit flight home, and there's an eviction notice hanging on my door."

And I owe Kami flowers.

Or chocolates.

Or—whatever you send a friend when you fuck up.

Not a *lover*. Not a *girlfriend*.

A friend.

We lost a bruiser of a game to Minnesota late last season when we were still fighting for a playoff spot. Kami showed up with pizza, beer, and brownies.

I forgot how much I like brownies.

And her dog. The little one that she can sneak in places because it'll hide in her purse. It's not yappy at all. It just sits in my palm and licks it. What's the dog's name? Feather? Alonzo?

Tiger. That's right. Her itty bitty purse dog is named *Tiger*.

"Nick? *Nick.* You're not listening to a word I'm saying, are you?"

"I missed Kami's birthday," I blurt.

Lavoie shakes his head while he bends over to inspect a chewed throw pillow on my floor. "Telling you, man…"

Felicity sighs. Without adding *you miss everyone's birthday*.

Which she tells me approximately every other month when I miss her birthday, or Mom's birthday, or Dad's birthday, or Coach's birthday, or now Ares's birthday or Loki's birthday, though I think she likes it when I forget their pet monkey, because they're not big fans of my style of gifts.

Especially gifts for monkeys.

She's not excusing me missing Kami's birthday. She's excused me from missing everyone else's birthdays for years, but not Kami's.

"You know what? You're right. You just got home. I can chew your ass out later at Mom and Dad's."

"Awesome."

She hangs up, and I look around my condo again.

The rug's ruined. My Gammy's gonna haunt my ass forever over this.

Something chewed on the stools at my island countertop. The

fridge door is hanging open, which explains the weird smell of moldy pizza mixed in with the cow piss and hay odor.

I step into my bedroom and realize there's no fucking way I'm sleeping in that bed.

Two weeks ago, I would've called Kami. Just to vent.

Because she was *there*.

She probably would've laughed, and *fuck*, that would've made it all better.

You know you did this to yourself, she would've said with a smile and a shake of her head, and I still would've been evicted, but she'd somehow make it okay, because that's what Kami does.

She makes everything okay.

"Need a place to crash?" Lavoie asks from down the hallway.

I press my palms into my eyes.

Clearly, I need a place to crash.

But if management finds out I'm staying with Lavoie, they'll probably evict him too.

I could call Frey, but I don't want to listen to him and Gracie fucking like rabbits, plus, their baby will probably be awake in a couple hours.

Zeus Berger's apartment is barely big enough to fit him—dude's weirdly minimalist, or maybe he's just saving cash before he leaves the league for good—and he'll be having phone sex with his wife.

And I'm not calling Felicity back to see if I can crash at her and Ares's place, for similar—but worse—reasons for not calling Frey.

And after my shit performance on the ice last night, I don't want to see any of the rest of the guys on the team who'd want to see me.

"Nah, I'm sick of your ugly mug," I tell Lavoie, who almost certainly knows what my other option is.

Heading over to my parents' place.

It's just for a few hours, I tell myself. I could get a hotel room, but I live in hotels enough during the season.

And there's not a hotel breakfast in the world that can touch my mom's cooking.

I'll only stay one night. Just long enough to get cleaners lined up to take care of my condo.

But then, everything's going back to normal.

Without Kami, but that's another story.

EIGHT

Kami

I'M NOT USUALLY A RULE-BREAKER. When you break rules, you get in trouble, and getting in trouble is conflict, and conflict and I are no more friends than anger and I are friends.

Which is why I've decided that the only way Sugarbear and I are going to survive her living at my house until I can locate a farm, zoo, shelter, or sanctuary that I approve of is to convince myself she's actually a dog.

It's been remarkably effective so far.

Kami, what's that weird noise in your carport?

Oh, that's my new dog. She has vocal cord issues.

Kami, what's the hay for?

My new dog's on a special diet.

Kami, why are you walking a cow?

That's not a cow, that's my new dog.

I've said that last one at least three times this morning as my three —I mean *four*—dogs and I have circled the block to get all of us some exercise. We're a few houses from home when I hear an engine approach and slow down.

I sigh, because there are only so many times I can repeat that Sugarbear's a dog before someone gets suspicious.

And I don't mean about her not being a cow.

I mean about my sanity.

"You ladies need a lift?" a very familiar, nerve-rattling, nipple-tightening, belly-flipping voice calls.

My vajayjay hears *you want a ride?*, and yes, it means *that* kind of ride, and it's also totally on board with this plan.

Clearly, I need to have a come to Jesus meeting with my vagina.

Or possibly I need to introduce her to something better than Nick's cock.

My three dogs all lunge for the road and the car, even Tiger, my teacup Yorkie, who tends to freak out at the sight of her own shadow.

Only Sugarbear stays calm, which is good, because I don't know how I'd handle being yanked down the road by a three-hundred-pound-and-growing calf.

I mean puppy.

"Down, Pancake. Back, Dixie. Tiger, stop." I hold tight to the leashes on my boxer and my spaniel, and I grab Tiger and pick her up.

"We're fine, thank you," I tell Nick.

"*Moooooooo,*" Sugarbear barks.

Yes, *barks.* I'm living fully in my fantasy, okay?

"It's no trouble," he continues. He coasts along beside us in his Cherokee while I pull my pack along toward home. "This car was built for hauling dogs and cows."

And it hauled a cow—*dog*—that pooped in it just a couple days ago. "That's nice, but I only have dogs."

For once, he's silent.

But only momentarily.

"I didn't mean for you to take the cow."

"Please stop calling my new dog a cow." I know. *I know.* I've lost my mind.

And then he laughs, and that rich, happy, intoxicating sound makes all of my determination waver.

He's not a *bad* guy. He's funny, even if some of his pranks push boundaries. He's loyal and protective to the people inside his circle, and generous in his own unique ways, even if he overlooks the little things. Though he *did* always make sure I got as much out of our physical relationship as he did.

And why did we stop that again? my vagina asks.

The engine stops, and his car door slams. Sugarbear stops too, so I tug on her leash. "C'mon, sweet girl."

She doesn't move. Pancake and Dixie are jumping all over Nick, and Tiger is straining toward him.

"Who's a good girl? Are you a good girl?"

I'm trying not to watch him love all over my dogs, because watching a man love on animals is almost as potent as watching a man hold a baby, and I need to be immune to Nick's charm, but I can't stop myself. He lets them lick all over his face and stick their noses in his crotch and put paw prints all over his track pants without complaint.

His light brown hair is disheveled, his green eyes are tired, and he's started growing his beard for the season, so he's extra scruffy in the cheeks. But he's still pulling off the panty-melting smile.

My dogs are even susceptible. Dixie just flopped on her back and spread her legs like she'd give him full access if he was interested.

"What do you want?" The question is harsher than I mean it to be, but I'm caving. I can feel it. I'm giving in to the magic that is Nick Murphy.

He straightens and hits me with those imploring green eyes that always flip my belly inside out. "I missed your birthday."

I steel myself against my body's instinctive reaction to full-blown eye contact with him. First there's the soda bubbles fizzing through my veins. Then the tightening in my nipples. The heat between my legs. And the extra hard thumping of my heart.

I tell myself someone reminded him, that this isn't *Nick* remembering my birthday.

It was right there on video screens on the scoreboard at the game the other night.

The Thrusters wish Kami Oakley a Happy Thirtieth Birthday.

The announcer even said it out loud.

I know Nick gets into the game and focuses hard on the ice, but it was *during a break*. While Ares was getting a new stick because his broke.

Nick was hanging at the net drinking water.

And he didn't even notice my name.

If we had a real chance at forever, wouldn't he have heard my name?

"Which birthday?" I ask. My palms are sweating. So are my boobs. And Sugarbear *still* won't move.

He frowns. "The one last Thursday."

"What *number* birthday? How old am I?"

His lips part, and his eyes get that goalie-in-the-headlights look. "You don't look a day over twenty-four."

"Thirty, Nick. I'm *thirty*. Your parents came to my surprise birthday at the game. Felicity was hiding thirty balloons in her office when you stopped in to see her that afternoon. *It was announced on the loudspeaker at the game.*"

"I—" He rubs his neck and absently scratches Pancake's head. "You're right. I should've remembered your birthday. I should know which birthday it was. I just got wrapped up in the season starting, and it's a big season, Kami. We could be repeat champions, and—"

He stops himself and looks down. "So I owe you more than a nice dinner out."

Dixie barks her agreement, and Tiger, who's still being denied Nick's affection, howls. It sounds sort of like an overinflated balloon with too much air rushing out the nozzle at once, and that howl is exactly the reason I took her home when I didn't really need another dog.

She was too precious to resist.

"You don't owe me anything," I tell him.

"You're my friend. I fucked up. I owe you dinner."

"No, you don't. Thank you for the sentiment, but you don't."

There's something I've never seen before flickering in his eyes as he searches my face.

Like—like he's *seeing* me.

Sugarbear moos and takes two steps forward to nuzzle Nick's thigh.

She doesn't even come up to his waist, and her brown eyes are so bright and content, and I could picture us all as a happy family, Nick walking our bovine dog, me holding the canine dogs, circling the block and picking up dog pop in cute little green bags and shoveling calf poop into cute large green bags and apologizing to the neighbors for the river of pee raining down on their rhododendrons from our growing several-hundred-pound puppy.

"Back, Sugarbear." I tug on her leash too—not that it makes any difference.

"You named the cow." He scratches her head and smiles at me again, the clouds part, and a million angels swoon and fall off their harps. "That's sweet."

Tiger whines mournfully in my arms. She's the only one of the three to ever visit Nick's place. He fed her plain popcorn, and she's basically his for the taking now, though I'm pretty sure she's not as easy as Dixie, who's now wagging her tail as she continues to lay belly-up at his feet. "We need to get going before someone mistakes my dog for a cow again and calls animal control. Excuse us."

I tug.

Sugarbear lifts her tail and gives me a *just a minute* look.

Of course she does.

"Are you keeping the cow?" he asks me.

"The *dog*," I grit out.

The cow-dog who's currently dumping a load on the sidewalk.

And here I am without my shovel.

He looks down at the patty. "Are you going to keep that?"

Oh, good gravy. "*You cannot have the cow's poop for a prank!*"

"A-*ha*! You admit it's a cow."

"She's a dog. Named Sugarbear. Nicknamed *The Cow*. And now I have to pick that poop up because I don't trust you to not shove it in Zeus Berger's locker."

"I was going to send it off to be made into Christmas ornaments for everyone on the team, but I like your idea better."

I sigh and shove all of my dogs at him while I whip a plastic grocery bag out of my coat pocket. Our fingers brush, and *dammit*, why do I always get that electric rush whenever he touches me?

He doesn't try to take the bag from me to clean up the poop himself, but then, he now has his hands full with a dog trying to lick his beard off while two more jump on him and the cow-dog nuzzles his hip. "Aww, who's a sweet puppy?" he croons to Tiger while I try to finagle a cow patty into a plastic grocery bag without actually touching it with my hands. "Kami, your dogs want to go out to dinner. They think you should let me make it up to all of you."

"Little up to my elbows in shit right now, Murphy."

"I could've gotten that for you."

"Kami?" Mrs. Ostermeijer, my next-door neighbor, pokes her head out the door. "Kami, is that a *cow*?"

"Afternoon, ma'am," Nick calls. "This is my dog. Her name's Sugarbear."

"Bless my stars, you look *just* like that handsome goaltender for the Thrusters," the sweet older lady says. "He's having an awful season, isn't he? Couldn't block a car rolling in at a mile an hour, could he?"

I snort when I should really defend his honor, which sends the scent of cow patty to the back of my throat, and now I'm choking on shit odor.

"Eh, he's an ass," he calls back. "He deserves it."

And that *right there* is why he's so irresistible.

Just when you think his ego can't get any bigger and more unbearable, he goes and deflates it himself.

"I heard his grandmother used to live down the street," Mrs. Ostermeijer says. "Back before I moved in, and everyone says the same thing. That he's an ass. My, you have such a good handle on that cow."

"She's a dog, ma'am. And thank you. And *everybody*? I heard at least half the neighborhood loved that goalie guy."

"No, everybody," Mrs. Ostermeijer confirms. "Some people were just nicer about it. Or so I heard."

I finally get the cow patty scooped into the bag and straighten. The thing must weigh five pounds.

"Here, let me," Nick says, and before I know it, he's swinging the cow poop bag and I have all four leashes—and Tiger—back in my arms.

"Put the shit down," I hiss.

"What a *sweet* gentleman," Mrs. Ostermeijer croons. "Kami, that one's a keeper."

He grins at me, still swinging the poop bag that he's undoubtedly going to shove into someone's locker. Or into their helmet.

I need to call Felicity and have her warn Ares.

"I'm a keeper," he tells me.

"I have a date tonight," I reply.

His brows crinkle and settle back into smirk mode almost as fast. "With who?"

"None of your business."

"Where?"

"Again, none of your business."

"You're going to the zoo, aren't you?"

"Yes. I'm going to the zoo. And we're going to ride the zoo train and make out in the tunnel."

His knuckles go white around the bag handles. I tell myself not to read into it.

"He probably kisses like an anteater," he declares.

"Have you ever kissed an anteater?"

I regret the question instantly, because he's smiling at me again, and I will never be immune to the magnetism and charm that oozes out of that smile. You'd think with the carved cheekbones and the square jaw and the growing stubble, that smile would look more predatory than boyish, but it's everything.

It's sexy and tempting and full of a promise that if I let him back in, I won't regret it.

My *body* wouldn't regret it. It's humming in anticipation of having those long, strong fingers stroking and teasing my skin and my breasts and my pussy and my ass.

I love it when he strokes my ass.

"I've done a lot of things I wouldn't do again," he says, now working that smoky bedroom voice too, "but I've done a few things I'd like to do more of."

I yank hard on Sugarbear's leash, and she finally moves. "I need to go."

Nick tosses the bag of poop into the back seat of his Cherokee. I cringe, because I can only imagine where it will end up.

My dogs are still overeager to love all over him, so they're tangling up their leashes to get to him as he joins us again.

"I miss you," he says quietly.

I miss who I always thought you could be.

I swallow hard before I can force the words I know I need to say. "It's time to move on."

"But we're friends. We can stay friends."

"Sure. We can stay friends." Friends who don't see each other. Who don't call.

Who don't go to each other's hockey games.

Dammit, I'm going to miss watching hockey. Maybe I'll cheer for the Seattle Badgers instead. They're all the way across the country. I'm in no danger of meeting and falling for one of *their* players.

"Are you brushing me off?" he asks.

"What? No. That would be rude."

"Kami."

We reach the short sidewalk leading up to my little two-story house with the powder blue siding and the white trim, and I do my best to rein in my dogs. "Treats inside!"

All three of the canine dogs bolt up the steps. The bovine dog looks at me like I've just run over her pet bunny.

Like she *knows* I'm trying to brush Nick off.

"Are you seriously keeping the cow here?" he asks again.

"I'm fostering her while I look for a more permanent solution."

"What about that place you took the goats over the summer?"

"Full."

"And the donkey—"

"It ate through three fences and they asked me to not call them again."

He tries to hide a grin, but he utterly fails. "Wasn't there some farm that took those baby bunnies?"

"The owner died and his kids sold the bunnies to be made into fur coats."

He has the decency to look horrified, so I don't tell him that I'm lying, and that all the baby bunnies were actually adopted by families, though the process took a couple months.

"So, yes, I have a new dog who needs a bigger home, but I refuse to let her go until I know she won't be turned into ground beef. And if *any* of you *ever* use an animal in a prank again, you'll have to deal with something way worse than penguins invading the ice."

His head jerks up, eyes wide, and I realize he needs to go.

Now.

"Did you—" he starts, admiration shining in his eyes, but I cut him off.

"Excuse me. I need to go wash my hair."

Before I realize what's coming, he grabs me around the waist and captures my mouth with his. His cheeks are scruffy, his lips firm and talented, brushing over mine, teasing the edges with his tongue, tasting like coffee and chocolate, and I could so easily melt into this kiss and pull him inside and beg him to take care of that ache building between my thighs.

And he would.

He's not selfish in bed. He'd go down on me if I asked him to. He'd worship my breasts. He'd trail his fingers down my spine and circle my ass with that light touch that sets my nerves fluttering.

He'd make me come so hard, I'd see stars.

He'd come too. Hard and fast and deep, with an *oh, fuck, yes* moaned out while he buries his head in the crook of my neck.

And then he'd leave.

Because it's what he always does. Even when I'm the one at his place, he leaves.

It's a mental thing. You can just *see* him leaving.

He pulls out of the kiss and tucks a lock of hair behind my ear. "Have fun on your date tonight. Call me if I need to buy any puppy food for you."

And while I stand there gaping, my cow-dog peeing a river down the sidewalk, he turns and strolls away.

NINE

Nick

OCTOBER IS my favorite month of the year. There's the start of hockey season. Halloween candy and pumpkin spice lattes. The weather.

Like tonight's weather.

Fifty degrees.

Overcast.

And dark early so I can pop a movie into the projector behind my parents' place, stretch out on a pool lounger, and watch *Miracle* outside.

Okay, fine.

I don't give two shits about the *weather*. I don't want to be hiding by a pool that's too cold to swim in, watching a movie by myself. I want to have a woman's feet tucked under my legs.

I want to hear her laugh when I crack a terrible joke and her moans when I talk her out of her pants and bury my cock deep inside her.

I want to kiss her again like I did when I left her house earlier today.

I could hit the bars, but I don't want some bunny offering to kiss my booboos over the game last night.

I want—

Fuck. I just *want*. And I want to not think about what I want, but since Lavoie brought it up, all I can think about is *want*.

And I don't want to want what I want, but I can't help myself.

So I'm hiding. From all of it. Including my sister's attempts to murder me with her eyeballs, because she doesn't want me to want what I don't want to want either.

Fuck, I'm a complicated mess.

The one thing I'm not complicated about?

This *date* Kami's on tonight.

She shouldn't be dating random dickheads. They're not good enough for her. They'll probably only tolerate her dogs so they can get a shot at her pussy, and that pisses me off.

At least I was honest with her about only wanting her pussy.

And to be friends.

I like being friends with Kami. She's easy to talk to. She bakes brownies. And she's the only person who laughs with me at the same inappropriate places in *The Mighty Ducks*.

Fuck, I'm thinking about her again.

This isn't good.

I've had plenty of friends-with-benefits relationships before. Usually they end when she finds a guy who'll give her something I won't—I'm not commitment material, which is something I accepted about myself a long time ago—and we're all cool with that.

But Kami—she doesn't have anybody else.

She just got sick of *me*.

It's unsettling. Is it age? Is it that I got a little fluffy in the off-season? Am I—

Fuck.

Am I losing my ability to make her come?

I look at my crotch. "We're *thirty-one*, dude. Swear to god, if you go soft on me—"

"There you are, you shithead," Felicity says in her happy puppet voice, which is about the hugest warning she can give me, because that happy puppet voice is about as likely to call me names as Kami is. "Ares, tie him up while I go get a lighter for his shoelaces."

I jump up, wishing I had that cow with me, because I know Ares wouldn't lay a hand on me if I were holding a cow. And while I'm dodging him, Felicity hits me with a sneak attack.

She grabs my ear and twists, and I go down like I've been hit with a triple-strength stun gun. "*Ow!* Let go."

"You know the rules," she says. "You don't sleep with my friends. Now you have to pay."

"Felicity. It's hockey season. You can't beat me up. Think of the team. Ares, man, tell her."

Ares doesn't tell her. Instead, he grips me by the arms and lifts me, holding me in front of him so she can rack me in the family jewels if she wants.

I don't thrash and fight it, because I've seen Ares squish a small sedan the way a normal man crushes beer cans. Fighting only makes it worse.

I do cover the family jewels though. "I didn't mean to hurt her," I tell Felicity, who's had to climb up onto the stone patio table to be at eye-level with me because of how high Ares is holding me. "And you should get down off that table before you fall and hurt the baby."

"You. Know. The. Rules."

"She was helping me with charm school, and things just… happened." I hold up my hands, realize I'm wide open for a racking, and cover my dick again. "I didn't sleep with anybody else while I was with Kami."

"That's level *one* of human decency, Nick. Level. One."

"I—"

"She called *her cousin Muffy* for matchmaking because of you. Do you know Muffy?"

I shake my head, do my best not to snicker at the name, and make a mental note to look up Kami's cousin Muffy.

"She's the worst matchmaker in *the entire country*. There's a *dog* with a matchmaker website who has a better success ratio than Muffy does. And do you know what the worst part is? The worst part is that she's determined to let Muffy set her up because *you* couldn't keep your dick in your pants."

Please note that I *don't* tell Felicity that Kami never complained about my dick. But I do angle a look back at Ares. "Can you put me down?"

"No."

If anything, he holds me closer to Felicity.

"What do you want me to do?" I ask.

"I don't know," she snaps.

Ah.

So *that's* the problem.

Felicity never doesn't know something.

"I apologized," I mutter. "For forgetting her birthday."

"*You talked to her again?*"

"I fucked up, so I apologized. Isn't that what I'm supposed to do?" Naturally, I don't mention the kissing part.

"*No.*"

"Women," I mutter.

Ares flips me upside down and dangles me by my ankles. I flail like a Muppet and he heads for the pool. I can't even try to rack *him* in the jewels to get out of this, because he's holding me facing away from his body.

"I'm sorry. *I'm sorry,*" I yelp, because that pool will be wicked cold this time of year, and if anyone can lift the cover with his mind, it's Ares. "I didn't mean it."

"Do you have any idea how long Kami's had a crush on you?" Felicity says behind us. "*Years*, Nick. *Years*. She would do *anything* for you."

I twist, trying to see my sister while all my blood rushes to my head. We're getting close to the pool, and I actually don't know that the cover's rated for the Berger twins either. "What? No, she hasn't. She's just nice to everyone."

"*No one* is as nice to *everyone* as Kami is to you."

Ares grunts in agreement.

And now I'm even more confused. And I apparently owe her another apology.

I know I probably shouldn't have kissed her today, but I wanted to prove to myself that I could do it.

That I could kiss Kami and not end up naked with her.

Because if I can kiss her and then *not* talk her out of her pants, it *clearly* means she's something more than my normal brand of friends with benefits.

Although I'm still not ready to face the implication that it might mean Lavoie's right.

That Kami might actually mean something more to me, and that her being mad at me is affecting my game.

Like maybe she's a *special* friend with benefits.

And that's as far as I'm willing to commit to, except I'm definitely down with committing to testing this theory that she could be my good luck charm.

"Do you remember the dick cookie incident?" Felicity demands.

I nod, upside down, because *everyone* remembers the dick cookie incident.

How many other older brothers could pull off having a thousand dick cookies delivered to his sister's ex-boyfriend's place? But for the record, I don't smirk with pride. Even though I want to.

"Kami was the only person who said you couldn't have been behind that."

"She clearly doesn't know me very well." Thank god. Because I was getting worried for a minute there that she was right.

That Kami might actually like me as more than a special friend with benefits.

Which is *way* different than a girlfriend.

And yes, I'm going to keep telling myself that.

"Dunk him?" Ares asks.

"That would be lovely," she replies.

Zeus comes flying from the side of the house, and I mutter a curse word my sister's unborn baby probably shouldn't hear.

Zeus must be done having phone sex with his wife, which we could all tell he was eager to get to throughout dinner. Since he's here alone, and since he's Ares's twin, Mom and Dad invite him over as one of the family anytime we get together.

"I got the pool cover!" he yells.

"I can't undo it," I yelp at my sister. "What do you want from me?"

"I want you to leave my friends alone."

That's a challenge if I ever heard one. "But your friends love me. That's not fair to—*erp*! Okay! Okay! I'll leave her alone!" For tonight.

But I still owe her an apology for her birthday, because saying *I'm sorry* clearly didn't cut it.

Zeus is hopping around the pool, flipping the cover off.

"Give me your phone," Felicity orders. She's stalking around the stamped concrete patio, fingers held out.

"No fucking way."

"I'm deleting Kami so you can't bug her. Not for vet calls, and not for booty calls."

"I don't need a vet anymore."

And that's the last thing I say before Ares releases me head-first into a fifty-degree swimming pool.

TEN

Kami

FORGET BUTTERFLIES. An entire herd of spooked antelope has taken up residence in my belly.

I'm at the bar in a farm-to-table restaurant in the Mulvaney Hill district, in an ivory sweater, knee-high boots, and a black pencil skirt that must've shrunk in my closet, because I have to keep tugging it down and sucking in my belly.

I'm waiting for my date.

And I keep waiting for Nick to walk in and sit down at the table across from me and make kissy lips at me. *That's right, baby. You could have me and Little Nicky all night instead of that loser with the pictures of his pet hamster from when he was a kid who keeps staring at your boobs and asking if you wax your cooch.*

I shake my head and text Muffy a picture of my boots to distract myself from letting the Nick in my head trash-talk my date before he even gets here, sighing when I realize my phone is once again at forty percent battery. I have *got* to quit putting off getting a new phone.

Kami: Are these too much? Do they say "I want you to fuck me tonight," or do they say "I'm putting my best foot forward?"

Muffy: Holy shit. Those are awesome. Can I borrow them the next time I need to crush a dude's balls? Those spiky heels will do some serious damage. And I love the fur top. Real cheetah?

Kami: Of course not! It's fake. And they're a size six. And you didn't answer my question.

Muffy: They say "I want to live in Muffy's closet."

Kami: Your feet are three sizes bigger.

Muffy: That's never stopped me before.

Kami: William is late. William, right? Did he ghost me? Do you think he showed up and saw desperation written in my face and decided to sneak into the coat closet for a quickie with the hostess instead?

Muffy: Stop fretting. He'll be there. He has a bum leg from his time in the Army.

Kami: So you're saying he probably wouldn't be comfortable having a quickie with the hostess in a coat closet?

Muffy: Definitely. He'd have to take her back to the kitchen and throw her on a prep table. But he's not going to do that because he's a very nice gentleman who was *very* excited when I called to ask him if he'd like to take you out. Deep breath, sweetie. You're going to have a wonderful evening. And I call dibs on maid of honor. I don't care how much you love your sister. You owe me.

I quit texting because I'm down to thirty percent battery now, and I blow out a slow breath and glance around the restaurant. Everything's warm honey colors with fresh herbs decorating the tables in mason jars. There's a beanie or fedora and a beard at almost every table, and there's an argument going on two stools down from me over which environmental engineering firm in Copper Valley is most likely to win the contract for upgrading City Hall.

It's classic Copper Valley outside the hockey zone.

There's a table near the front window where a young couple is feeding avocado toast to their toddler. Those big brown eyes and black curls tug at something deep in my belly. He smiles a toothy green grin, showing off his food, and both his parents smile and shake their heads. Mom leans in to wipe his mouth, and the little guy smushes avocado into her mouth.

It should be gross, but it's adorable. And sweet. And perfect.

And everything I want in my future.

"Kami?" a rough voice asks.

I look up to see an elderly gentleman with a shock of white hair and a cane peering at me over his glasses. He's in a stained pink polo and khaki pants, and if he grew a beard, he'd look like Santa Claus with that bright pink nose.

"Hi," I say hesitantly. "Can I help you?"

His brown eyes light up. "Muffy said you were pretty, but she didn't say you were *this* pretty."

I blink once.

Then twice.

"M-muffy?" I repeat.

He winks. "Didn't tell you how experienced I am, did she? I'm William. And it's my pleasure to be on the arm of a live one tonight. You wanna blow this hippie joint and go get some oysters?"

It takes me a full three breaths to find words. "Um, yes. But can you excuse me for a minute? I need to use the restroom."

"You're not plannin' on disappearing out the window, are you? Muffy promised me you're not the disappearing type."

"No, I really do just need to use the restroom." And call Muffy and chew her out.

He frowns, and my heart squeezes. I wonder how many times he's been left behind.

If Muffy's in charge of his dates, undoubtedly too many.

"I can use the restroom at the oyster bar," I tell him.

His face lights up, wrinkles and all. He looks down at my feet and whistles. "Yeah, you're dressed up good for the oyster bar. Right this way, darlin'."

I slide a twenty onto the bar to pay for my kombucha, then take William's arm and let him lead me out of the restaurant.

And then I have to readjust his hand when it slips to my ass.

"You like to dance?" he asks me.

"I do."

"Oooh, honey, that's a good thing, because I sure do like to watch."

Then again, maybe his problem *isn't* that Muffy's in charge of his dates.

"I used to watch my late wife dance in the kitchen all the time," he adds.

And there goes my heart squeezing for him again. "I'm sorry for your loss," I say instead while we navigate around a group of teenagers taking up the whole sidewalk.

"Eh, better her than me." His hand slips to my ass again, and I sigh as I once again right it.

Muffy is going to die.

ELEVEN

Kami

I'M BEGINNING to get used to conflict.

Take this morning, for example. Muffy has refused to answer a single one of my calls since last night, so I'm leaving home early, after walking all four of my dogs—yes, Sugarbear is still a dog, and I swear she's getting more dog-like every hour—to go visit my dear cousin Muffy at her house.

Which also happens to be my Aunt Hilda's house.

I park around the corner and sneak through the backyards of the other 70's-style brick homes so Aunt Hilda won't see me coming. It's been a long time since I climbed the trash cans out back to shimmy up onto the sun-room roof to get to Muffy's room, and thirty is apparently already zapping my muscle mass, because it's a lot harder on my arms and legs to get up on the roof than it used to be.

I scramble over the rough shingles to the window and pull out the screen. The curtains are only partially drawn, and I can see Muffy sleeping in her childhood princess bed.

Sliding the window open takes more effort than I remember too. The house must've settled since we were teens. But I manage it, and I'm slipping inside when Muffy rolls over, looks at me, and screams.

I dive for the bed and cover her mouth. "*Shush*. It's me. It's Kami."

"I know. That's why I'm screaming," she says against my hand.

"You set me up with a horny old dude who could've been my *grandfather*!" I whisper-shriek.

"Muffy? Honey, did you have another one of your nightmares?" Aunt Hilda calls.

I glare at her and pull my hand away.

"Yes, Mom," she calls dutifully.

"What was it this time?"

"The one with the goat claw," she replies without even having to think about it.

"Oh, at the car dealership with the inflatable cars?"

"Yes, Mom."

"I'll go make you an omelet. Omelets cure everything." The hallway floor squeaks and I sit back on Muffy's pink, not-so-fluffy-anymore comforter.

"Not only did he keep grabbing my ass, I almost got *arrested*," I hiss. "He's not supposed to leave the nursing home. They thought I kidnapped an old man so I could harvest his sperm!"

"Did you dance with him?" she asks.

I blow out a breath. "Yes. Six times."

"Aww, you big softie." She leans over and hugs me. "He doesn't get to dance very often. I knew you'd dance with him. That probably made his entire month."

It's hard to stay mad when she puts it like that. "What's he in a nursing home for anyway?"

She pats her crazy brown morning hair and grimaces. "It's a center for elderly criminals."

"*What*?"

"Of the harmless variety." She waves a hand and starts scooting off the bed. She's in a Thrusters T-shirt and bikini briefs, and she picks her underwear out of her butt while she heads to her closet and pulls out a robe. "He got sucked into a scheme where he was calling women pretending to be their long-lost grandfather in need of gas money to come visit. He thought he was calling on behalf of real grandparents whose grandkids were ignoring them."

"That's…"

"Exactly like something my mom will do one day." She yawns and scratches her stomach. "You want omelets for breakfast? Or do you have to get home and feed your cow?"

"You still owe me a *real* date," I grumble, but I follow her downstairs for egg white omelets with Aunt Hilda, who's in a pair of pink silk pajamas that she wore back before gastric bypass surgery a few years ago. She's swimming in silk.

Almost literally.

"Kami, honey, can you introduce me to that nice Canadian boy on the Thrusters?" Aunt Hilda asks when I walk into the kitchen. She doesn't seem surprised to see me, which makes me wonder if she had a role in my date with William last night. "I'll add some turkey bacon to your omelet if there's any chance you can get me his number."

"Which Canadian?" I ask, because there are at least three.

"Duncan Lavoie, of course. The only one who matters."

"Felicity won't even give *me* his number. I don't think I'll be able to get it for you." Never mind that I have it anyway because of a potbellied pig incident, and yes, that was *also* Nick's fault.

"The other Canadians?" she asks hopefully.

"One's married and the other's gay."

"I don't mind just watching if the gay one's down for it."

"You know you're the reason I have nightmares," Muffy tells her mom.

Aunt Hilda grabs her in a hug, and they're like one big giant silk monster floating together in the kitchen. "And I'm the reason you can't find a boyfriend or get a real job. I know, honey. I know. I also pay your therapy bills."

"I don't go to therapy."

"Everyone should go to therapy. It's good for you. Kami, you go to therapy, don't you?"

"No, but I probably should." Hypnosis therapy would be good.

Then I could forget Nick.

Because even while I was explaining the situation to the police at the oyster bar last night, I couldn't help thinking about Nick.

He'll be a dirty old man one day. Sneaking out of nursing homes to hit on women a third his age.

Unless the right woman finally snares him. The one who will finally mean more to him than hockey. Than pranks. Than everything.

And that one won't be me.

"Cheer up, Kami." Muffy hands me an egg white omelet with spinach and kale and mushrooms and I'm honestly afraid to ask what else. "I know last night wasn't exactly what you had in mind, but I have the *best* date lined up for you tonight."

"Is he under seventy?" I ask.

"Yep."

"Single?"

"Uh-huh."

"Average intelligence or better?"

"Yep."

"Does he tell knock-knock jokes?"

Both Muffy and Aunt Hilda frown at me. "I...don't think so," Muffy finally says.

"Impotence problems?"

"Kami. Don't you think you're getting a little picky?"

"You set me up with a member of a senior citizen crime ring."

"Oh, did you go out with William last night?" Aunt Hilda claps her hands. "I'd do him if he were ten years younger."

"*Mom.*"

"Sorry, sweetie. It's the hormones. Menopause is no joke."

I eat my omelet quickly, because I'm actually at risk of being late to work. Again.

"Come through the front door next time, hon," Aunt Hilda calls as I dash away.

I make it to the clinic with five minutes to spare before my first patient of the day. I rush in the back door and swing into the break room to toss my coat onto the rack and my bag in my cubby, except I can't get more than a foot into the door.

Because the break room is piled with at least two dozen giant teddy bears with red ribbons around their necks, all of them holding helium balloons that read *I'm sorry*.

"Whaaa...?" I start.

"That's exactly what I was going to ask you," my mom replies dryly behind me.

"I don't..." I trail off, because I think I *do*. "How many bears are there?" I ask weakly.

"Thirty." Mom sips her coffee and gives me the look of all mothers suspicious of being denied a glimpse into their children's dating lives.

You know the one.

The *does this mean you're going to give me grandchildren of the human variety soon too?* look.

"Was there a card?"

"Was a card necessary?"

Nope.

Not at all.

I rub my chest, right over my fluttering heart.

I've never seen Nick Murphy apologize for anything, but I've seen him pull a prank or seventeen.

And if there's one thing I know about Nick, it's that he never does anything small.

I might be in trouble.

He loves himself first, I remind myself.

It doesn't help.

Forget *might*.

I am most definitely in trouble.

TWELVE

Nick

SINCE WE DON'T HAVE another game until Wednesday, and since my agent is a worthless shit when it comes to solving my living problems—although he's a god when it comes to endorsement deals and milking the hell out of things like that self-published book I wrote about one of Felicity's dick ex-boyfriends a few years ago— half the team joins me Monday night to move my shit out of my condo.

Along with my parents.

Who are *delighted*—Mom's words—to have me moving back into their basement.

I'd get a hotel room, except the last thing I need is to be black-listed from all the hotels in town, which might be inevitable given that I fully intend to pay Zeus back for the cow.

"This is temporary," I remind my mom. "One week. Tops. I'm meeting with a real estate agent before practice tomorrow." Because apparently my reputation precedes me, and none of the building supervisors at my buddies' places have returned my calls. One even hung up on me.

Mom smiles over a box of stuff she pulled out of my cabinets. "Of course you are. By the way, honey, butter goes in the fridge," she says. "You'll have to remember that when you use my kitchen."

Fuck me. I knew I blacked out bad enough after the season

opener last week that I put my popcorn in the fridge, but I didn't know I put my butter in the cabinet.

"Here. You take this." I shove a full bottle of Jameson at Klein, my backup on the team, because I need to not drink it. "Happy birthday."

Happy birthday.

That hollow hurt in Kami's eyes yesterday—she thinks somebody told me.

Of course she does. Why shouldn't she?

Guilt is one emotion I do my best to avoid at all costs.

One of many, actually.

But I can't stop thinking about Kami. About the idea that she's hurt because of me.

About all the ways I'm going to prove to her that we shouldn't end our friends-with-benefits relationship just because we hit a few hiccups.

She hasn't acknowledged today's offering yet, but that's okay.

I have twenty-nine more ideas to go.

"You could stay at my place," Jaeger, one of our newer offensive linemen, tells me, "except you couldn't bring your girlfriend since my building doesn't allow cows either."

I flip him off, because charm school apparently worked.

Normally I'd put him through a window.

But today, a finger is all I have.

It's possible I needed that dunking in the pool last night.

Zeus too.

Ares dunked him when he wasn't expecting it, then frowned down over both of us, said, "No more shit pranks," and stalked off to take Felicity home.

Now, both Berger twins are among the guys here helping me pack up my stuff.

The cleaners come tomorrow.

And I'm turning in my key on Wednesday.

And soon, Zeus Berger will find out what fucking with Nick Murphy means.

I wouldn't be pulling my weight on the team if I didn't get him back.

And one good prank deserves another.

"I moved back in with my parents once," Zeus tells me while we load up his truck, since my Jeep's already full. Ares's Escalade is already loaded down too. "'Course, I was nineteen, home for that first summer after college, and I only lasted about three hours before Ares got home too and we rented out this cheap-ass apartment in Wishberry Lake. You ever been to Wishberry Lake?"

"You have a point?" I ask him.

He grins. "Yeah, basically that if I can find an apartment in Wishberry Lake, and you can't find one here, you're a big loser. *Ow.* Fucker."

He punches the air, trying to hit Ares back—nice of the big guy to defend my honor there—but Ares is quicker. Probably because of all that vegan food Felicity has him eating. I swear the dude's getting lean without losing any muscle mass, which only makes him more dangerous.

"Say sorry," he says to Zeus, who's fighting—unsuccessfully—to get out of his twin's headlock.

"Sorry, Murphy," Zeus says dutifully.

Ares releases him. "Now hug."

"Aw, that's not necessary, man," I say while Zeus and I eye each other dubiously.

"*Hug*," Ares repeats.

He's getting that look on his face again.

The one that says if we don't hug, he's going to enjoy the hell out of shooting practice tomorrow when I'm at the net.

I don't know what he's threatening Zeus with, but the two of them are clearly communicating something.

Zeus awkwardly goes for the one-armed shoulder hug. Fucker's so tall, I'm left to one-arm him under his armpit.

"More," Ares growls.

"Fuck," I mutter.

Zeus grabs me with both arms, and I loop mine around his back. I can hear his fucking heart beating, and I swear it's shouting *Let me go! Let me go!*

We both jump back in time to see Felicity high-five Ares. "I got six pictures," she tells him.

He slips an arm around her and bends down to kiss her head. "Good job."

Fuck pranking Zeus.

I'm getting *both* the Berger twins.

"Mom's offering a pizza party for everyone at home," Felicity tells me. She's dwarfed next to Ares, but she's so smiley and happy all the time, it doesn't look weird anymore. "I told her the guys already had plans to hit Chester Green's. You're welcome."

It's like being seventeen again. *Nick, honey, invite your hockey friends over so I can make sure you're not out getting any girls pregnant. I'll get some nice PG-13 movies for you to watch too.*

I grew out of being embarrassed by my parents a long time ago. Most of the guys on the team like being mothered—in moderation— because it's so rare to play in the same town as family.

But visiting my parents across town for a home cooked meal and having the guys swing by because *I live there* are two different things.

"You are an angel," I tell Felicity.

"Yeah, don't get too comfortable thinking it's all because I'm a good sister."

"There's always a catch, man. *Always*." Zeus shakes his head while Ares nods in agreement.

"What?" I ask.

"I told my boss I'd get you to do a video with Sugarbear," Felicity replies. "And that it'll be *adorable*."

"Kami's new dog? Sure. Done." Especially since it means I'll have to see Kami again.

"Good. Because the other half is that I'm interviewing you both. With Thrusty. As soon as Kami finds her a new home." She smiles at me and adds, "And Sugarbear has this really cute voice!" without moving her lips.

She's so freaky.

And so cool.

Some of the best and worst moments of my entire life have come courtesy of my sister's weird talents.

Also, *fuck* waiting for Kami to find the cow a home. "Why can't we do it tomorrow?" I ask her.

"Because you're a dick and I'm not giving you an excuse to bother Kami," she replies sweetly.

"She's got you there," Zeus says.

Felicity smiles, and yeah, fine.

I'd do just about anything for my sister.

Right now, I'd do just about anything to get back in Kami's good graces too. I wonder if Felicity knows about this morning's delivery.

"You're about cleaned out, so we'll go get a table," Felicity says. "Not like we have to hurry to unload anything."

Right.

Because we'll just have to load it back up when I get a new place in a few days. "Thanks."

She smiles again. Nice to see her smiling so much. Even I can't deny Ares has been good for her, even if it pissed me off to find out he was sleeping with her when he was supposed to be guarding her against a crazy ex-boyfriend.

"Better go make sure Mom's not trying to give away anything. I think she has a crush on Jaeger."

"That's…"

"Disgusting?" she asks with a big grin.

"My mom has a crush on Hulk Hogan," Zeus offers.

"You mean you do," Ares says.

They're still laughing when I head for the elevator.

This isn't so bad, I tell myself. Things will get normal again. I'll have a new place within a week. We're playing the Boston Blades at home on Wednesday, and they'll be tough, but I know we're tougher. And Kami will forgive me, and I'll get my game mojo back.

Life is about to be perfect once again.

THIRTEEN

Kami

THE BUTTERFLIES ARE BACK, and not just because I got called home from work early to deal with Sugarbear getting through the fence in my piddly backyard and eating Mrs. Ostermeijer's mums. Placating my neighbor was fairly simple, but if Sugarbear gets through the *other* fence, it won't be so easy.

And it's not like I can just call up doggy daycare and ask if they take extra-large varieties for while I'm at work.

Maybe tomorrow, I'll take her to work with me. We do have a parking lot. And she loves my dogs.

So tonight's butterflies are once again due to a date.

A *real* date. With Douglas. A man who *isn't* a hockey player. And who wears *glasses*, and who Muffy assures me is no more than thirty-five. And who wants to meet at a wine bar downtown.

Nick knows wine exists, but he's more of an Irish whisky kind of guy. Or Irish beer. Or sometimes a mix of the two.

Not thinking about Nick tonight, I remind myself.

Tiger howls when I dance into my slingbacks. Like I'm cheating on her for having a date. "It's a work night," I tell her. "I won't be out late. Promise."

Pancake rolls her eyes and flops to the ground in front of my couch. Dixie tries to trip me and bounces all over the living room.

She's a pinball, leaping off the couch, missing the recliner, bouncing off the wall, skidding to a stop before the TV stand.

"You three are *fine*." They got an extra-long walk with Sugarbear after work, and then we played fetch in the front snip of a yard for half an hour while Sugarbear ate her grains in back, during which I only thought about Nick and the thirty apology teddy bears approximately three million times. "Dates are good for me. And so they're good for you. Don't you want someone else to play fetch with?"

Tiger flops on her back next to Pancake and makes her goofball howl again. Dixie skitters out of the room and dashes back in two seconds later with her stuffed monkey that she likes to play tug of war with. She drops it at my feet and pants up at me.

"After my date."

She, too, flops mournfully onto the rug beside Pancake and Tiger. I unplug my phone, snap a picture of the three of them looking pathetically adorable, and send it to my mom. Then I head for the door.

Half an hour or so later, I'm being seated in a suede-lined booth big enough for two beside the exposed brick wall at Noble V, one of the trendier wine bars in downtown just down the street from Chester Green's. Muffy made the reservation for us, claiming she owed me for dancing with William. My date hasn't arrived yet, but I wonder if Muffy's men are just the late kind. Plus, I'm ten minutes early, which is unusual when I'm heading into downtown at rush hour.

I guess the city's campaign to get more people on public transportation is working.

I fiddle with the menu, glancing at the fine writing on the thick linen paper tucked into the leather menu cover. The wine is easy— they have my favorite Riesling from a small winery outside the city near the Blue Ridge Mountains—but too many things on the food list sound great for that to be an easy choice.

Nick would go for the hamburger, but I—*dammit*.

I don't *care* what Nick would go for.

The salmon sounds good. Fish is good. Healthy. Sophisticated. Undoubtedly delicious here. I flop the menu down and glance around again.

Everything's dark wood. High, exposed-beam ceilings. The bartender's young and hot and wearing a black button-down, and the servers are all in total black too. And *oh my god*, that's Doug Dobey, Felicity's ex-boyfriend, talking to the hostess.

I duck my head over the menu again, because now I'm thinking about Felicity.

And Doug.

And the thousands of cookies printed with dick pics that Nick sent Doug, who then dumped them on Felicity's lawn, when they broke up.

Nick does *not* do anything small.

Also, Doug went a little stalker nutso after that. We haven't had reason to talk since the break-up, but I'd still rather not see him.

Who wants to see their friends' psycho exes? Especially when he was ultimately the reason the entire Thrusters team got sent to charm school?

Heat surges across my neck, and I lunge for my cell phone, because my date's name is *Douglas*.

Muffy wouldn't.

She *wouldn't*.

But did she know?

I'm failing to unlock my phone because my hands are shaking so badly when the hostess's black shoes stop beside my table. "Ms. Oakley, sir."

I whip my head up, and *fuck*.

Doug's lips part as we make eye contact. He's in pressed jeans and a blue button-down. His brown hair is neatly trimmed. So's his beard. His glasses reflect the candlelight on the table. And if I didn't know better, I'd think he wasn't a psychotic crazypants.

"Is this some kind of a fucking joke?" he demands as he looks me up and down.

"I think there's been a misunderstanding," I stutter.

The hostess glances between us, then shoots a look toward the bar.

"Did Murphy set you up to make me look like a fool?" he snarls.

I pull my phone out and aim it at him. "I'm recording every word you say. You're going to back away and let me leave, and never, *ever* talk about this *huge* mistake again, and I won't show this to Ares Berger."

"Fucking—"

"Ma'am?" The gentle-voiced manager joins us as I'm scurrying out of the booth. "Is everything okay?"

"Blind date gone wrong," I tell him, because that's simpler than *my idiot cousin set me up with my friend's psycho ex*. "May I please have an escort to my car?"

"I can't fucking *believe* this," Doug seethes. "My first date in a fucking *year*, and it's this bitch. Fucking *Muff Matchers*. I'll put them the fuck out of business for this."

"Sir—"

Whatever else the manager says, I don't hear, because there's a hollow *whoosh* in my ears and the entire dimly-lit restaurant takes on the hues of hell. "Oh, you better take that back *right now*," I growl.

"You're a *bitch*," he repeats. "And this dating service is run by retar—"

Everything after that gets a little hazy.

I know I take a swing at him. Someone screams. Maybe a few someones. I definitely connect with something, because there's a sharp sting radiating from my middle knuckle to my elbow. Hands grab me. I thrash about. I'm shouting. Something about dicks not calling other people names. Something about Nick chopping off Doug's nuts if he gets in my face again.

It's not like I can threaten that *my* brother's going to do it.

A wall of mist hits my face, and I realize I've just been tossed out of Nobel V and into the night. Streetlamps illuminate the wide sidewalks and couples in dark jackets and groups of single women laughing together walk past.

"I don't know what he did to you," the hostess tells me as she hands me my coat and purse, "but damn, girl. I want you on my side next time my boyfriend pulls a dick move."

"Can I escort you to your car, ma'am?"

The manager is outside the bar too, watching me as though I'm a lit stick of dynamite.

"I'm sorry." I shake my hand out—did I break it?—and realize my sinuses are clogging and my cheeks are wet. "I don't usually—"

I swallow hard, because *I don't usually lose my flipping mind at wine bars* is just too weird to force out. I don't even know myself right now. "No, thank you," I finish.

The manager shifts a look over his shoulder, and I realize he's asking just as much for my safety as for Doug's.

Probably more so for mine.

Maybe.

My heart's still pounding like it's in a boxing ring.

"I have friends just down the street," I tell him, gesturing at the glowing neon sign for Chester Green's. I doubt my friends are there —it's not a game night—but I know the bartender and several regulars.

Plus, there's no way Doug would walk in there.

Everyone in Chester Green's knows who he is, even if Muffy apparently doesn't.

And after that, I definitely need a drink.

And *then* I'm going to kill Muffy.

Again.

FOURTEEN

Nick

IT'S NOT OFTEN that half the team descends on Chester Green's at once, but we're doing it in spectacular fashion tonight. We're taking up the entire back wall of the bar between the team, girlfriends, and wives. Zeus has claimed Frey's baby and is telling everyone that she gets her good looks from her mother's side of the family. You wouldn't think a baby would turn half a hockey team into sappy dorks, but we're all making funny faces at her and fighting over who makes her smile the biggest.

"I can't wait until you and Joey have babies," Gracie, Frey's wife and Zeus's sister-in-law, tells Zeus. "It'll be good for your ego."

She grins while she says it, and everyone laughs.

Everyone except Ares, who's shaking his head like *nothing* will ever cure Zeus of his ego.

We're on our second round of drinks when the door flings open and a familiar brunette hustles inside, head bent over her phone. She pauses just long enough to talk to the hostess and point to the bar, then ducks her head again and charges for an open seat.

I track her movements, sliding a glance at Felicity, who's whispering and laughing with Gracie.

Felicity's back's to the door.

Kami hasn't spotted us.

So unless the two of them are texting—which isn't likely, seeing as Felicity's not making any move to grab her phone—then I'm the only one who realizes we're all in the same building.

And I don't like that Kami's all dressed up, or that she's frowning, or that she just threw back a shot.

I stand up so fast my chair tips and clatters, which makes everyone look at me.

"Gotta piss," I announce.

Felicity rolls her eyes.

Zeus stands. "Yeah, me too," he says.

My lips part and my eyes bulge, because we don't go to the fucking bathroom together like a flock of women.

The entire table busts up into laughter, and he lowers himself carefully back into the seat, still holding the baby. "Just shitting you, Murphy. Should see the look on your face."

Fucker's going *down*.

But everyone goes back to talking, and nobody pays any attention to me walking off toward the john. Or any attention to me switching paths and sliding onto the stool next to Kami.

"Don't tell me some fucker stood you up," I say.

She jumps, hand to her throat, and her eyes fly to me.

And then they go even wider than they already were.

She moves to hide her phone, but not before I get a quick look at her text messages. Every cell in my body freezes, and my muscles tense like I'm getting ready for a fight.

"Why the fuck are you texting someone about Felicity's ex-dick?"

"Mind your own business," she snaps.

She shoves her phone in her coat pocket and grimaces like she's in pain. When she pulls her hand out again, I realize her knuckles are red and swelling.

"Kami?" Fury is washing through me, because I don't know what happened, but *something* did. And whatever the fuck happened, I'm going to make sure it *never* happens again.

"Just a mistake," she mutters. "I handled it."

She flinches when I touch her hand, but she doesn't pull it back while I lift her knuckles for closer inspection.

"This is how you handled it?" I growl.

She tosses her hair back and straightens her shoulders. "Maybe."

I feel somebody watching me, so I glance back at the team table. Jaeger's staring. He pokes Lavoie, who looks at me too.

"Come here," I grunt, and before she can object, I'm pulling her into the back hall. I stop outside the women's restroom.

"I handled it, Nick," she repeats, but she's cradling her injured hand, and I'm seeing red.

"Where is he?" I demand.

"Probably nursing his ego and getting his nose realigned. It was a blind date, okay? Neither one of us knew, we both agreed it was a mistake, and *I handled it.*"

"Did your cousin set that up?"

"My dating life is *none of your business.*"

"The fuck it isn't."

There's nothing sweet in her brown eyes now. It's all lightning and suppressed fury. "Do you want kids, Nick? I want three. And I want a little house in the country where I can have chickens and goats and *cows* if I want to, and I want to go to PTA meetings and soccer games and buy matching outfits for our annual Christmas picture. And I want to fall into bed every night with a man who worships me, not someone who settled for me because I'm convenient. And that man, Nick Murphy, is *not* you."

I've never wanted to settle down in my life, but there's no fucking way I'm letting Kami go. I can't explain it. Not to her. Not to myself.

But I *want* her.

I grab her at the waist before I realize I've moved, and I capture her mouth with mine. I'm devouring her lips, gripping her ass in one hand, her hair in the other, tasting the tequila still lingering on her tongue. She whimpers, but she's kissing me back and gripping my shirt like she'll drown if she doesn't.

Kissing Kami is like having an ice cream sundae for dessert. Like watching the sun rise in paradise. Like holding the cup after winning the championship.

Glory. Beauty. Perfection.

Her skin is silky soft. Her tongue so eager. Those little moans and gasps when I rake my fingers over her ass utterly enthralling.

The idea that she might've let someone else kiss her like this tonight is enough to make my blood boil.

The idea that it was Felicity's stalking asshole ex makes something else entirely hammer through my chest.

But Kami's safe.

She's with me.

She's—"*Oof.*"

The sucker punch to the gut takes me by surprise.

But it's nothing compared to the disgust curling her lip as she backs away, rubbing her hand again. "Do. Not. Kiss. Me."

"I—" I stammer.

But I stop.

Because her chin is wobbling, her eyes are going shiny, and the disgust is giving way to pain.

Something sears my chest and leaves a hollow ache behind as she turns on her heel and marches back down the hallway. I trail after her in a daze, and even watching her march up to Ares, tap him on the shoulder, and whisper something doesn't immediately snap me out of it.

Ares leaps to his feet. Felicity whips her head around until she finds me, her eyes going first round, then narrowing into such narrow slits that half the guys at the table squirm.

I'm pretty much a dead man.

And I don't care.

FIFTEEN

Kami

I TURN onto my street a while later, my veins still buzzing and the taste of Nick still lingering on my lips.

Why does he have to be such a good kisser? And so overprotective? And so—so—so *Nick*?

He didn't kiss me because he loves me. Or because he *ever* sees me being the love of his life, or because he wants to settle down and have babies with me.

He kissed me because it's always gotten him what he wants.

And that's me.

Hiding in a hallway where no one else can see.

His dirty little secret.

I pull to the curb in front of my house and realize Maren and Alina aren't the only ones waiting for me.

"This cow eat my vines!" Mr. Varga, my neighbor on the other side, is pointing angrily at Sugarbear, who Maren is holding on her leash, when I step out of my car. "Ten years! Growing ten years, gone in hour by cow!"

"I'm so sorry," I sputter out. "She's just a puppy. She didn't know any better."

Maren and Alina share a look under the street lamp.

"I'll pay for the damage," I add. I have no idea how much it's going to cost me or how I'm going to pay for it, but I will.

"Pruning is good for grape vines," Maren tells Mr. Varga. "It promotes new, fresh growth. We'll give you some of the dog's poop to fertilize them, and you'll have the best grape crop of the century next summer. Organic fertilizer. Can't beat it."

"And it eat my trellees!" he shrieks.

"Art," Alina declares. "I have a photographer friend. She'll do a photoshoot of your trellis with the co—dog, and we'll get you in *Virginia Vineyards*. You subscribe, right?"

"She just pooped," Maren whispers to me while Alina works her charm on my irate neighbor. "Maybe we should take her inside for a little bit?"

I take the leash with a resigned nod. "Sugarbear, want a treat?" I ask.

She barks.

Mr. Varga scowls at me, because her bark still sounds like a moo, and I take the puppy into my house, fully aware that he's probably ten seconds from calling animal control.

Alina joins us a few minutes later with Muffy in tow.

"I talked him down," Alina tells me. "But you probably need to find a better place for her. Like yesterday."

"I have an idea!" Muffy announces.

"I'm not talking to you," I inform her from my recliner, where all three of my dogs have piled on top of me, though Tiger keeps dashing over to lick Sugarbear's face on the couch before coming back to lick me on the face too. My phone's plugged in next to me.

It's a sign I have a problem that I have phone chargers in every room of my house.

Muffy holds her hands up. "He registered as Douglas Dobermeister, not Doug Dobey. I swear I didn't know. Also, do you happen to have any lawyer friends? He's threatening to sue me for false advertising or something."

"Ares will take care of it," Felicity says, poking her head into my house too. "Holy shit, that's a cow on your couch."

Muffy glances back at Felicity. "How many more of your exboyfriends do I need to avoid? I'll need a list," Muffy says to her.

"Forget it. I'm done," I tell them all. "I'm going online and hitting all the dating apps."

Alina, Maren, and Felicity all seem relieved, but Muffy's face falls, and my guilt ratchets up to new highs to battle with the utter fury I'm feeling toward Nick tonight. Dixie licks my sore hand, and Tiger bolts to climb all over Sugarbear on the couch again.

"You know the odds of me accidentally setting you up with any more of your friends' former stalkers is approximately 483,000 to one," Muffy says quickly. "Even lower if you widen the geographic area around Copper Valley to include the farthest suburbs."

"The odds are much higher than that," Maren argues. "You can't use the whole male population in Copper Valley, because they're not all looking for love, and they're not all your clients."

"I'm just saying, even if I did a random sampling of men who *aren't* my clients, the odds are seriously stacked against this happening again."

While they argue math, Alina carries in a full wine glass and hands it to me before settling on the floor and rubbing Pancake's ears.

And that's when Maren turns to me and says the last thing I ever expected Maren to say. "There's a speed dating event at Wreck'n'Roll next Tuesday."

"Speed dating? So the pain is over sooner?"

"I'll go with you."

I tilt my head at her.

Her deep blue eyes don't blink back.

"I thought you were too busy to date," I say slowly.

She shrugs. "Sometimes you have to scratch an itch. And sometimes you realize you don't want to wake up in your forties after putting so much into building a career that you forget to build a life."

She *is* the oldest of our group, so I shouldn't be surprised. "You think we can find our someones at a game bar?"

"No, but it's a good start."

"Kami. Give me one more chance." Muffy gives me the puppy dog eyes, the ones that say *you know I'm trying, and I can't move out from living with my mother until my business gets more successful, and you have to throw back a lot of worms before you catch the shark,* which is an odd thing for her to say, except it's Muffy, so it kind of makes sense.

"The odds are against us," I tell Muffy. "Even at speed dating, we'd probably come away more disappointed than excited."

"That's ridiculous," Alina informs me. "I'm no math genius, but you've barely started looking. Plus, you're smart, you're pretty, and you're sweet. You're like the holy grail that all men are looking for."

Some of the adrenaline from the wine bar rolls back onto the shore, with a few extra surf crashes added from the residual fury I'm feeling toward Nick. "I don't *want* to be wanted for being smart, pretty, and sweet. That's so…so…*generic*. And it sets expectations really high that I'll stay smart, pretty, and sweet. I don't *feel* sweet. I don't want to be *sweet*. Sweet is passive and gets stepped all over because sweet never fights back. And one day I'll have crow's feet and liver spots. Which means all that will be left is *smart*, which we all know is code for *boring*, because who wants to sit around and listen to Aunt Kami talk about how she made *smart* decisions all through her twenties and thirties and that's why she's alone with just her sixteen dogs and her four cats, two parakeets, and a token sloth?"

"Oh, can I have a sloth too?" Alina asks. "They're stupidly cute. Did you see the stuffed ones at—never mind."

"There's also the not-normal factor working against us," Maren points out.

"Did you just say we're not normal?" Muffy asks.

Sugarbear moos—I mean, barks like she, too, is offended.

"No, I'm saying we have a skewed version of *normal*," Maren replies, quite politely, because I think we'd all agree that Muffy isn't normal, though I've always loved her for marching to the beat of her own kazoo. "We're so far from normal, we wouldn't know normal if it knocked on the door and informed us it was normal."

I open my mouth to argue, except I started my week by finding a home for a calf that was put in a professional hockey player's condo, and I just punched one of my best friend's ex-boyfriends for calling me a bitch and insulting my cousin on a blind date.

"That's crazy," Muffy says. "You four are all totally normal." She shoots a glance at Felicity, the ventriloquist married to a giant of a silent hockey player, and adds, "Okay, most of you are normal."

"How many women do you know who have half of a profes-sional hockey team in their contact list?" Alina asks, clearly agreeing with Maren's assessment.

Muffy opens her mouth, peers at the four of us, then closes it with a frown.

"Exactly," Alina says with a sigh. "That's *not normal*. And Maren's two degrees of separation from Beck Ryder."

"Former boy banders who are now underwear models don't really count, do they?" Maren wrinkles her nose.

"Boy bands totally count," Muffy says eagerly.

Maren rolls her eyes. "*Everyone* on the entire planet is at *most* six degrees of separation from some kind of celebrity. But I'll give you that we talk to more men with six-packs and swollen bank accounts in any given week than most women do in a lifetime."

"I see tons of normal men at work," I say.

"Would you date any of them?"

"It's really not right to date patients."

"Your patients are animals," Alina points out. "I don't think it's unethical for you to date doggy daddies. You're making excuses."

I sink lower in my seat, disrupting all three of my dogs, because she's right.

Brown-haired, green-eyed hockey goaltenders are my biggest weakness, and they're in short supply. Which means if I'm serious about finding a future, I need to get out there and look more.

Dixie climbs out of the pile to lick my face while Tiger dashes for another round of playing with the sleepy cow-puppy.

"Do you think hypnosis would help me get over him?" I ask.

"I think speed dating will help you take the first few steps," Maren replies. "Plus, we get to do it over Skee-Ball. Even if the dudes are duds, we get to have some fun."

"All right. Speed dating it is."

Felicity gives me a funny look but stays silent.

Actually, she's been really silent for most of the time since she walked in the door.

"Are you firing me?" Muffy asks.

"Yes," my three friends chorus together.

Now I'm wincing. I'll text her later and tell her she has one last chance, but I want to know his full name and see a picture before I agree to it this time.

"The Badgers are playing the Blades tonight," Alina announces. "Who's up for watching?"

All of us are, naturally.

We're a little crazy like that.

Not that I should be watching hockey right now. But at least it's better than thinking about the growing problem with Sugarbear.

And the growing problem with Nick.

Felicity settles on the other side of my recliner. "I might have an idea for Sugarbear. But I don't know if I like it."

I look at the cow-puppy, who's drifting off to sleep on my sofa with Tiger sprawled across her snout. "Will she be safe?"

"Definitely. And it's not permanent, and you can still see her. Let me look into it tomorrow, okay?"

"Thank you," I whisper.

I don't add *for everything*, because it's Felicity.

She knows.

SIXTEEN

Kami

TUESDAY MORNING, after a covert early morning walk for all four of my dogs, I get to the clinic just as a flower delivery truck is pulling out of the parking lot behind the building. I'm trying to remember if I've forgotten anyone's birthday when my mom meets me at the back door, cup of coffee in hand and eyebrows even higher today than they were yesterday.

"Oh, shit," I mutter. "What now?"

"I don't know who your mystery man is, but when I was your age, I wouldn't have been rolling my eyes over thirty bouquets of roses. Actually, when I was your age, I didn't know anyone with the money to send thirty bouquets of roses."

I'm cringing before I walk into the break room, where, sure enough, vases overflowing with pink roses are covering every vertical surface. There are still three teddy bears left that we weren't able to find homes for yesterday, and now I'm wondering if there's symbolism in the pink.

It's not red, so it's not *love*.

Not that I'm operating under any delusions that Nick loves me.

He just can't do anything small.

Including apologize.

But he also didn't drop to his knees last night and offer to marry me and give me babies and worship me every day for the rest of his life.

No, he did the *Nick* thing and distracted me with what he *can* offer—physical pleasure.

I sigh.

Maybe I'm being too hard on him.

But I'm not asking him to change. I'm just asking him to let me go so I can find someone who can give me what he can't.

Mom's watching me over her *World's Greatest Vet* mug.

"Why do I feel like the bad guy when all I want is someone to love me?" I ask the room of roses, because it hurts too much to look at my mom when I ask it.

Dad adores her. He's an astrophysicist—yes, my brother followed in his footsteps—and he thinks she hung the moon, that there's nothing she can't do. She's the only person in the world he'll put aside articles on groundbreaking discoveries in astrophysics for.

"This isn't love?" she asks gently, gesturing to the pink roses in the crystal vases.

"This is guilt."

"So...these aren't from any of your dates that Muffy found you?"

And now I'm cringing harder. My hand is a little bruised, but nothing so bad that I can't do my job today.

I'm spared answering and explaining all about Nick by my phone ringing. I pull it out and check the display.

It's a local number I don't recognize, and I actually have enough battery to get through a conversation without having to plug in to Mom's charger in the corner, so I swipe to answer and head for my locker to put my coat and purse away. "Hello?"

"Ms. Oakley?"

"Yes?"

"This is Officer Badcock with Copper Valley Animal Control. I need to ask you a few questions, please."

Oh, shit.

Oh, *fuck*.

I give Mom the *I gotta run* gesture and take off for the parking lot.

Fifteen minutes later, I'm pulling up at my house just behind an animal control van. Mr. Varga is looking on from his front window. Mrs. Ostermeijer is peering out too, and I have no idea how many neighbors across the street are watching.

I text Felicity quickly before I get out, asking if she's looked into that temporary solution for Sugarbear yet.

The animal control officer climbs out of his truck, and I hop out of my car too.

The next thing I know, I'm blabbing my entire life story to him.

At least the part starting with finding Sugarbear in Nick's apartment—hell yes, I'm name-dropping—and improvising the part about being the Thrusters' official vet and ending with the part about how she's such a good cow, I refuse to let her be made into ground beef.

Once I get past talking about the donkey, and the ducks, and the pygmy goats, I can't tell if I'm losing him or if he's making a note to visit the Thrusters' management.

"The penguins?" he says on a sigh.

"I, erm, heard that was the last straw with the coaches," I offer. "There shouldn't be any more animal pranks."

With the press release they put out yesterday about the players volunteering once a week for the next four weeks at various pet shelters around the city, I'm almost positive this really is the end.

"I'll take her to work with me and find her a forever home by the end of the week," I promise Officer Badcock.

And that's how I end up with Sugarbear riding along in my Mazda, her head hanging out my back window, on my way back to work for the second time that morning.

Mom just shakes her head while I tie the cow puppy to the *Employees only* parking sign at the back of the lot near the only patch of grass we have.

My phone dings, and I glance down to see another text from Nick.

I'm sorry.

I ignore it—and the lump in my throat and the hot sting in my eyes—and shove my phone into my back pocket.

Nick never says he's sorry. Never.

"No chance of patching things up?" Mom asks while she scratches Sugarbear behind the ears.

"I just don't see us with a real future."

Not one where we both get what we want.

My phone dings again, and this time, I ignore it.

I'm sorry too.

I'm sorry that I can't see anything clearly when he's around. I'm sorry that I forget my own name when he kisses me. And mostly, I'm sorry that I ever thought he could feel the same way about me.

SEVENTEEN

Kami

BECAUSE FELICITY IS FREAKING MAGIC, she calls just before lunch with good news. She definitely has a place Sugarbear can stay for a week or two. After work, I load up my temporary puppy in the back of my car again—using Nick's Cherokee is out of the question so long as I'm trying to get over him—and head over to the Belmont district.

Felicity's gaping as I pull into the long drive of her parents' house with Sugarbear hanging her head out my back window.

"That cow really does look like a dog," she says, as if she doesn't have a pet monkey at her place. Yep, a real pet monkey. Long story.

"You saw her with my real dogs last night. Wouldn't surprise me if they taught her to play catch too," I tell her.

She cracks up, and the tightness in my chest loosens. "The neighbors will love that."

As for me, I'll love that the neighbors are all at least a quarter mile away, and that Mr. and Mrs. Murphy have enough land that they can legitimately raise a cow here.

She steps closer and rubs Sugarbear's cheeks. "You're such a sweet girl, aren't you?"

"Felicity! Honey, don't touch the cow. Not in your condition. You don't know what kind of germs it has."

"It's okay, Mrs. Murphy," I call to her mother, who's coming out the etched glass front door in a pink tracksuit. Probably on her way to or from the gym. "So long as she washes her hands good, she'll be okay."

"Go on, you heard her. Go wash your hands." Mrs. Murphy marches down the steps. "How old is this cow again? And how long does it need to be here? *Felicity*. Go wash your hands."

"She's carrying *Ares Berger's* baby," she mutters to herself in one of her puppet voices. "The cow germs don't stand a chance."

But she dutifully heads for the house.

Probably because we both know her mom won't stop until she's sure the baby isn't in any danger, even if the baby's father's genes are most likely as indestructible as he is.

Mrs. Murphy stops in front of the car and shakes her head. "A cow. What will they think of next?" She's smiling, though. I know that smile. It's the same smile Nick has. "It's so nice of you to be the team's vet, Kami. I'm so glad Felicity and Nick have friends like you."

Wow, that wasn't a fireball straight from a guilt monster at all. I smile weakly as I busy myself helping Sugarbear out of the car. "Where do you want her? I promise this is a short-term thing. Just until I can find a petting zoo or something that will take her."

According to Felicity, who cornered Zeus last week, the cow came from an auction somewhere outside the city. Apparently they knew I'd find her a home.

I hope every one of them gets sprayed by a cat with anal gland issues when they do their shelter volunteer days.

Kami will take care of it. She's so sweet. She won't let anything happen to these poor innocent animals we use. She's so dependable. She's so fucking boring.

Felicity joins us again as we get Sugarbear set up in the grass behind the pool, which is thankfully covered. "Do you have the yard treated?" I ask.

"With organic fertilizer."

I smile at her wry tone. "Your insistence?" I ask Felicity.

"No, Nick's," Mrs. Murphy answers. "Do you have dinner plans? We're having tacos, and we haven't seen you in forever."

Pew pew goes the guilt blaster. "You saw me just last week at my birthday party."

"But you were so busy, we didn't get to talk."

"Actually, I need to go get ready for a date," I lie, because Felicity was kind enough to let me know that Nick's living here while he looks for a new apartment, and I don't want to be around when he gets home from afternoon practice.

She pinches her lips together and frowns. "You don't date much, do you, honey?"

"*Mom*," Felicity hisses.

"What? I never hear about *any* of your friends having boyfriends."

"We're just waiting until we know they're good enough to bring them home to you, Mrs. Murphy," I tell her.

And then I realize what I've just said.

Your son wasn't good enough to bring home to you, Mrs. Murphy.

Felicity makes a strangled noise, green eyes dancing.

"I need to get home," I blurt. "My dogs…walks…potty time… hungry. I'll just get those grains out of my trunk. Felicity knows how much to feed her. I'll drop by again later to make sure Sugarbear's comfortable."

There's that lump in my throat again, but this time I know exactly what it is.

I'm going to miss my cow-puppy.

I turn and hustle back to the front of the house, with Felicity on my heels. "Kami. Whoa. Hey. Slow down."

"I didn't mean that," I whisper.

"*Stop*." She grabs my wrist, and because I don't want to trip my friend, I pause.

And that's when she tackles me with a huge Felicity hug. "I'm sorry my brother's a dickhead," she tells me. "I wouldn't bring him home to meet my mother either."

"He's not…" I swallow, because he *is* a dickhead. I've defended him for as long as I've known both of them, and I need to stop.

"He is," she assures me. "He has his good points too, but he's a total dickhead sometimes. He can't help himself."

"This is so messed up," I sigh. "I'm sorry. I made everything weird."

"No, you didn't. Actually—" She stops herself and shakes her head.

"What?" I ask, because that's the same look she was wearing yesterday at my house after the double disasters downtown.

"You deserve someone fabulous. And if I can do anything to help—"

"No!" I shake my head quickly, because my date with William the other night looked positively normal compared to some of the dates Felicity went on before she married Ares. "I mean, no, thank you."

She's cracking up again. "Yeah, I wouldn't take my help either."

"She's a *terrible* judge of male character," she says in her grumpy puppet voice.

"Utterly awful," her pragmatic goat voice replies.

"But we still love her!" her cheery cat voice chimes in. "And we're so glad Ares picked her and took her out of that awful dating pool. Full of dick sharks! All dick sharks!"

"You are such a nut," I tell her.

"And I'm exactly the kind of nut who's not going to let my brother get between me and one of my very best friends in the entire world."

I cannot stop cringing today.

"What?" she asks.

"Do you know—is he planning on sending me thirty of something *every day*?" I ask in a rushed whisper.

She frowns. "Thirty of what?"

"Teddy bears yesterday, bouquets of roses today…"

I trail off, because there's that pensive look *again*.

"I might've overreacted to him forgetting my birthday," I tell the driveway.

She doesn't say anything again, and I glance up at her once more. Her cheeks have gone a shade pale, and there are worry lines at the bridge of her nose.

My heart thumps hard against my ribs. Part of me wants to show her the text message.

The part where he apologized. She'll be just as surprised as I was.

But the other part of me knows that getting over Nick is the best thing I can do for all of us.

"Felicity, sweetheart, you're not touching that cow grain, are you?" Mrs. Murphy calls.

"You have to call me as soon as you get home and fake being stood up by your date so I have to leave, because that's literally the only thing that could get me out of dinner here tonight. If my mother gives me one more list of grandma-approved baby names, I might explode."

"She's just excited."

Felicity grins, and she doesn't have to say a word.

I know what she's thinking.

That's the Kami we all know and love. Always making excuses for people. Always finding the silver lining.

But I can't keep doing that with my love life.

I can't keep doing that with Nick.

"I'm getting the grains," I call to Mrs. Murphy.

"Does she have any dog toys?" Mrs. Murphy replies. "A pet needs toys."

Felicity's phone buzzes. She doesn't look down, but instead hustles me back to the car. "Practice is over. The boys are on the way. Let's get this done."

Two weeks ago, I would've made an excuse to linger.

But today, I rush through unloading my car.

Because she's right.

I don't want to be here when the boys arrive.

Nothing good can come of me seeing Nick again.

Nothing.

EIGHTEEN

Nick

I CAN'T STAND STILL Friday morning.

We're in Arizona for an away game before we hit the road for the Canada circuit half of the week, and everything's wrong.

Klein's starting tonight.

We lost Wednesday night. I can't stop a puck to save my life.

And I can't get the image of Kami's bruised knuckles out of my head.

Who's she with right now? What's she doing? Fuck, I should've called her cousin and warned her not to fucking *dare* set Kami up with any more losers. What's her name again? Misty? Megan? Georgina?

"Bro, you need to get laid," Jaeger says to me. "Take the edge off. Got a number last night. Don't mind sharing if you want it."

We're all hanging out in Frey's suite before practice this afternoon. Because of that whole *royal* thing, he travels with a bodyguard and gets upgraded.

Every time.

So every time, we invade his suite and play video games.

Except I'm not feeling like playing hockey on a PS4 today.

"Fuck the number," Zeus says without taking his eyes off the screen where he's skating circles around Jaeger. Seriously. They're playing the Thrusters in the game, and their little cartoon figures are

88 PIPPA GRANT

skating circles around each other. "I got a bucket full of charm. All I gotta do is lean out this window, and I'll get you a whole room of women."

Jaeger's shaking his head. "Your wife know you talk like that?"

"She knows it's the truth."

"So very odd, she actually agrees with him," Frey chimes in, looking up from his phone. Dude's clearly getting baby pictures, because he keeps grinning that dorky grin, which is even bigger than his normal grin. "It's astonishing."

"Fuck this," I mutter. "I'm hitting the weights."

I'm not starting tonight.

Might as well.

Lavoie and Ares follow me to the executive gym in the hotel.

"Have you talked to her?" Lavoie asks.

I ignore him and head for the treadmill, because the puny weight machine isn't going to cut it, especially if I want to be in peak shape by the time we face the Indies.

Not that I'll be starting at this rate. Fuck, I hope Klein's up for it. Their front line is killer.

Ares gets to the treadmill first and sits on it.

Lavoie hops on the other machine.

I grunt and head for the bike.

Ares grabs it and holds it in his lap on the treadmill.

Dude's a fucking *beast*. And he's pissing me off.

"You like her," he says.

"What'd you do to fuck it up?" Lavoie asks.

I'm almost certain Ares knows as much as Felicity does, which isn't the whole story, because I don't even know the whole story.

All I know is, she hasn't texted, she hasn't called, and she's been to my parents' house every fucking day this week to visit the cow.

Always when I would obviously not be there.

She hasn't acknowledged any of my apology gifts either.

This isn't like Kami. She's always overly polite. Sweeter than sweet tea. Nice to the point of pain.

Which means I've fucked up *bad*.

"She wants forever," I tell them both, because I don't know how else to explain this weird neverland I'm in with her. I want her. She wants me. But she doesn't want me. And she won't talk to me.

"So?" Lavoie says.

"I don't do forever."

They both stare at me, Ares still holding the bike while he sits on the treadmill.

"Would you get up and let me use that thing?"

"You like her," he replies. Again.

"Do you know anyone who doesn't like Kami?"

"You like her *more*," he corrects.

Lavoie drops his hands between his knees. "You ever had a slump before?"

"Slump? This isn't a fucking *slump*. It's just…" *Fuck.*

I'm in a damn slump.

"Happened to me after my divorce," Lavoie tells me. "Can't fight it if you don't face it."

I look at Ares. He's never had a slump in his life. Sat out half of last season with a sprained ankle, but he worked his ass off in PT to get back on the ice, and he was always there cheering the team on.

As much as Ares ever makes any noise.

"Love got Z too," he says.

I blink.

Right.

Zeus got traded from Nashville to New York a little over a year ago. In the middle of a slump.

Right about the time he met his wife.

He almost quit the league for her, but she wouldn't let him.

The idea of quitting the game makes me break out in a cold sweat. I've lived and breathed hockey since I strapped on my first pair of skates. I stepped in front of the net as goalie in a peewee league game at five, felt an immense *safety* that had been missing from my life, felt a power I was too young to understand but desperately needed, and I've never looked back.

Being on the ice, pads on, stick at the ready—this is what I do.

It's what I *am*.

The ice has always been my first love.

It fucking saved me.

I'm not ready to give it up.

I shove Lavoie. "Maybe I'm getting old."

"Growing ear hair and getting bunions already?" he deadpans.

"I'll still be blocking your shots when I've got ear hair and bunions. I just need to adapt a little."

"You need to admit what's really wrong and accept the fact that you're not in control when you're on the love boat."

"The love boat? What are we, an eighties hockey show?"

I'm not in love with Kami.

I just like hanging out with her.

Maybe she's right. Maybe I *do* owe her some space. Probably too late to cancel the singing telegram I ordered for her office today.

Shit.

"What's the last thing you think about every night before you fall asleep?" Lavoie asks me.

Fuck.

I think about Kami. About her smile. About the taste of her pussy. About the way she wrinkles her nose when she's picking mushrooms off her pizza.

"Popcorn," I lie.

I have a serious fucking problem.

"Call her," Lavoie says.

Ares growls.

Lavoie ignores him. "Bet if you talk to her, you'll play a hell of a lot better."

"That's bullshit." Fuck, if Kami's my good luck charm…if she's what's missing in my life…

My stomach dips, and I feel the hollow pain where it lands in my nuts.

I'm not ready for kids. I'm still basically a kid myself. I can't even handle a pet.

But I miss Kami. The Kami who smiled at me and didn't judge me for losing my temper with reporters or get mad when I was a dumbass pranking my teammates with animals.

Not the first seven times anyway.

She wants a farm.

For all the animals she's pulled out of all of our places the last few months, how didn't I know she wanted a farm?

Lavoie shakes his head and hops off the treadmill. "Call her, dumbass."

Not so sure that's a good idea.

I turn and head for the door. "Going to see Coach Ferrera," I tell him. If anyone will know a better way to get me out of this slump, it's the goaltender coach.

He's been around and seen it all.

He'll know this isn't about a woman, and he'll know how to fix it.

I hope.

NINETEEN

Kami

FOR ALL THE animals I've had to rescue thanks to the Thrusters, my second favorite is one I check on now and again. And Sunday afternoon, I'm hanging with him at Felicity and Ares's place.

"Have you been a good monkey lately?" I ask Loki, the capuchin monkey who adopted Ares shortly after he arrived in Copper Valley last year.

Loki screeches, leaps off the couch, and grabs a stuffed llama to rock it like a baby.

"Aww," Maren, Alina, and I all say together.

Felicity has her feet propped up in Ares's lap. She smiles at the monkey. "Loki, show them your new trick."

Loki flashes a toothy grin at all of us, then gives us all the middle finger.

"My uncle Zeus teaches me the best things!" Loki says.

Okay, Felicity says it, but she uses her monkey voice and doesn't move her lips.

"Where *is* Zeus?" Maren asks. "I thought he'd be hanging out with you guys."

"Joey flew up for the day."

All three of us collectively reply with a knowing *Oh*.

If Zeus's wife is in town, they're busy.

And I do mean *busy* in the *getting busy* sense.

I stifle a sigh.

I miss sex.

It hasn't even been two weeks since I cut Nick off, and I've never really missed sex after a break-up like this before, but he was *good*. I'd never had a double orgasm before. Or that thing he did against the wall the one night—

I shake my head and realize everyone's watching me.

Including Loki, who's also sneakily backing toward the cozy galley kitchen off the spacious living room. I glance down and rub at the soft leather on the couch, because I don't want to answer the questions.

"Tough road trip," I say into the silence.

Nobody answers.

Probably because it involves saying, *yeah, Nick's game is total shit this year*.

"Did Kami tell you about the thirty dog treat bags from that gourmet pet bakery downtown?" Alina asks Felicity.

"I'm more interested in hearing about this singing telegram she got at work on Friday," Maren interjects.

"How do you know about that?" I ask.

"Saw the pictures on your clinic's Facebook page." She grins. "And the note that the message was too risqué for a family vet to share publicly."

I wince, because there was definitely some mention of *pussy* in that song the dozen costumed singers delivered.

"Was that one guy really dressed up like a wiener dog wrapped in a bun?" she adds.

"Yes."

"And the kitty—"

"I don't want to talk about it."

"What else has he sent?" Felicity asks. She's going for casual interest, but there's something more than curiosity in her voice.

Ares hears it too, I'm certain, because he slides her one of those looks that I can't read, but that makes her squirm.

"Pizza for the entire office," I tell her, and I don't add *without mushrooms*, because she'd know what that meant, and I refuse to get my hopes up that Nick's finally paying attention.

I want to move on. I don't want to be on this up-and-down tilt-a-whirl that comes with wondering if he cares about me as much as I've always been obsessed with him.

And that's what it was.

An obsession.

I didn't really *know* him. Well, not until we started hooking up in February.

"Did he send thirty?" Maren asks.

"Naturally."

"I never knew he could use his powers for good," Alina muses. "This is fascinating."

"No, it's not. It's annoying. He's only doing it because he feels guilty."

Felicity opens her mouth, then closes it again.

"Murphy doesn't do guilt," Ares says.

I get chills, because that's one of the longer sentences he's ever said in our presence.

And he doesn't mean Nick doesn't feel guilty.

He means Nick's never felt guilty *before*.

"Maybe Kami has a magic pussy and he wants it back," Alina suggests.

Loki screeches and throws a dish rag at her.

"He doesn't like the p-word," Felicity stage-whispers. "Is anyone else starving? I could eat an entire bag of those chickpea puffs."

Loki leaps onto the counter, flings open a cabinet, and starts throwing spice jars all over the marble countertops.

Ares gives him a look, and he hangs his head and starts shoveling it back in.

"He's okay with your pregnancy?" I ask Felicity, because it's a legitimate concern.

Her brows crease. "Mostly." She lowers her voice. "I think he might need a special friend."

"He's getting to that age," I murmur back.

Loki turns big, suspicious monkey eyes on us.

"Can I borrow your monkey for one of my videos?" Alina asks. "He's fucking adorable."

My phone rings while Felicity laughs. "Sure. But you're only getting one take and you have to use whatever he does."

"Deal. Whoa, that's a face."

I rise and tilt my head toward the hallway. "Mind if I use your spare bedroom for a minute?"

"Yes," Felicity answers.

"Is that Nick?" Maren demands.

"Is that Muffy?" Alina asks.

"Sit," Ares orders me.

I sit while I swipe to answer, because if I don't, they'll all follow me back to the bedroom. And if I don't answer, they'll ambush me for my phone to figure out who was calling. "Hey, Muffy."

"I know it's last minute, but you can't say no, because I've really got it this time. He's *perfect*, Kami. He loves animals and he speaks French *and* he's very well-endowed."

"Wait. How do you know that?"

"Hang up," Maren hisses.

"You are *not* going on another Muff Matchers date," Alina agrees.

I have to dodge the monkey, who's been sent to sic my phone.

"And how did he come to hire you?" I add.

"He's my neighbor!"

While I process *that* information, I pause long enough that Loki manages to get on my shoulder and shriek right into the phone.

And my ear.

"Whoa, are you on a date you didn't tell me about?" Muffy demands.

I twist, trying to grab Loki while holding the phone, which means I'm basically dancing solo over the living room rug, or possibly playing charades single-handedly with no idea what I'm acting out. "No, I'm hanging with Felicity. Are you talking about the cute neighbor? The one with the black truck that he washes without his shirt on every Saturday through the summer?"

"*Yes!* And he needs a last-minute date to a wedding."

"A wedding?"

"Yeah. Like *right now*. You have to get changed *right fucking now*. Where are you? Are you downtown? I'll bring a dress."

"You're not going to a wedding on a first date," Felicity orders.

"Absolutely not," Alina agrees.

Loki screeches again, steals my phone, and dashes for the hallway.

I chase after him, shrieking, "Yes! I'll do it!" to Muffy, and "No! Not in the toilet!" to the monkey.

I'm suddenly three feet in the air, gripped by my arms, while Ares picks me up and sets me aside. He races into the bathroom—he's quick for a big guy—and rescues my phone at the last minute.

So there I am, standing in a bright, cheery bathroom with Ares, Loki, and Muffy still squeaking on my phone. "Stay right where you are! I'll be there in forty-five with everything you need!"

Ares pins me with a look. His reflection does too.

"What do you want?" he asks.

I gulp, because even though I know he's a big ol' teddy bear, he's almost a foot and a half taller than me and that's not his friendly face.

It's not his *I eat weak hockey players for breakfast* face either—I've seen that plenty on TV and the videoboard at Thrusters games—but it's not harmless.

"More," I tell him. "I want *more*."

He studies me another minute with bright blue eyes that are way more intelligent than most people would give him credit for.

"He misses you," he finally says.

I resist the urge to roll my eyes, and Ares gives me a small grin.

"But you should go," he finishes.

He hands me back my phone, picks Loki up and hands him a cookie—no, I don't know where he got a cookie, and since it's Ares, I'm not going to ask—and I back up so he can get out of the bathroom.

"On the date?" I ask.

"No what-ifs," he replies as he heads down the hallway back to join Felicity, Maren, and Alina. "Go."

Well, that's not confusing at all.

Nick misses me, but I should still go on this date.

I'd ask him what Felicity would think of his advice, except I think I know.

She'd say I should go too. I've met Muffy's neighbor. He's always been kind, he's attractive, and he's age-appropriate.

I dial her back quickly despite the warning signal my phone battery is flashing at me. "You mean your neighbor Josh, right?"

"The one and only."

"Great. I'm totally in."

TWENTY

Kami

MUFFY AND AUNT HILDA both show up to help me get ready. Maren and Alina are still strongly objecting, but quietly with just dirty looks after Ares tells them to knock it off.

And soon, I'm in a sleek black dress with my hair swept back in a simple knot and my makeup a tad on the overdone side.

"It's Josh's boss getting married," Muffy whispers to me as we stride through the lobby and toward the Lyft waiting outside. "I'd personally never do a Sunday night wedding, because people have to work on Mondays, but I guess that's when the bride's family could make it."

"You look so beautiful," Aunt Hilda gushes.

She said the same thing to Felicity, Maren, Alina, and Loki before she told Ares she used to be as big as he is, except without the height. He gave her a fist bump, and now she swears she's never washing her knuckles again.

"I know this is going to work out," Muffy tells me. "Josh is like the prime beef in my menu. With a side of golden potatoes roasted to perfection."

"I miss potatoes," Aunt Hilda sighs.

"And crème brûlée for dessert," Muffy adds. "I can't believe I lucked out in being there right when he needed a date. And I *never* thought he'd come to Muff Matchers, but he *did*. You're going to have the best time. Do you think it's too late to hook up a GoPro to your dress so I can live vicariously through you all night?"

I pin her with a look.

"Right, right. But at least record something with your phone. Even if it's smushed between you while you dance at the reception. Please? Pretty please?"

I pause. "Muffy...did *you* want to go with Josh tonight?"

Her face goes cherry and she shakes her head so hard her braids whip at her cheeks. "What? No. He's not into my type."

"Energetic and entrepreneurial?"

"She's too much woman for him to handle," Aunt Hilda interjects, gesturing to her boobs.

"*Mom.*"

"What? It's true. He goes for the smaller-chested women. And he's not creative enough to truly appreciate your art."

"You do art?" I ask Muffy.

"She means my matchmaking art. My client list is a little...different. It turns men off sometimes."

"And women," Aunt Hilda chimes in.

"If you like Josh—" I start.

"I like matching misfits better," she declares in her *this matter is closed* tone.

I don't ask if that means I'm a misfit, because the fact that I was hung up on Nick since high school and settled for a friends-with-benefits relationship with him instead of asking for more pretty much qualifies me for needing special help.

She shoves me into the Lyft, and she and Aunt Hilda wave as we pull away.

Ten minutes later, the driver drops me at the aquarium, and now I understand the Sunday night wedding. When you want to get married at the aquarium, you take what's available.

Josh is at the base of the marble steps leading up to the fountain outside the glass building, checking his phone. He's in a black tux, his sandy hair trimmed neatly, freshly shaven, and while he's no Nick Murphy, he's still a catch. I smile as I approach. "Josh? Hi."

He glances up and does a double-take. His hazel eyes make a quick scan up and down before settling on my face. "Wow. You look—hi."

He grins a lopsided smile, and my heart melts a little at the edges as he offers me his arm.

Maybe this is it.

Maybe this is finally exactly what I need.

"Shall we?" he says, his gaze still darting from my face to my dress.

"I'd love to."

There's something so different about being led up the steps of a public building with a man who's not trying to keep me a secret.

I like it.

Inside the aquarium, the staff directs us to the Deep Blue gallery. We walk through the glass tunnel beneath ocean wildlife, and emerge into the theater with the floor-to-ceiling window into the giant tank where everything from grouper to stingrays to sharks live.

It's a small wedding, no more than seventy-five people, and the groom immediately strolls over to greet us. "Josh, Caroline and I are so glad you could make it."

He's an older gentleman, maybe in his fifties, and as Josh shakes his boss's hand, his arm goes tense beneath my fingers.

"Wouldn't miss it, Bob," he says, though his tone is tighter than I expected.

I guess maybe Josh doesn't like his boss.

"This is Kami," he adds, extracting my hand from his elbow and wrapping an arm tightly around me.

Bob's graying brows lift as he surveys me. "Well. Hello there, Kami. I was…unaware that Josh was dating anyone."

"Seemed prudent to keep her under wraps," Josh replies with something heavy laced in his words and a smile that has more bite than I've ever seen on him.

Not that I've seen him often, but he's always smiling when I see him washing his truck with his golden retriever watching on.

Bob laughs nervously, and the bride—a woman closer to my age than Bob's age—rushes over in an ivory scoop-neck satin gown. There's nary a jiggle in her slender thighs under the tight material, and I don't think she's wearing Spanx to keep her stomach that flat.

"Josh. You made it." She kisses him on both cheeks, then turns to me and takes both of my hands in hers. There's something vaguely familiar about her high cheek bones, the thick blond hair, and the upturned nose. "Oh, my, aren't you precious. I'm so glad you could be here for Josh today. I know this has been hard on him, but when it's love, it's love."

She kisses both my cheeks too, then waves to someone behind us. "Oh, Aunt Marge! Excuse us. The seating chart is over by the door."

Bob hustles to keep up with Caroline, and I shoot Josh a curious look. "You know your boss's fiancée?"

"We dated once," he says briefly, and I suddenly realize *that's* why she's familiar.

She was at his house more than once when I stopped by to say hi to Muffy and Aunt Hilda over the summer.

"Once?" I press.

"Let's go figure out where we're sitting."

We've been relegated to one of the back tables, which is still an awesome view of the tank, because there's no *bad* view when the whales and eels and schools of every kind of ocean fish imaginable swim past the huge wall of windows. I take a seat beside a bird-like woman in black who already has three empty drink glasses in front of her.

"Get you something before they start?" Josh asks, dipping low so he can whisper directly in my ear.

"Ah, a glass of red, please."

He disappears after bestowing a heated smile on me, and the woman in black with the salt and pepper hair gives me a once-over before following Josh with her eyes. "Can't believe she gave up *that* for an old cheating geezer."

I snap my jaw shut when I realize I'm gaping. Because it sounded like—

The woman chuckles. "So you're the ringer." She slides glossy eyes over me. I'm starting to feel like a slab of steak in a meat counter. "The boy has taste, I'll give him that. Wait until you see my —*hiccup!*—date." She lowers her voice and leans in until I can smell the gin on her breath. "He's *twenty*. And I paid him to give me a lap dance halfway through the ceremony. Those college boys will do anything for a couple grand. Don't tell—*hic!*—Bob that that's where his alimony's going, mm-kay?"

So, it's going to be one of *those* weddings. "Your secret's safe with me," I tell her.

She winks. "I like you."

"I like you too."

Josh returns with an easier smile and two glasses of wine. "Mrs. Smith," he says to the woman.

She snorts. "Call me Sarah. Mrs. Smith is about to be that floozy. No offense."

He darts an uneasy glance at me, but I just give him an amused *I know what's going on* smile.

"None taken," he tells her.

Another man, this one tall, olive-skinned, with short dark hair and a suit that seems to be custom-fit, approaches the table and pulls a chair away from the black linen tablecloth. "Water for you, Sarah."

"Honey, say it in Spanish and use that accent," she says.

He obliges, his youthful face lighting up as she slips him a hundred-dollar bill.

Bob's watching, but I'm pretty sure he missed the money under the table.

"So, your ex is marrying your boss?" I murmur to Josh.

"Prefer to think of it as him saving me from making a big mistake." He's smiling, but his voice isn't.

Yep.

Definitely that kind of wedding.

"Don't suppose you want to make out?" he asks while Sarah's date—whom she's calling Enrique, but who is apparently actually named Sean—pulls her up for an impromptu slow-dance.

Without music.

Before the ceremony starts.

Actually— "Is this the whole wedding, or just the reception?" I ask.

"The whole fucking wedding," he replies on a sigh.

I scope out the rest of the wedding guests and decide Bob and Caroline aren't so much popular as they are generous, because nobody seems to be interested in much more than staring at the fish and whispering to each other.

"Just how broken-hearted are you?" I ask.

"Why?" Josh wants to know.

"If we have another date, will it be about us, or about them?"

His eyes dart to the side.

And weirdly, I'm not so disappointed.

Or maybe not weirdly.

"I just broke up with Nick Murphy," I tell him, because why the hell not? Josh and I clearly aren't going to be each other's soul mates. We might as well be honest friends.

His eyes go round. "The hockey player?"

"Yep."

"Holy shit. And now you get *this*? That's a serious demotion in the dating world."

"Nick Murphy who's having a shit season?" Sean asks, suddenly stopping. "Is he having a shit season because you broke up with him? Dude. You gotta get back together. He's my *boy*. And we gotta win that back-to-back championship. I already bet next year's tuition on it."

"When did you break up with him?" Sarah demands. "Was it before or after that horrible game in New York?"

"We weren't actually *dating*," I say quickly.

"It was before!" Sarah shrieks.

Sean shakes his head at me. "I don't care what you want to call it, you need to give that man more love. We need him stopping pucks."

"He really is having a shitty season," Josh says.

"Dearly beloved, we're about to begin," a man calls at the front of the room. "If you could take your seats, please?"

"How long were you dating?" Sean whispers around Sarah, who's also watching me with eyes *way* more alert than they were a minute ago.

"We weren't—eight months," I whisper, because I'm not interested in explaining the entire situation.

"You got him through the championship!" Sarah shrieks.

"I—"

"Wait. Wasn't that when the whole team was sent to charm school?" Josh asks.

"You know about charm school?"

He nods, all the tension gone. "Yeah. I read that blog—you know, the *This Chick Loves Hockey* blog?"

I gasp. "That's my friend Maren's blog."

"Whoa, you know Maren? She's fucking *hot*," Sean says.

The minister clears his throat, but it's hard to see his glare with him backlit by the lights coming through the ocean water.

"Could you introduce us?" Josh whispers.

"You get your booty on your own time," Sarah hisses. "We need to get Murphy back to the top of his game. Now, why did you break up with him?"

"The wedding's about to start," I whisper.

"Fuck them, cheating bastards," Sean says. "What did he do? He didn't cheat on you, did he? I'll put him through the fucking wall if he did."

"He forgot my birthday, okay?"

Both men stare at me like I've sprouted a unicorn horn, but Sarah nods. "Good for you, honey. Good for you. Bob forgot every one of my birthdays for thirty years, and now look where we're at."

"We're talking about the Thrusters winning," Josh reminds her.

"You can't ask a woman to screw a guy just so a sports team will win," Sarah shoots back. "What's in it for her?"

"Uh, diamonds?" Sean says. "Unless he's cheating. Is he cheating?"

"I don't think so," I sputter.

"Is he at least smart enough to realize you're his good luck charm and he wants you back?"

I pause.

To the best of my knowledge, Nick has *never* apologized to *anyone* voluntarily.

And in addition to the teddy bears, roses, singing telegram, pizza, and dog biscuits, I've gotten thirty sets of tickets to Thrusters games —including a few at *other* arenas, and those came with hotel vouchers and plane tickets—and when I switched on the radio the other day on my drive into work, the DJ kept announcing that every song that morning was dedicated to Kami, from the dum-dum-head who forgot her birthday.

"Oh, he does want you back, doesn't he?" Sarah says.

Someone at the next table shushes her. Caroline is walking down the aisle, which is really just Caroline walking through the door from the tunnel.

"Did he send flowers?" Sean asks.

"And…then some," I reply.

"He knows he fucked up?" Sarah brightens. "Oh, honey, you have a chance. You really have a chance. Plus, you'd get *way* more in alimony than I am if it ever goes south."

"Would you all *be quiet*?" someone in front of us hisses.

Sarah flips him off. "Father of the bride," she murmurs to me. Louder, she replies, "If you didn't want us here, you shouldn't have invited us."

"Mom," a young woman in pink hisses three tables to our left.

Sarah shrugs. "Sorry, honey. You know your father's a dickweed."

"Getting what he deserves," Josh adds.

And three minutes later, we're all being shuffled out the door.

"You guys want to go get some drinks at Chester Green's?" Josh asks.

"And we'll steal Kami's phone and call Murphy to see what it'll take to get his game back on," Sean agrees.

I shake my head. The last time I was at Chester Green's didn't end so well, and I don't care that the team's supposed to be boarding a flight to Canada this evening and Nick definitely won't be there, because other people there still know me.

And *everyone* there will be interested if they hear this insane theory that me dumping Nick is why he's having a bad season.

He's a professional. He's not thinking about me on the ice. He never did.

Whatever's going on with him, it has nothing to do with me.

I fake a swoon and sway into Josh. "Oh, wow, I think there was something in that wine," I say. "I'm suddenly not feeling so good."

All three of them stare at me.

Crap.

I'm going to have to puke.

I'm going to have to make myself puke, right here, outside the aquarium, before they'll believe I don't feel good.

Or maybe I could just fake a faint.

It might hurt, but it'll get me out of going to Chester Green's.

"Or it might've been that dog I ate earlier," I improvise.

"You mean hot dog?" Sarah asks.

"No, dog-dog."

Suddenly all three of them are leaping back.

"You ate a *dog*?" Josh says.

"It might've been monkey."

They all take one more step back.

"You brought a chick who likes to eat *animals* to the aquarium?" Sean hisses at Josh. "We're lucky we got out of there without her diving in that tank and taking a bite out of the stingrays."

"Stingrays are delicious," I confirm.

I'm most definitely going to be sick, because I'm disgusting myself now.

But they're far enough away that I feel comfortable pulling my phone out and ordering a Lyft, which is all the battery power I have left. "I'm going home," I say. "Nice to meet you all."

And before they can argue, I dash off.

Could this date have been worse?

Yep.

But it could've been better too.

A whole fuck-ton better.

TWENTY-ONE

Nick

IT'S BEEN over a week since I started my apology campaign, and I've gotten *nothing*.

My text messages to Kami still show as unread. She hasn't called. Felicity hasn't passed any messages.

Neither has Ares, but I know he saw her, because he told me so. *Saw Kami.*

That was it. No mention of how she was doing. If she asked about me. Where they were.

If she was alone, or if she had any other dates.

Zeus improvised a story when he realized I was too curious, but I didn't believe the thing about her getting caught having sex in the zebra enclosure, because she told me once that the only zookeepers she's friends with are female, and she wouldn't have sex at the zoo anyway because it would be mean to the animals to introduce unsanitary conditions into their living environment.

Pretty sure she was trying to dissuade me from taking advantage of her behind the gorilla enclosure because she didn't want to get caught having sex in public, but then, I don't want to screw around where goats or chickens have been screwing either, so I didn't question it.

We're getting dressed for our game in Calgary. Klein's starting again. I'm just sitting the bench in case he gets winded or hurt.

I don't play every game—coaches don't think it's good, and while it might seem like we're the laziest motherfuckers on the ice because we don't go anywhere, we take the most hits and sweat the most under all those pads—but I don't sit out as many as I have this season so far either.

I stare at my phone before I tuck it into the locker, but on second thought, I pull it back out.

What the fuck could it hurt?

The phone's ringing before I remember we're two hours behind Virginia because of time zones. She should be getting ready for bed.

But it's already ringing.

She'll just let it go to voicemail if she doesn't want to answer. She's stubborn enough to ignore my texts, she's probably stubborn enough to ignore my calls too.

But to my utter surprise, there's her voice. "Hello?"

"Kami! Kami. You're—you answered."

Lavoie catches my eye, then drops his gaze like he's not listening.

Ares isn't as polite. He watches me while he stretches.

"Hi, Nick," she says warily. There's noise in the background. People. Bowling balls? Definitely buzzers and bells.

"Are you out on a date?" I blurt before I remember I'm a fucking hockey player who doesn't get tongue-tied and insecure over my sister's friend being on a date.

Oh, fuck it.

My heart's about to pound out of my chest, because if she's out on a date, she might be meeting the man of her dreams right now.

Fucker probably couldn't find her clit with a map and a flashlight, but if that's what she wants, *fine*.

That's her business.

"I'm out," she says slowly. "Did you need something?"

"On a date?" I press.

Swear to god, I hear her roll her eyes. "Not at the moment, no."

Fuck, *this* is what relief feels like. I'm jelly-kneed and wobbly-thighed. I sink down on the bench in front of my locker and stare at Calgary's logo on the carpet. "I just—just wanted to see how you're doing," I say.

"Aren't you supposed to be playing a game right now?" she asks, and the concern in her voice is a life raft.

She still cares.

"Yeah. I mean, no. In a few minutes. Not yet. Klein's starting. I'm —" I'm stuttering and stammering like I'm a freshman in high school asking the head senior cheerleader if she wants to come watch a cartoon movie with me and my family. "Your cousin Judy still setting you up on dates?"

"You mean Muffy?" she says dryly.

Muffy. I knew it was something funny. I grab my wallet and look for a piece of paper to scribble the name on. "Just making sure you're paying attention."

"You are utterly ridiculous."

There's a smile in her voice. I can hear it, and knowing I put it there lifts a weight I didn't realize I was carrying.

Muffy.

I'm googling her as soon as I hang up.

"I like to think the ridiculous is part of my charm," I tell her.

"You really need to stop with the gifts. It's not necessary."

"Bet nobody else you've dated would've thought of today's."

"That's because normal people don't buy thirty Heifers for Humanity in another person's name. Or ask for all thirty of the gift goats that they give with the heifers to go to the honoree. I have enough stuffed animals for a goat orgy."

I'm grinning now, because that was fucking brilliance.

Maybe not the part where people in third world countries will be eating Sugarbear's cousins, but the part where I got cows into her apology gifts.

"It's too much, Nick. Please. I get it—you're sorry. You don't have to keep sending presents."

I've never had a real girlfriend, but I've dated casually plenty, and there's one thing I've never found in another woman—the desire for me to *not* spend my cash on her.

How can I *not* like Kami?

She's just good people. Selfless and shit.

"Maybe I just want to send my friend birthday presents. Maybe it's not all about an apology."

"Nick…"

"I can't send people farm animals anymore. I have to channel my creative energy *somewhere.*"

Lavoie snorts. Frey outright laughs. Zeus is smirking.

Only Ares shakes his head like we're all three bananas short of a fruitcake.

There's a shriek on her end of the phone, and then a roar of people cheering. "Where are you?" I ask.

"Whoa, dude. If I can't have phone sex in the dressing room, neither can you," Zeus says.

"Wrap it up, Murphy." Coach walks in and scowls at me.

"Gotta go," I tell Kami. "I'll call you later."

"Nick—" she starts, but Lavoie snags my phone and ends the call for me.

Or maybe in spite of me. Because I didn't want to hang up.

I wanted her to tell me she was having a miserable time and answered because she wished I was with her.

I wanted her to ask me to call again soon instead of me just telling her I would.

I wanted to her *want* me.

"Oh, fuck," I gasp.

Lavoie rolls his eyes. Frey grins. So does Zeus.

Ares, though, pins me with a *yeah, you idiot, and you've got your work cut out for you, don't you?* look.

Because they know. And they're right.

I'm in love with Kami.

TWENTY-TWO

Kami

THE PHONE GOES DEAD, and after checking to make sure it was Nick hanging up and not my battery—nope, I have twenty-three percent left, so it was definitely a hang-up—I pocket it while Maren gives me the *you are in so much trouble* glare.

"It was game time. If he's calling at game time, something might've been really wrong." I turn back to my Skee-Ball game and toss a ball up the wooden lane.

And totally miss even the biggest ring.

"Was something wrong?" Maren asks.

"Just the fact that he'd call me right before the game."

There's a huge shout, and we both glance over at the table of men at Wreck'n'Roll who are still arguing over the greatest football players of all time. Maren and I agreed before we got here that we'd pretend to be football fans tonight, because it seemed safer than getting dragged into another Thrusters conversation like at the wedding Sunday night.

But we sold it a little too well, especially Maren with the trash-talking, and now all the men we were supposed to be speed dating are bonding over beers and yardage statistics.

"Maybe we should become domestic partners and both head to sperm banks," Maren says.

"Will you buy me a farm in the country and let me have pygmy goats?"

"Can I install solar panels and wind turbines and a satellite wifi receiver?"

"Of course."

"Done."

We finish up our game, sneak around the guy who wanted to show us pictures of his ceramic clown collection—hello, childhood nightmares—and head for the door.

"If Nick pulled his head out of his ass and realized he loves you, would you take him back?" Maren asks nonchalantly, as though she's not inspiring that stupid hope that pokes its head up like a baby bunny out of a fluffy blanket in spring.

"Why would you say that?"

She eyes me.

I eye her back, but harder, which means I'm totally going to win, because none of my friends can stand it when I'm not sweet and congenial.

She totally breaks first and looks away while we troop into the parking garage. "It's just—he doesn't apologize. Ever. To anyone. And he keeps sending you presents. And calling. And putting in *effort*. Nick doesn't do effort. And if this season is any indication, he's about done with hockey. Because it would be too much work to get better."

"That's not fair. He works hard."

"Doing the bare minimum. He's getting old for a goalie. He can't skate by on natural talent anymore."

"Hockey is his life. He's not going to fade into obscurity because he's getting older."

I'm not arguing because I think she's wrong. Not exactly, I mean.

It's more that if I start to consider that Nick *could* be approaching retirement, and if he's realizing it too, he'll need something in his life to fill the void.

And maybe that'll mean he's finally ready to settle down.

But if I let myself think there's hope, then I'll quit looking for someone else. I'll put my own dreams of a family on hold, and he'll stay in the league another five or six years, and I'll be approaching forty before we have any babies.

I know it's not trendy or modern city woman-ish or whatever to want babies, but it's biological to want to belong, to want family, and

I refuse to apologize for wanting something beyond my career. And my pets. And my friends.

And now I feel guilty for wanting more when I actually have a really good life.

Maren shakes her head. "This would be so much easier if there were some legitimately interesting men in this dating pool."

"You don't know anyone at work?" I ask her.

"Nope."

I mentally run through my patient list. Just because *I* don't want to date someone who brings their pets to the clinic doesn't mean I couldn't set Maren up.

But the only person coming to mind is a client with a particularly testy cat, and Maren's allergic.

A red sports car screeches to a halt next to Maren's Bolt. The driver rolls down his window, whistles, and then flicks his tongue at us.

"Dude, you've got broccoli stuck in your teeth," Maren says.

His eyes go wide and he flings himself back in the car to check himself out in the mirror.

She passes her Bolt and heads down the aisle, possibly on her way to pretending like the jacked-up truck is hers, but more likely, just hoping the dick will get bored before we head back inside.

Felicity dated enough weirdos before Ares that we all got a little paranoid about even letting guys know what kind of car we drive.

Luckily, this guy actually *does* have something stuck in his teeth, so he speeds off before we're more than two cars past Maren's.

"I'm getting more serious about that domestic partners thing," she tells me.

I squeeze her hand. "So long as you don't sing in the shower."

We both laugh, but I'm not feeling all that light-hearted.

The sad truth is, I miss Nick.

And hearing the hesitation in his voice tonight—I think he misses me too.

But how do you find forever with a guy who doesn't even know it's an option?

We climb into Maren's car, and she starts the electric engine. "You going to the game Friday night?" she asks me.

"I...kinda have really great tickets," I admit. "You want them?"

She studies me with a wry smile. "How many tickets?"

"Four."

I have *thirty* sets of four tickets to Thrusters games. All courtesy of Nick.

All practically front-row.

He had to have paid a fortune to resellers to get them. It would be absolutely shitty of me to *not* make sure they got used.

"How great?" Maren asks.

"Close enough to smell their blood in a fight."

She studies me for a minute before she turns her attention to backing out of the parking spot. "I have not-so-great tickets. What say you give yours to Muffy and your Aunt Hilda and those two guys you met at the wedding the other night, and we hang out in the nosebleed section?"

I contemplate the conversation between Muffy, Aunt Hilda, Josh, and Sean, and then I contemplate Nick watching it all, since the seats he got are practically extensions of the Thrusters' bench, and I crack up. "I love you," I tell Maren.

She smiles. "May we someday find men who love us as much as we love each other."

"Are you sure that's not aiming a little too high?"

"Have you seen the way Ares looks at Felicity?"

I sag in my seat, because yeah, I have.

And I've seen the way she looks at him.

And even if Nick *does* miss me, I can't see him ever falling so desperately in love with me that he ever thinks of me before hockey.

"Maybe we're looking too hard," I say quietly.

"Or maybe we're not looking hard enough."

Or maybe we're just not the kind of women who inspire men to fall that hard.

Maybe I *should* settle for being number two in Nick's life.

It's not like I'm going to get a better offer.

TWENTY-THREE

Nick

LOSING SUCKS.

Losing a home game on a Friday night after losing a game on the road Thursday night sucks worse.

The worst part, though?

It's my fucking fault again. We were up by one with four minutes left on the clock tonight. Want to guess what happened?

I happened.

I fucking happened.

"Shake it off, Murphy," Zeus says as we head out of the dressing room after the reporters have finally cleared out. "Shit happens. We'll get 'em next time."

Says the guy who did everything short of blocking the shots for me. Dude's sporting a busted cheek and probably a few bruises in places he won't talk about.

"Yeah," I grunt.

Ares claps me on the shoulder. He's in a purple T-shirt with a cartoon dinosaur trying to grab its own tail with its short little front legs, and a message that says to *Always Tail Your Keep Up*.

Dude has the weirdest wardrobe, but Felicity digs it, so whatever.

"Let it go," he tells me.

On cue, the entire offensive line bursts into that song that gets stuck in my head for days on end.

When you can't beat 'em, join 'em, so I sing along louder than all the rest until Coach pops his head out into the hall and threatens to institute mandatory cartoon princess movie night once a week if we don't find better music.

Dude's pretty relaxed most of the time, but his daughters' taste in movies gets on his nerves sometimes.

We all split as we hit the parking garage, but Lavoie catches up with me before I get to my Jeep. "Grab a drink?" he asks.

No, I don't want to grab a drink. I want to go home, to my condo, and text a friend who'll read my mood and suggest a movie and then randomly whisper *your feet are prettier than daisies in a garbage disposal* because she has this hilariously twisted sense of humor that catches you totally off-guard just when you need a distraction from yourself.

But I don't have a fucking *friend* tonight, because she's ignoring my texts and calls again, and she wasn't sitting in the seats I got her, but her cousin and her aunt were.

Nor do I have a home, unless you count my parents' basement as *home*. And I haven't had any luck in getting any leads on new apartments downtown either.

My real estate agent tells me I've been blacklisted. It's going to take a fucking attorney to get me a place downtown.

"Yeah," I say. "Let's get a drink."

Jaeger, Klein, Sokolov, and The Bear catch up to us, and we book two Lyfts to get the four blocks to Chester Green's.

We could walk, but it's not always safe on game night.

Win *or* lose.

The first thing I see when I walk into Chester Green's is Kami. She's bent over laughing at something, her brown sugar hair tied up in a messy bun, simple diamonds sparkling in her ears, a Thrusters jersey swallowing her slender shoulders. She's sitting between her cousin and Maren at the round gold couch in the back corner. Two guys are smushed into either end, all vying for her attention with blatant lust in their eyes.

I swear the one in the Thrusty shirt is drooling.

My chest clenches like it's a gong taking a bruising from a hammer.

The cousin. Muffy.

I need to pay her a visit.

Find out what it'll cost me to get her to set me up on a date with Kami.

Lavoie grabs me by the back of the shirt and hauls me down the bar to where a half-dozen bunnies are already making room for us. We wade into the crowd, and the six of us are suddenly separated by a sea of perfume and jerseys so small, they'd fit better on toddlers than on full-figured women.

"Hey, honey." A bottle blonde with a plunging V-neck pushes her boobs to my bicep. "Tough break tonight. You'll get 'em next time. I'm Anni with an I. Want me to make it all better?"

"I'll help too," a redhead says in a throaty voice on my other side, also now under boob attack, though so is her Thrusters' shirt, which looks like it might pop under the strain of being too small to contain her knockers. "I'm Jami with an I and a heart for a dot."

"I have a heart too." Anni winks. "Two, but you can only see one if we go somewhere private."

"Buy me a drink?" Jami bats her lashes at me. "I *really* like sex on the beach."

Kami's giggle carries through the room, and I look across the wooden bar to watch her in the mirror. She and Maren are whispering together. Reminds me of last New Year's Eve, when we all got together at Mom and Dad's place for Cards Against Humanity.

Some of the words out of her mouth that night—just because *I* use them doesn't mean I expect to hear *Kami* say them.

Kami.

With an I.

And she's *all* heart.

Fuck, such a sweet heart.

But other than a fuck-ton of gifts she doesn't even seem to want, what the hell do I have to offer her? I don't know the first thing about being a boyfriend, much less a husband and father. And I'm about to bring my home team down in flames.

"If you're not interested in a drink, do you want some financial advice?"

My fingers have somehow become entangled with Jami's—or is it Anni's?—and they're both leaning so close we could be sharing clothes.

"I just finished my CPA degree this spring," Jami—definitely Jami, the redhead—tells me. "I come with the body *and* the brains."

"And I'm a nurse." Anni grabs my ass. "I know all about taking care of booboos. And that puck you took to the shoulder looked like it hurt."

My skin suddenly prickles like it's raining feathers, and I glance in the mirror again.

Kami's smile is gone.

Three of the dudes with her are pointing our way. Superfans. Which should be awesome, except tonight, it's not.

"Not even a little bit of a grin?" Anni asks.

"Oh, honey." Jami sighs. "It's one game. We're gonna help get you all fixed up."

My gaze flits back to the two women. Jami's flagging down the bartender. When he doesn't immediately reply, she stretches, pushing her ample bosom out until it could serve as a shelf for about six whisky bottles.

"Yes, ma'am?" the bartender calls.

"We need a Jameson for Nickie-poo." She blows him a kiss, and he grabs a bottle from under the shelf, shaking his head with a grin.

"You wanna talk about it, sweetie?" Anni asks.

"I—no."

The familiar ripple goes through the bar—the one that says *everyone* knows we're here—and I take quick stock of my teammates. Klein and Jaeger are entertaining six women with beers and war stories, their backs to the bar. Sokolov and The Bear have their own fan club on my other side, both of them head and shoulders taller than everyone around them.

Lavoie's leaning by the dartboard, talking to three women, with a clear view of the room.

"We heard rumors you were seeing someone." Jami strokes a hand down my chest. "Guess you're single now, hm?"

"Nice to see you out again," Anni adds. "I learned a new trick with my tongue since the last time we talked. Wanna see?"

"Sex helps the body heal," Jami agrees.

"Lots of sex helps it heal faster," Anni adds.

"Unless you pull a nut or something."

"That's really not possible."

"Nickie-poo, did you pull a nut? We can help rub your nuts."

Maren's talking to the dudes, and Kami's gathering her things. Muffy gives me one of those older sister-slash-overbearing-cousin looks that would scare the shit out of me if I wasn't a hundred times better at being an overprotective big brother than basically anyone on the planet.

"He definitely pulled a nut."

"You want me to take a look and see if I can lick it all better, baby?"

"I'm a good nut-licker too. Just because I'm not a nurse doesn't mean I don't have experience."

The dickopotamuses and doucheasauruses aren't letting Kami and Maren out. Muffy either on the other side of the round couch table, and with those guns, she looks like she could take them, but she's not using them to her advantage.

I can't hear whatever the twatnuggets are saying back to the women, but I don't have to.

I know the look.

Seen it enough on Felicity's ex-boyfriends' faces.

No, baby, you don't want to leave yet.

Stay, sweet cheeks. I'm gonna buy you another drink.

You know you want to come back to my place with me.

I'm crossing the floor before my brain remembers I'm supposed to be reformed from charm school.

And before my teammates realize I've moved.

Because if they saw me, there's no fucking way they'd be letting me out of arm's reach.

"Whoa, whoa, you're Nick Murphy," the head dickopotamus says.

"Oh, fuck," Maren says.

Too late.

I'm pulling the first dude out of the booth. "Did the lady ask you to move?" I growl in his face. He smells like cheese fries and piña colada, and his nose hairs are three months past needing a trim.

"Murphy!" Lavoie barks from across the bar.

I point to the second guy. "Move. *Now.* Before you learn what happens when you talk to my girlfriend."

"And here we go," Maren sighs.

The other guy's not moving, so I grab him too. "What do we do when ladies ask us to move?"

"We were moving!" the first guy says.

I'm in real danger of actually getting my nuts dislocated, and my body's sore and tired after a long game, and my biceps are straining, but I don't put either down.

"Are we *ever* going to have to have this discussion again?" I growl.

"We didn't know she was your girlfriend, swear we didn't."

"I didn't touch her, man. I'd never touch your girlfriend."

"Put them down, Murphy," Lavoie orders.

"Nick, please," Kami says quietly.

It doesn't matter that everyone around us is shouting and barking and pushing. She talks, and I can hear her.

Doesn't mean I want to listen.

But the truth is, she's trained me. *Felicity can handle herself. How many times have you hit a guy for her, only to have it happen again? This. Doesn't. Work.*

You need a better method.

Next time you get mad, think of Loki hitting the asshole who's pissing you off. Imagine that fuckshit getting taken down by a twelve-pound monkey. And then just smile.

I'd always smiled. Partly because Kami said *fuckshit*, and partly because yeah, the image of Ares's emotional support monkey sticking his fingers up some fucker's nose and then biting his nuts off *was* a damn good image.

"Nick," she repeats.

My arms are shaking, and not just because I don't usually lift four hundred pounds at a time.

Not after a game anyway.

I give both men a strained shake and put them down, and that's when I realize Kami's looking at me.

Not looking at me like she used to, like she's happy to see me.

No, there's a ghost between us now.

And there are stress lines in her forehead.

I'm fucking this up.

Dammit. I'm fucking it all up.

"Kami—"

Lavoie, Jaeger, and The Bear shove between me and the four guys who were sitting with the ladies, offering autographs and tickets and apologizing for me.

I'm not fucking apologizing.

Not to the dicknuggets, anyway.

"Sorry," I mutter to Kami.

I hate saying *sorry*.

But it's all I seem to be able to say around her lately.

Ever since I missed her birthday.

She's not wrong.

I should've remembered. I shouldn't have to make it up to her by sending her thirty presents a day for thirty days.

She saved me from missing my mom's birthday. She helped me pick out Felicity's wedding present. And reminded me about Felicity's birthday.

She remembered *my* birthday.

Maren pushes between me and Kami. "You are *so* lucky Felicity's not here," she mutters.

Muffy gives me a stink eye too as she and Maren push Kami toward the door. "Your genome sequence is incomplete."

"Dude." Jaeger's head whips around and his jaw parts while he watches Muffy and her overalls and her twin braids walk away. "Who's that?"

I fumbled for half a second, processing that Kami's walking away, that she's serious, that she's *done* with me, before I find the *right* answer. "Felicity's friend's friend. She doesn't speak English."

"She just called you a Neanderthal," Jaeger says reverently. "In *nerd*."

I ignore him, because all I can see is Kami.

Looking back at me before Maren and Muffy hustle her out the door.

I don't know what that look means, but I know something else:

She's *the one*. And I've fucked it all up. Again.

TWENTY-FOUR

Kami

THE LOOK on Nick's face haunts me all night.

I've never seen him so lost. Or so intense. Not off the ice anyway. Even when he's doing something that he *knows* is a bad idea, he barrels in without hesitation, without question, without doubt.

But last night, his green eyes seemed to be asking me for everything I've ever wanted, but I don't know if I can trust myself, because maybe I'm just seeing what I want to see.

Or maybe, he's finally seeing *me*.

But does seeing mean *wanting*? And if he wants me, does he want me because he cares about me and wants me to be happy, or does he want me because of everything I did for him?

It's a complicated question without an easy answer.

But it's an answer I need nonetheless.

I pack my dogs up and leave Dixie and Pancake with my parents' aging Dalmatian lab mix, Isaac Woofton, and head the few blocks over to the nicer neighborhood where the Murphys live.

The roads are foggy, and I don't call first—partly because I'm trying to conserve the battery in my phone—but I've been dropping by daily to check on Sugarbear anyway. Mr. and Mrs. Murphy won't mind.

It's Nick who might have something to say.

At least, I *hope* he has something to say.

Because I'm not entirely certain what I want to say, even when I get to the end of the long driveway to the brick mini-mansion.

Tiger grins at me from inside my purse. She's completely in favor of visiting Nick. It's like she knows where those gourmet dog bones came from. They might be almost as big as she is, but that doesn't stop her from enjoying the hell out of them.

I step out of the car, pulling Tiger and my purse with me. She licks my hand, but happily settles inside the giant bag because she loves the rocking motion of being carried.

Crazy dog.

I love her to pieces.

We walk around the pristine landscaping, following the curved walk to the backyard in the thick fog. I don't expect anyone to be up, and certainly not to entertain me. Once I check on Sugarbear, I'll call Nick and ask him to meet me back here. I know he's still staying in the basement, because Felicity let it slip the other night that he can't find a new apartment downtown.

I like the fog this morning.

It's giving me a sense of privacy, even here in the Murphys' yard, to let me have just a few more minutes to gather my thoughts before I call Nick.

I turn the corner, straight into the path of a charging three-hundred-plus-pound cow.

A charging cow who materializes out of the fog and who could toss me into the air and take me for a joyride that would undoubtedly end with every bone in my body in crumbles.

"Aaaah!!" I dive, stumbling as I try to flatten myself against the house. Sugarbear's flank brushes my hip, and I throw my arms out. Hard, wet concrete rushes toward my face. Tiger yip-howls and tries to dive out of my purse. A sharp pain radiates from my hands to my shoulders, and my left knee hits a rock before my body jolts to a stop.

"Tiger," I gasp, rolling to cradle my shaking pup.

"Kami!"

The deep, panicked voice hits me straight in the heart, and a moment later, the familiar scent of dark chocolate and sandalwood soap fills my nose as heat envelops me.

"Are you okay? Where does it hurt? Can you turn your neck? Oh, shit. Hey, Tiger."

I'm scooped up in two strong arms before I realize the world's moving again.

"I'm okay," I say weakly. Tiger howls indignantly as I clench her with the arm that's not gripping Nick's neck. I need to check her out. Make sure she didn't break anything.

His hold tightens around me. "Fuck, I thought the cow was going to run you over." He buries his nose in my hair, and he slows as he approaches the patio table, like maybe he doesn't want to put me down.

My heart's racing, but it's not the terror of narrowly missing going for an unexpected joyride in the sky courtesy of a calf. The sting is already leaving my hands, and if it hurt to land on the sidewalk, I don't remember it now.

Because the thrill of being this close to Nick will always override anything else. Pain, frustration, worry—it all fades away.

I can't help myself. I've never been able to help myself.

He doesn't set me down, but instead holds me in his lap as *he* sits at the table. "Are you hurt? Did she step on your feet?" He's gingerly touching my arms and legs, prodding like he's feeling for swelling or breakage.

"I'm okay. Just startled."

Tiger barks, and I carefully check her over. Her whole body's vibrating, but she seems more eager to stretch toward Nick than she does to be upset over almost getting trampled by Sugarbear.

"We were playing fetch," Nick says.

Over his shoulder, I see Sugarbear trot through the fog and around the pool, kicking a giant blue yoga ball. She's grinning like she's proud of herself, and a surprised laugh huffs out of my lungs.

"You taught her to fetch?"

"Well...yeah. What else are you supposed to do with a dog?"

He grins. I laugh again, and *god*, this feels so *right*. His smile widens, his eyes going crinkly at the edges and some of his normal confidence coming back.

But not all of it.

"I've missed that laugh," he tells me quietly as he tucks a strand of hair back behind my ear.

"You're up early," I reply, because my hopes are floating on a cloud, and if I say the wrong thing, they'll tumble ten miles back to earth and splat into nothingness. *Did* he realize he lost something the last couple weeks?

He doesn't look at Maren or Alina like this.

And I've never seen him defend anyone but Felicity the way he defended me last night.

And then there was the whole *my girlfriend* thing last night.

You deserve better than a one-way relationship, I remind myself. Because I *have* to.

His brows bunch together while he studies me, and I realize I'm still sitting in his lap, and he's petting Tiger, who's in *my* lap.

"I'm an ass," he says slowly.

Sugarbear moos indignantly. Tiger howls her goofball balloon howl. And I do my best to keep my expression neutral, but the utter disgust and surprise on his face coupled with the unexpected confession is actually really damn funny.

"Says who?" I ask.

"C'mon, Kami. You know it's true."

"You're very…focused on what's important to you."

He's very focused on *me* at the moment. "Can I take you to dinner Tuesday night?"

There was a time when *Yes!!!* would've sprung off my tongue like the word had a life of its own, but I manage to suppress my easy side and watch him watching me.

He seems to be holding his breath. Hope and a plea implore me in his unguarded expression. Part of me wants to say yes just because I need him to be the overly confident one here, just like he always has been.

But something snapped that morning he called me with Sugarbear in his condo, and even being this close to him again can't turn me back into the girl who would do anything for a little bit of his attention.

"Why?" I finally ask.

He squeezes my thigh. My body still remembers what those fingers can do.

"I miss you." The husky tone in his voice sends a delicious shiver washing over my shoulders and spine. "I just—you get me. I want to get you. To know you. Not—fuck, Kami, I've never done this before."

"You've never told a girl you liked her before?" I whisper, and I can't mask the raw hope making my voice shake.

"No." He visibly swallows. "I've never…*dated* before."

My heart flutters harder, like a butterfly fighting a hurricane, and Tiger tries to leap up to lick Nick's face.

"How is that even possible?"

"I…I've more just hooked up. Not *dated*. I never wanted to. I always had…"

"Any girl you could ever want?" I supply for him.

He goes pink around his ears and glances down. "It's just been you. This year. I don't want—nobody else makes me—*please*, Kami? Dinner. Tuesday. And if I'm good, maybe you'll let me take you out again after that?"

Now it's not just my heart fluttering. There's a delicious tingle sparking to life between my thighs too. "When you say *good*…"

And *there's* that cocky, smoldery smile I love so much. "More good than I've ever been."

"*More good*?" Am I stroking his hair? Oh. Look at that. I think I am. "You mean better?"

He angles his head, and his nose brushes my cheek while his beard tickles the corner of my jaw. "You make me forget my right words."

I laugh, because *nothing* makes Nick lose his head. "You are such a flatterer."

"I mean it, Kami. I'm falling apart without you."

He brushes his lips over mine, a whisper of a touch, slow, like he wants to take his time memorizing the imprint of every bit of me.

"You got along fine without me for years," I whisper against those full, soft lips. My breasts are getting heavy, and that tingle between my thighs is turning into a full-on demand for attention after two weeks of neglect.

"Say yes to Tuesday."

His fingers dance up my thigh, and if he dipped his fingers anywhere near my clit, I'd probably combust.

"Yes," I whisper.

He makes a noise that's somewhere between desperation and relief, and the gentle, hesitant kiss becomes insistent and hard and demanding.

I wrap both arms around him and part my lips, and he doesn't wait for a second invitation to devour me. Tiger yelps, but it's a distant, tinny sound, behind the rough growls coming from Nick's throat. He fists my hair in his hands and angles deeper, his cock springing thick and hard against my leg.

If all he wanted was sex, there were *plenty* of options for him.

But he wants *me*.

Which makes this kiss ten times as heady as all of our previous kisses combined.

"Fuck, Kami, I missed this," he breathes. He trails kisses from the corner of my mouth to my jaw and down my neck, his hands releasing my hair to go exploring. "I missed *you*."

I can't answer, because I'm too busy gasping as he palms my

breast and squeezes. My head drops back and I close my eyes, because *ohmygod*, no one has ever lit my body and soul the way Nick does.

"I want you so bad," he breathes against my collarbone.

"*Yes*," I gasp.

Pancake nudges my arm, but I push her away while Tiger growls and tries to climb between me and Nick.

I start to laugh—a breathy, heady laugh that makes my clit throb harder—when Pancake nudges me again.

And I remember I don't have Pancake with me.

"Wha—" I start, but I'm interrupted by a giant sneeze.

A giant *cow* sneeze.

A giant, *productive* cow sneeze that slimes Nick, Tiger, and me together, and not with plain old slimy cow snot, but with thick, wet cow snot full of bits of grain and grass that's now dripping down the side of Nick's face and into his beard.

I start to wipe it off him, realize my face has much of the same, and Tiger's so coated that she looks like a Christmas jelly dog tree.

Or something.

Tiger howls indignantly.

Sugarbear sneezes again.

And all of us scatter.

Me flying off Nick's lap and grabbing Tiger. Nick darting around the cow's other side.

Sugarbear looks at all of us and sneezes again.

Then she licks her snout, moos, and harrumphs as she kicks the yoga ball.

Nick and I lock round eyes over the calf.

He starts to grin.

I crack up so hard Tiger yelps again.

And Mrs. Murphy sticks her head out the back door, which we can barely see through the fog. "Nick! What on *earth* are you doing to that poor girl?"

We both jump, me because I wonder if she saw us kissing, and Nick because—hell, who knows? His mom pretty much thinks he hung the moon, and he's always taken advantage of her adoration.

"It's okay, Mrs. Murphy," I call. "Sugarbear told him quite clearly that he needs to quit hitting on her."

His eyes go comically wide and his lips part like he didn't see that coming.

Like he didn't know I was capable of throwing him under the bus.

But Mrs. Murphy laughs, and the shock on Nick's face is making me giggle too. I don't *have* to stroke his ego. He has enough of it without my assistance.

But I'm not going to hold back the other parts of my personality around him anymore.

Not if this is going to be *real*.

A slow grin creeps over his features as though he's catching on.

And I realize I might be in trouble.

Because he *does* have a little more experience in one-upmanship than I do.

"Come in here and get a cup of coffee," she says. "Felicity and the crew will be here any minute."

"The crew?"

"Oh, yes. Thrusty's interviewing Nick and Sugarbear. After that video I took of the two of them playing fetch last night went viral on Snap-whatchamacallit, the Thrusters decided to move up the promo. And you can use my bathroom to wash up."

Nick comes around the cow and steals Tiger from me. "I'll get her," he offers. He lowers his voice and adds, "And you could join us both in the shower if you wanted."

My nipples offer a plea of *yes, please*, but my brain is dialing back into the conversation.

Do I want to have sex with Nick?

Yes.

But I want more than an offer of dinner before I strip for him again.

I want to know he's serious. That he's willing to give us an actual chance, and that we're not going to just slip back into the old patterns of hanging out *just* so we can have sex.

I want to know if he's in this for real, or if he's in this because I'm easy.

"We'll see how Tuesday goes first," I murmur back.

His eyes narrow, but not in suspicion.

No, I just accidentally challenged him.

"I mean—" I start with a stutter, but he's full-on grinning now.

"No take-backs," he replies, heading to the door with my dog. "And you won't regret it."

"She won't regret what, honey?" Mrs. Murphy asks.

He grins at his mom. "Being my girlfriend."

TWENTY-FIVE

Nick

PROBABLY WASN'T nice of me to leave Kami to my mother after dropping that bombshell, but if we're going to do this—if we're going to *date*—then it's probably not the worst thing I'll ever do to her.

Not that I'll be a dick on purpose.

It just happens.

When I get back upstairs after showering all the cow snot off both me and Tiger, who was a very agreeable shower companion and now smells like my shower gel, Kami's sipping something out of a mug while Felicity grills her at the table.

"You *swore* you were over him," my sister is whispering. She's worried—you can tell because she's leaning really close and gripping Kami's arm so hard, she's probably leaving a mark—and I have a moment of panic.

Because I don't want to hurt Kami.

And I *haven't* ever done this committed-relationship thing.

Kami doesn't blink, just shrugs a little. "Something feels different," she tells Felicity, and my heart starts beating again.

She's right.

Something *is* different.

"Tell me he didn't send you thirty of his bobbleheads for one of his daily presents," Felicity whispers. "Because if that's what's different—"

"Good idea, sis." I drop into the seat beside her still holding Tiger, so Kami's across the table from us. "Who wouldn't want thirty Nick Murphy bobbleheads?"

Kami smiles as she sips whatever's in her mug. Tea? I don't think she drinks coffee. Or maybe it's hot chocolate.

I need to find out.

"I'd take thirty Nick Murphy bobbleheads," Felicity says sweetly.

"Only because you'd make them say terrible things," Kami points out.

Ares stifles a laugh behind me. Dude's always sneaking up. Walks quiet for a big guy.

"Holy shit, where's your beard?" Felicity suddenly yelps.

I rub my chin, because yeah, it feels weird, and probably will for a few days. "It didn't survive the cowpocalypse."

"But—but—but it's your *lucky beard*."

"Not doing me a lot of good this season, is it?" I pass Tiger over to Kami, who I'm hoping will be a much better good luck charm. "Think I got her clean."

"She looks beautiful and snot-free. Thank you."

I don't like the surprise she's trying to mask in her eyes.

Like I'm not supposed to do little things for people.

"You washed a dog? In your shower? Voluntarily?" Felicity asks. Her hand goes to my forehead. "Are you sick? Do you have a fever?"

"Knock it off, smart ass."

"Have you *ever* bathed a dog in your life?" she presses.

"I used to give you baths."

Ares and Kami both eye me like they'd be willing to team up to make sure someone put powdered mango in my underwear every day for the rest of my life if I'm about to make a joke about Felicity doing *anything* bad in the bath when she was a kid, and I almost start itching just *thinking* about the last rash I got before I realized I was allergic.

"And it was such a pleasure to take care of you that I thought I'd try it again with Kami's dogs," I add quickly.

Tiger barks. Or something. It's like a cross between the sound of a fart and a semi horn, except smaller.

I realize Mom's missing, and I glance around.

"She's out back with the camera crew," Felicity tells me. "Which is exactly where we need to be if we're going to get your interview done before you guys have to leave for practice." She nudges Kami. "Want to watch?"

Kami slides me another look, my skin goes hot all over just from having her attention on me. "Do you have a voice for Sugarbear?" she asks Felicity.

"Of course."

"Does Sugarbear secretly think Nick's a total goober?"

"Hey!" I object.

Both women ignore me. "Only way to find out is to stick around," Felicity tells her.

"But can I sneak out before your mom realizes it's a good chance to grill me?"

"Ares has you covered."

Ares grunts in agreement.

"Then I'm in," Kami announces.

We all head out back, where the fog is slowly lifting. The Thrusters' camera crew is setting up in front of the table. I try to slip beside Kami, but Felicity blocks me and lowers her voice so low that it only registers because she's fucking terrifying.

"I swear to God, Nick, if you hurt her—"

"Good job, Nick," I interrupt in my own low voice. "Way to grow up and try to be a bigger person. It's about time."

"I'm not saying you don't have it in you," she hisses back. "I'm saying Kami's my sister. You're committing incest."

"Now you're being ridiculous."

"Fine. You're committing *friendcest*. And you better marry her and be ready for all the blood and gore of childbirth because if you're serious about her and this isn't just some test to see if she's your hockey good luck charm, then you're going to give her as many babies as she wants and change all the diapers and clean up the yard of all the dog poop because that's exactly the sort of thing people in committed relationships do. And if this *is* just a test to see if she's your good luck charm, I will *end* you."

A sliver of guilt jams itself under one of my fingernails, but it's on my left hand, and I can still play with the guilt sitting there, so I just stare my sister down.

I *do* think I'll play better with Kami not mad at me anymore.

I'm already feeling better about practice this morning, knowing she's having dinner with me Tuesday night.

But more, I'm really fucking selfishly glad I get to see that smile again. Even if she does keep hiding it behind her mug.

And it has nothing to do with hockey, and everything to do with just wanting to be near her.

Also, I'm pretty fucking certain I don't deserve this chance, but hell if I'm going to waste it.

I cut around Felicity and slip an arm around Kami's waist. "Hot chocolate?" I ask with a nod at her mug.

"Cow snot soup," she replies.

I recoil for half a beat before she cracks up at her own joke. "Oh, your face," she says on a giggle.

Sugarbear moos in amusement. Tiger tries to run in place, her feet dangling since Kami's holding her under the chest.

"Nice," I tell Kami. "You know the difference between me at the net and me here?"

"Careful," she warns me, her eyes going playful, that smile so bright it's doing more than the sun to melt off the fog. "You don't score unless I say you can."

"Well, fuck." She beat me to my own *I block the shots on the ice, but I score all the goals here.*

"Get over here, Romeo," Felicity calls in mock exasperation. "My bratwurst needs to mortify you."

"In a minute," I tell Felicity, but suddenly my pants are tight around the middle and I'm two feet higher in the air than I was a minute ago, feet dangling just like Tiger's.

"Now," Ares says from behind me, where he's lifted me by my waistband.

I shrug at Kami while I squirm in my pants.

Not the first time Ares has tried to give me a wedgie, and it won't be the last.

Mom's leading Sugarbear over on her leash. "Here you go, sweetheart," she says to me. She licks her thumb and rubs at a spot on my chin. "Oh, you cut yourself. Hold on."

"Mom—"

I try to duck her second attempt, but Ares grabs me by the shoulders and holds tight while my mother licks her other thumb and rubs my chin again.

"There. Now it won't show on camera."

"Wow, Murphy, your mom is hot," Thrusty the Bratwurst says, courtesy of my ventriloquist sister. "Think she'd lick my chin next?"

"Oh, hush," Mom tells Felicity, but she's blushing, and she tries to smooth her hair down. She skitters out of the way, lavender track pants swooshing.

"Come back, Mrs. Murphy," Thrusty calls. "We want to hear about how excited you are to be a grandma to a cow!"

"She's such a good grand*moo*," Felicity vents in a dopey cow voice.

I choke on a snicker and try to glare at her. "Really? That's your cow voice? Sugarbear sounds way more intelligent than that."

"Says the guy with the hairless face," she replies as Loki, her pet monkey, who adds an indignant shriek behind me.

Because the monkey's sitting on the cow's back, and they're both giving me twin looks of *who's the dumbass?*

"What happened to your beard, Murphy?" Thrusty asks before I can interject a single word, because that's how Felicity rolls.

She's fucking hilarious, and I know she's improvising every word out of her mouth.

"My cow sneezed and it fell off," I tell Thrusty.

"Weak-ass whiskers," Thrusty says.

"Strong-ass sneeze," I reply. "She would've blown you all the way to Kentucky."

Loki screeches like he's laughing, and Sugarbear moos.

"You think shaving's gonna improve your game?" Thrusty asks.

Felicity's not being mean. It's just what everyone wants to know.

"Nope, but I'll tell you what will."

The bratwurst leans in conspiratorially. "You got a plan, Murphy?"

"Fetch," I tell it.

"With the cow?"

"Sugarbear. And you know what she likes?"

Thrusty suddenly flies to Felicity's other side. "Bratwurst?" he says sarcastically.

I shrug. "I was going to say me, but sure. I'll bet she likes playing fetch with bratwurst too."

Kami's giggling, and fuck if the sight of her happy doesn't put a spring in my heart.

Is Lavoie right? Is this what love's like? Because I'd give my right nut to keep her smiling like this every day.

I look back at Felicity, and I see something I haven't ever seen before.

At least, not directed at me.

It's *happiness*.

Not that I don't make my sister happy—we snipe at each other, yeah, and I get why she doesn't want me dating one of her best friends—but this is a different kind of happy.

It's an *I'm happy for you* smile.

An *I'm happy for you* smile that disappears as fast as I caught it.

"If the cow likes you, she must not have any better options," Felicity quips as Thrusty.

"He's a package deal," Sugarbear replies. "I get Felicity too. She's *moooootiful*."

"Can we back up a minute?" Felicity says as herself. "Sugarbear, how did you end up moving—I mean, *mooooov*ing in with Nick?"

"She was a gift," I say quickly, because I know Felicity too well to let her answer that as herself, or as Thrusty, or as Sugarbear, and especially as Loki.

"Someone likes you that much?" Thrusty asks.

"They didn't know I have a thing for cows."

Felicity's eyes take on a spark, and *fuck*.

I'm going to be getting cow shit for *years*. Possibly actual cow shit. Which I'll still save for use against Zeus Berger just when he's starting to get comfortable.

"When you say you have a thing for cows…" Felicity says as Loki, who's now climbing onto my shoulder and picking at my hair.

"They're cute." If I'm going to dig a hole, might as well dig it deep. I rub Sugarbear's snout. "Who wouldn't love this sweet face?"

And I do like the cow. She's a really good substitute for a dog.

"You heard him, ladies. Nick Murphy likes cows." Thrusty grins at me, which is disconcerting regardless of the number of times I've done interviews with the puppet since Felicity started with the Thrusters last year, because a sausage with a rocket pack coming out its ass *should* be disconcerting. "The cuter the better. Think maybe you need a stuffed cow to fit inside your pads next time you start, Murphy?"

"Got a nice warm spot in my armpit just the right size for a bratwurst," I reply.

"You have issues, dude," Loki says.

I probably do.

But Kami's bent over with her face stuffed in the sleeve of her jacket, trying not to laugh, and I suddenly don't care if I get a thousand stuffed cows sent to me at the arena.

Kami likes me again.

I don't know where I'm taking her Tuesday night, but it'll damn sure be somewhere spectacular.

I'm not about to fuck this up again.

TWENTY-SIX

Kami

THERE'S nothing like a real first date to inspire yet *another* case of the butterflies.

Or possibly I mean a case of the hummingbirds, because those suckers can really beat the air, and they're vicious when they fight, and I'm pretty sure all those nerves in my stomach are dueling right now, because I might be close to throwing up.

It's not that I don't want to go on a real date with Nick.

It's more that I'm terrified we'll actually start dating, for real, and then one of us will spend the whole night sleeping over with the other, and he'll snore, or I'll talk in my sleep. Or we'll try to cook a meal together and he'll insist it's the man's job to grill and he'll end up burning everything and we'll order pizza instead and he'll forget about the mushrooms again. Or I'll ask if we can watch one of those new romantic comedies on Netflix, and he'll pretend he didn't hear me and put on some movie about hockey players who go to war in space, and then all the magic will be ruined and I'll realize I should've just gone along with Maren when she suggested we get sperm donors and make our own commune.

My phone dings, and I unplug it and grab it off my dresser while Dixie and Tiger race circles around me.

It's Muffy.

And the six texts that follow tell me she's made friends with my friends, and she's pulling them into this conversation.

Muffy: Kami, where's he taking you? Don't say to the zoo. That's so stereotypical for a guy to think a vet must want to go to the zoo. Unless he finagled a private tour so you get to pet the tigers.

Alina: Pretty sure there will be tiger petting going on tonight.

Muffy: Yeah, I want details on THAT too.

Maren: Oh, yuck.

Felicity: Why am I in this conversation?

Muffy: Because you can tell us what Nick's present today meant.

Felicity: What did he send now?

Muffy: I don't know, but I bet it was thirty of something REALLY good.

Kami: He sent thirty keys. I don't get it.

Muffy: Oh my god. He bought you thirty cars!

Kami: No, they look like house keys. Mostly. A few look like they go to padlocks.

Alina: You mean handcuffs?

Felicity: You know every time I think of my brother using handcuffs and petting...I can't even type it, my blood pressure goes up, and that's really bad for the baby.

Maren: Nice try, but your baby is half Berger. It'll be fine. Your cooch after birth though...

Muffy: How big was Ares when he was born?

Felicity: This is why there are drugs and vaginal reconstruction, but I'm sure everything will go back to normal just like it's supposed to. Except maybe with floppy boobs and a layer of belly fat I can't shake. Kami, I have no idea why Nick sent you keys, but feel free to rack him in the nuts if he tries anything that would make me demand brain bleach. He needs to woo the shit out of you. Woo. The shit. Out of you.

Alina: Uh, is this Felicity, or did Zeus get hold of your phone?

Felicity: Dammit. It's the Berger effect. I'm carrying Berger spawn, and he-she is infecting me with Zeus thoughts. I'M SUPPOSED TO BE HAVING ARES THOUGHTS. Ares thoughts would be so much nicer than Zeus thoughts. Whatever Nick's planning for vengeance against Zeus for that cow, he better triple it on my behalf.

Kami: I promise I will NOT tell him that tonight.

Maren: Thank you.

Alina: On behalf of all of Thruster Nation, I second that. Thank you.

Muffy: Does anyone else think it's funny that it's called Thruster Nation? No? Just me? My mom's giggling. She thinks it's funny.

Muffy: Oh my god. I'm turning into my mother.

Felicity: Kami, I sincerely hope my brother realizes how much he doesn't deserve you and how hard he's going to have to work to earn you, because you would make the best sister-in-law, and I'm not saying that just because you perfected vegan brownies last winter. Which sound delicious, by the way, and you can send a pan or three my way anytime you want to. Also, I know Nick can be an ass, but I honestly believe he could be a really good boyfriend if he put half as much effort into a woman as he puts into looking good.

Maren: This isn't getting any less weird.

Alina: I asked around at Chester Green's last night. There's not a single regular who can remember the last time Nick left the bar with a woman. I think he's already domesticated, he just doesn't know it yet.

Maren: So, basically, we're saying have fun, guard your heart, and remember that the commune is still an option if he sends you dick cookies.

Kami: Um, thanks. I think.

Muffy: Oh my god. I just looked in the mirror. I went to my mom's beautician, and OUR EYEBROWS ARE PLUCKED THE SAME NOW. I need to go lie down. Or possibly get a third job so I can afford to move out.

Kami: Third? What's your second job?

Muffy: I mean second job.

My doorbell rings, and I sign off the group text and silence my phone while I follow my dogs to the door. I just charged the stupid phone, and five minutes of texting took the battery down to seventy percent. I really need to get one of those portable battery packs.

Or a new phone.

Except do I really need a phone on a date?

Nope, I definitely do *not*.

Tiger's howling her adorable deflating-balloon howl. Pancake's *aroof!*-ing, and Dixie's wagging her back end off.

I smooth my hair back one last time before I swing the door open, and there's Nick.

In dark jeans and a wool coat with a maroon button-down peeking through. He's freshly-shaven again, though with a serious five-o'clock shadow going on, which I expected since he texted me a picture earlier today of him, Duncan Lavoie, and Tyler Jaeger in Thrusters T-shirts, all holding up kittens at a pet shelter.

I'd forgotten it was the first of their mandatory volunteer days today.

He smiles, his eyes lighting up and all of the hard angles of his rugged jaw and sharp cheekbones softening. "Hey," he says, just like he has every other time I've seen him the last eight months, but this *hey* is different.

It's softer. More thorough, if a *hey* can be thorough. Like he's saying *hi, thank you for giving me another chance, I hope I can talk you out of that sweater tonight,* and *wow, you look amazing* all at once.

Which is crazy, because it's just a *hey*.

"Hey," I reply, and I just stand there, in the doorway, gawking at him like a total nincompoop. He got a haircut. And—oh, he's wearing that aftershave I couldn't get enough of back before the season started when someone set off a cologne bomb in the dressing room.

I showed up at his apartment and the whole thing smelled like a metrosexual lumberjack, and I swear I spent two hours with my nose just buried in his neck, sniffing.

Apparently I have a thing for metrosexual lumberjacks.

Which explains why I'm still drinking in the sight of him in his custom-fit coat and the pants that hug his thighs. When I realize his fingers are twitching like he's facing down an opponent on a break-away, like he's nervous, the dragonflies buzzing around my stomach settle down.

He wouldn't be nervous if he didn't like me too.

Maybe this *will* work.

"Did you want to come in?" I ask.

He shakes his head. "I got us a table at—it's a surprise. Do the dogs need to go out?"

My heart's getting melty again, because that's one of those little questions I never thought he'd ask. A detail I always assumed he overlooked, like me not liking mushrooms. "They just came in. Let me grab my coat."

Two minutes later, we're hopping into his Cherokee, which smells like it's been freshly washed too. There's a hint of lemon in the air, and the leather seats are cushy and warm.

"How was the shelter?" I ask him as he pulls away from the curb.

He grins again. "Awesome. Those animals are so cool. I took home three cats, a dog, and a ferret."

"No," I gasp.

His grin turns to a smirk, and I bat at his arm. "Not funny, Murphy. Because we all know who'd be taking care of your pets."

"There was a kitten that followed me everywhere. Loud little cat. I couldn't tell if she was chewing me out or asking me to take her home."

"Probably both. You can't pick a cat. It has to pick you. And now she'll never be adopted since you didn't get her."

He darts a quick glance at me. "Seriously?"

I just smile.

Odds are relatively good the kitten's just social and will be adopted in no time, but it's fun to make Nick squirm.

"You have an evil side." The blatant admiration in his voice makes me laugh. "What other secrets are you hiding?" he asks.

"According to your sister, my cousin, and all of my friends, my secrets are things you have to earn."

We've barely gone three blocks, but he pulls the car over into the parking lot of my favorite breakfast diner and looks at me. "Why didn't you ever call me on my bullshit before?"

Answering that question makes me feel more naked than I ever did when I actually took my clothes off for him. "You know that feeling when you're on a winning streak, and you don't want to change anything, you don't want to shave, you don't want to need new laces on your skates, you don't even want to turn in a jersey that's getting beat up for a fresh one that looks so much better, because you don't want to mess with what's working?"

He nods, not breaking eye contact.

"That's how I felt about finally being close to you," I whisper.

"What changed?"

"Me." I lift my shoulders, because I don't know how else to explain it. "I always thought I'd have a family by the time I turned thirty. And then…"

I trail off, but he finishes the sentence. "And then I was a dick on your birthday."

"No, you were *you*. I just decided it was finally time I was *me*." I don't mention still wanting a family, because it's pretty early in the date to freak him out.

But he wouldn't have asked me out if he wasn't willing to consider some of my hopes and dreams…would he?

I ignore the little voice in the back of my head that sounds like all of my friends combined sighing, *It's Nick,* and instead, I smile at him. "So, are we going on a date to a parking lot?"

His smile returns, and he shuts off the engine. "Nope. We're going to breakfast."

"Here?"

"Here."

"Elmer's is…" I trail off, because Elmer's is usually closed by noon. They're breakfast-only, and it's six in the evening. Elmer's *should* be closed. But there are a few lights on, and two cars are parked at the back of the small lot.

He grins wider. "You like their waffles."

I'm speechless for half a second, and then I do the only thing that makes sense.

I launch myself across the center console at him. "That's so—so —*thank you.*"

His arms circle around my ribs. I kiss his cheek, and he turns so our lips meet, kissing me gently again, like he did Saturday morning, but I don't want gentle.

I want *Nick.*

His stomach rumbles loudly.

"Don't listen to it," he says, angling back for another kiss, his hand sliding down my back toward my ass. "It can wait."

My belly rumbles too, and we both crack up. Nick swats me on the butt. "All right, all right. Let's get going. If I don't feed *your* hungry tummy, I'll never hear the end of it."

"From who?"

"Felicity. She *knows* things."

"She didn't know about us for eight months."

His stomach grumbles again, and we once again dissolve in a fit of laughter.

"Okay, okay," I say. "If I *have* to eat waffles, I guess I have to eat waffles."

"That's the spirit."

He grins, and if we laugh this much through our entire date, then it's already shaping up to be the best date of my life.

TWENTY-SEVEN

Nick

I STILL DON'T KNOW shit about being a good boyfriend, but I know that rubbing my foot up and down Kami's leg while we devour waffles and bacon and she tells me stories about her family and her patients doesn't feel like a *date*.

It feels like hanging with one of my best friends.

And I like it.

"Do you ever feel like the dumb one in your family?" Kami asks as she pushes away a mostly-empty plate and sighs happily with her hands on her belly.

"No way. I have like, four entire hockey plays up here *all the time*." I tap my temple. "Bet you Felicity doesn't even understand one of them."

Kami shakes her head and laughs. "Sorry. Forgot I was talking to Ego Man."

"You feel dumb?" I ask. "You're a *doctor*."

"I have *one* doctorate to Atticus and Brynn's two *each*."

I don't know her brother or sister well, but I know one's some kind of astrophysicist who writes bestsellers and the other does something with DNA that's so over my head I don't even try. Neither one lives in Copper Valley now.

"You still have one up on your cousin," I point out.

"No making fun of Muffy. She started Muff Matchers after having a nervous breakdown in medical school."

"I'd have a nervous breakdown in medical school too."

"No, you wouldn't. You'd bluff your way through it and convince people the heart actually pumps urine to help the kidneys out when they're stressed."

I grin. "You really do know me well."

"No, you're just simple."

I laugh over my orange juice, and she slides *her* foot up *my* calf.

I'm hard in an instant. Raging, uncomfortably hard. So hard I can barely swallow the mouthful of juice I'm almost choking on.

She grins at me, and *fuck*, if I'd known she had this devious side, I would've just married her eight months ago.

Whoa.

Whoa.

I sputter out a cough and catch her ankle under the table. "Gonna have to wait," I tell her as I stroke the ball of her foot, since she slipped her shoe off. "We still have plans."

"If you're taking me to the zoo, we can skip it and head back to your place."

I scoff. "The zoo? Totally unoriginal. And we could head to *your* place."

"But I like hanging out with your parents."

Her eyes are sparkling, her cheeks flushed, and that smile—*god*, it's so radiant.

For a dumb old puckhead like me.

"C'mon," I say, rising to my feet and offering her a hand. "We don't want to be late."

"Is this what the keys were about?"

It totally is. "What? No. I just ran out of ideas. Tomorrow you're getting paperclips."

"Nick."

I wave to Elmer, who waves back from the kitchen. I paid him two days ago when I talked him into opening up just for us tonight.

"You need paperclips at the clinic, right? For paperwork and shit?"

"Not the size or quantity of paperclips you'd send if you were actually sending paperclips."

She might be right. I might be pretty simple to understand.

We leave the building and a blast of cool fall air swirls leaves around the parking lot. She shivers, and I take full advantage of the opportunity to wrap an arm around her shoulder. "You don't really feel dumb, do you?"

"No, but...I do feel less smart. I thought you might —never mind."

"What?" I press.

She sighs. "I always thought your ego was overcompensation for being the *dumb* one too. Not that you're dumb. Or unsuccessful. You're just...not Felicity-smart."

"Or talented," I agree. "I tried talking without moving my mouth once, and I strained my tongue."

"You did not."

She's hiding a smile as I unlock her door and boost her into the Cherokee. But instead of shutting the door, I lean down so we're at eye level.

"I didn't want to be smart," I tell her, and my heart gives a weird jolt, like it knows what's coming.

"Not even a little?" she teases lightly.

"Smart kids get bullied. I—" *Fuck.* I have to clear my throat, because even though it's been twenty-something years since it happened, it still feels like yesterday.

But if Kami needs to hear why I'm a shithead, then I'm going to tell her.

No matter how much I don't want to think about it.

She tilts her head, brows drawing together.

"I was little," I tell her. "For my age. It's part of why my mom's so...like she is. I was short and scrawny and I never gained enough weight for the doctors. And the other kids noticed."

"Did you get picked on?" she asks softly.

"Well...yeah." And shoved. And kicked. And mocked. Crazy the things the right first-grader will say to make you feel like shit. Especially when you're a little peewee and your dad's a huge fucking retired hockey player. "A little."

"Nick."

I roll my shoulders back. "Kids are mean. And my dad was fucking huge. Not just tall and built, but *known*, you know? So I asked to play hockey when I was four so I could learn to be huge too, even if I was little. So, no, Felicity being smart didn't bother me. Me being a pipsqueak bothered me. I wasn't gonna be a nerdy pipsqueak on top of it. Especially once I realized how much Felicity needed a tough older brother to protect her, no matter how big I wasn't. But *you*—" I squeeze her arm. "You're perfect. So quit thinking you're not. Okay?"

She doesn't answer right away. Instead, she studies me with serious dark eyes until she asks, "Is it true you don't practice hard?"

The cocky grin is automatic. "Says who?"

"You want the whole list? Keep in mind, I have half your team-mates programmed into my phone."

"I…could probably practice harder," I concede.

That earns me a raised brow.

She's fucking adorable when she's grilling me. "Ask my mom sometime how awful I was the first couple years I played."

"Your mom would *never* say you did anything wrong."

Probably true. "She has awful embarrassing pictures though."

"Your mother thinks you're practically perfect."

Also probably true. "She used to take me to the skating rink for two to three hours a day to practice. Not because she made me. Because I wanted to."

Her brows knit together. "You'd practice three hours *a day*? In *grade school*?"

"Yeah." I shrug, playing with her hand, because I'm getting a little warm in the cheeks. "I was fast. I had a stick. And then I had all the goaltender pads. It was my safe place."

"Oh," she says softly.

"So, yeah, it probably looks like I'm slacking off a lot," I admit. "But when you do it right the first time, you don't have to spend hours doing it again."

"You have muscle memory."

"Not quite good enough this year though." I brush her cheek and pull back. "Time to go. Can't be late."

Because she's Kami, she doesn't push it. But she does start asking questions when we pull up to the warehouse in Copper Valley's revitalized downtown thirty minutes later. "Is this a haunted house? I swear to God, Nick, I might be an animal doctor, but I still know how to use a scalpel on your testicles if you even *think* of tricking me into going to a haunted house."

"You don't like haunted houses?"

"No."

"That sudden chainsaw sound doesn't rev your engines?"

"Don't make me use your middle name."

Fuck, that's a legitimate threat. "It's nothing any scarier than being alone with me for an hour," I promise her with a brow wiggle.

We head inside, and she goes from suspicious to amused. "Are you serious? The keys make total sense now."

"I picked the zoo theme," I tell her on our way to the check-in desk.

And then I crack up at the scowl she gives me.

"Okay, okay, I didn't pick the zoo-themed room. But you're gonna love what I did pick."

We get to the check-in desk, and the dark-haired woman behind the desk gives me a once-over.

And not the *good* kind of once-over.

Nope, this woman's wearing the frown of pretty much every Thrusters fan I've met this season. "Murphy…Murphy…Murphy…" she murmurs as she scrolls through the computer. "Oh, right. There you are. You can join your group over there."

She points to a ragtag bunch in overalls sitting on benches lining the opposite wall in the lobby. Their scowls don't entirely mesh with the black tile floor and gray walls covered with huge posters of the various escape room themes.

"No, I had a private reservation," I tell her.

"We're going to need to search you for contraband animals," she adds.

Kami turns around and coughs into her elbow, but I'm pretty sure she's actually laughing, which is the only thing keeping me from getting irritated with the receptionist. "We're in our own room, right? Just the two of us?"

She shakes her head. "Your reservation is for a group event with that family right there."

Fuck. "What other rooms do you have available tonight?"

"They're all booked."

She flashes a diabolical smile. No point in asking to talk to the manager.

She *is* the manager.

"*All* of them are booked?" I ask.

Kami squeezes my hand. "It's okay. We'll make new friends."

I look across the way again and realize one of the older guys in overalls is glaring at a younger guy with earbuds in, who's scowling back like he hopes the lights go out and our escape room experience turns into a live-action version of Clue.

I'm about to suggest we skip it when Kami adds in a whisper, "I have bad date karma. It's my fault."

"What are you talking about?"

"I had a date with an old guy who kept grabbing my ass two weeks ago. And then that…thing…with someone we all used to know that you're not allowed to think about. And then Muffy set me up with her neighbor, who is *super* hot, but it turned out he needed a date to his ex-girlfriend's wedding to his boss, and I mean *old* guy boss, and we all got thrown out because… that's not important. The point is, I think I just have bad date karma."

My blood pressure is rising by the millisecond as I think about all the other men who've been within kissing distance of Kami since her birthday.

"Or Muffy's a really bad matchmaker," I point out with a scowl. "You're with *me*. This is supposed to be a *good* date."

"It could be, if you don't act like a spoiled child."

Now the receptionist is having a coughing fit.

A woman in a black T-shirt with a name badge around her neck steps out from behind one of the doors leading to the escape rooms.

"Wankers and Murphy?" a voice calls.

Kami and I both do a double-take and simultaneously choke on snorts as the entire contingency of overall-clad guys—and token woman in jeans, boots, and a sweater—all stand.

"I've got the Wankers," the woman announces.

"Oh my god, Nick, we *have* to," Kami whispers. "How often do you get to spend a first date with a bunch of Wankers?"

I can't talk because I'm still choking on snorts, so when the woman calls, "Murphy?" again, Kami tugs my hand and pulls me toward her.

"We're here," she says. "Sorry. My boyfriend inhaled some dust. He has breathing problems sometimes. It's a congenital condition."

I should be threatening to pay her back later, but seeing her eyes sparkle and shine like that—she can make up stories about me anytime she wants.

I wouldn't even care if she said I had a small dick, because first of all, she knows better, and second of all, so long as she likes my dick, I don't really care what anyone else thinks.

Especially if she keeps calling me her *boyfriend*. I'm more like a full-grown man-friend with fucking awesome cock skills, but I can work with *boyfriend*. But only if it's Kami calling me that.

I put extra effort into pretending I'm hacking up a lung, because it's what I'm supposed to do, and I'm going to be the best fucking boyfriend to ever walk the earth.

Bonus, Kami rubs my back and uses her free hand to grip my arm like she needs to guide me.

Fuck, I missed her touching me. The things we take for granted, man.

We're led down a long hallway and into the prep room. I did one of these escape room things with the team just before training camp started, so I pretty much know how it goes. Kami's listening with rapt attention while our hostess explains how to find clues and how much time we have to figure out the combination on the lock out of the control room before we lose the game.

"If we lose, it's the Johnson-Wankers' fault," the old guy grumbles.

"Shove it, old man," the younger guy with one earbud popped out replies.

Kami's lips twitch, but you have to be looking close to see it. The hostess asks if anyone needs to use the bathroom one last time before we're all locked into our room for an hour, and Kami nudges me.

"I'm good," I whisper.

"You have a respiratory problem," she whispers back, so softly no one else can hear. "Count to five and cough. You have to sell this."

She pecks my cheek while the old guy grumbles about how stupid this is and the woman—his daughter, maybe? Or grand-daughter?—forces a bright smile. "It's been thirty years. We're going to bond, we're going to get out of this room together, and we're going to *let this all fucking go*. Or else you'll never see Alex and me again."

For the first time, Kami frowns. "Do you all need to do this alone?"

"No," the left half of the group answers while the right half all reply, "Yes."

I fake a coughing fit.

"Are you smart?" one of the middle-aged men asks Kami.

"She's a doctor," I answer for her. My voice is raspy, and she scoots closer to me while she shivers.

I'm no expert in shivers, but I think that was a *she likes my voice like this* shiver.

"An animal doctor," she explains. "Not an astrophysicist or anything."

"Good enough. I'm John. My brothers, Joe, Jim, and Jake, and Jake's son, Alex, who's not smart at all. You're on our team and I'll give you half a cow if you can get us the hell out of here in fifteen minutes or less."

"Aren't we all on the same team?" Kami asks, ignoring the half-a-cow thing.

"No," all but the woman and Alex answer.

"I don't team up with Johnson-Wankers," the old man mutters.

"I'm Jordan," the woman tells us, "and this is my dad, Jeremiah, and his brother, Jerry."

"Jesus," I mutter. I'm just calling them the J-squad. Numbering them might be easier.

Kami's lips twitch again. "I'm Kami. This is Nick. He'll be mostly useless thanks to the respiratory issues, but he's often lucky, so there's that working to our advantage."

She pats my back again.

So maybe I'm not going to get to make out with her in the magic escape room, but despite the lingering ache in my dick, I don't mind.

She said I get lucky.

I can have patience.

"Great, so now you all know each other, and the rules, and how to hit the panic button," our hostess says brightly, "let's go rescue some kittens in space."

Groans and mutters of "Some *what*?" go through the room.

Except for Kami.

She tips her head back and laughs while she claps her hands. "You're amazing," she tells me, and I just grin.

I could block six thousand pucks in this moment.

Lavoie's right.

I've got it *bad*.

Our hostess herds us into the actual escape room, tells us to look for our first clue "in outer space," and pulls the door shut behind her.

"What the ever-loving fresh hell is *this*?" the old dude, officially now known as Cranky Grandpa, says as he looks around. Guy would've gotten along great with my Gammy.

"We have to rescue the kittens from the Gooz, and then escape the ship within an hour," Jordan tells the J-men of Team Wanker. "Start looking for clues!"

She rushes to the captain's chair and controls set up in the middle of the fifteen-by-fifteen room. Half the walls are windows to outer space which would only be cooler if they were lit by a projector and the stars were actually moving. I make a mental note to do this *right* if I ever buy an escape room company when I retire.

Of the remaining two walls, one's lined with a control panel of buttons and screens and chairs at the long counter, and the other is painted with cells holding kittens in space suits.

That cat at the shelter was fucking adorable today.

I should go back. Just to visit.

And take Kami.

Except she gets to see little animals all day long. Maybe she doesn't want to go.

"Where's that panic button?" Cranky Grandpa mutters.

"If you hit that panic button without even trying to find a clue, I'll hide all your reading glasses and *I'll* steal your chickens," Alex announces.

Kami and I share a look, and we both head for the control panel along the far wall. "We have to find the keys to the holding cell and also crack the code to make sure there aren't any Gooz guards between us and the kittens," Kami says.

"I'll beat them up for you," I offer while I squat under the control panel and search for clues.

"But the noise might attract the Grand Gooz Emperor."

"No wonder he can't block a puck. He's fucking nuts," one of the J-Wankers mutters.

Kami rolls her eyes. "So you're fighting over chickens?" she asks while she picks up the keyboards and looks under them.

"That dickhead shaved penises into my cows," Cranky Grandpa replies, pointing at the oldest of the Johnson-Wankers. "My *prize* cows. Right before I took them to auction."

"Thirty years ago," Alex sing-songs.

"He wouldn't be so upset if he didn't have a tiny pecker," the Johnson-Wanker with the earbuds says.

"If I *had* shaved penises into your cow, you would've deserved it for stealing Ma's chickens," the J-Wanker who apparently is denying his involvement says.

"Wait, are you all cousins?" Kami asks suddenly. She points between Jordan and Alex. "And you're...involved?"

"I'm adopted," Alex tells her.

"You're just as much a Johnson-Wanker as the rest of us," one of the J-men says.

"They always hid him from view of Grandpa's farm. We met in the engineering department at school," Jordan explains. She smiles at him, and he smiles back with a blush.

"They're getting married over my dead body," Cranky Grandpa

announces.

"They've been feuding for *thirty years*," Jordan tells us with an exasperated sigh. "Before I was even born. It started with the cows and chickens and now they all think the others are sabotaging their tractors and contaminating their seed. If they don't call a truce, Alex and I are moving to Italy."

"I hear the gelato's good," I offer.

Kami gives me the *wrong answer* eyeball.

"I have a cow?" I correct.

"You a farmer in your spare time?" one of them asks. Fuck, I can't remember which side of the feud that guy's on. Whatever.

I shake my head. "Nah. Got pranked. Almost lost Kami over it. Really sucked. But the cow's cute. I ordered her this special harness with unicorn cows on it for when we go for walks."

Every last J-man—including Cranky Grandpa—gives me identical *you're a fucking nutjob* eyeballs.

"Aww, they agree on something," Kami murmurs. "We're doing a good deed on our date. Go, us." She stops, and a wide grin spreads over her face. "Oh my gosh, I think I found a clue!"

She flips over the keyboard, and there's an envelope taped to the bottom.

"You got yourself a meat cow or a milk cow?" Cranky Grandpa asks me.

"She's a pet," I reply. "I moved back home with my parents so we can live together all the time."

Kami's trying to read the new clue, but her lips are wobbling.

"Fucking dumbass," one of the J-men mutters.

"Oh, no!" Kami announces dramatically. She throws the back of her hand to her forehead and collapses to the floor in mock horror. "No, *it can't be!*"

"What? *What?*" Jordan exclaims.

"The kittens..." Kami pauses dramatically, and dude. She's a terrible actress. But fuck if watching her get into it isn't spreading warm goopy happiness all through my chest. "They're going...to be... *gassed!*"

"Noooo!" Jordan cries equally dramatically. "How do we stop it?"

Alex and I share a look, and if I think *I* have it bad, that guy's so whipped he probably can't put his own shoes on without asking permission.

You fucking go, dude.

"Where's that fucking panic button?" Cranky Grandpa says again.

One of the J-men that I think is on his side holds him back. "Hey, Jordan's having fun. Stop it."

"We're going to enter a talent show," I tell the men. "Me and Sugarbear. My cow, I mean. She can tap-dance."

"At least she's not marrying *this* weirdo," another of the guys mutters to Cranky Grandpa.

"We have to find the switch to disable the poison chambers," Kami announces.

"There are switches here!" Jordan points to all the controllers at the console next to the captain's chair in the middle of the room, and both women dive for them and start flipping switches.

"Alex, go help Nick," Jordan hisses.

Her fiancé dutifully obeys. "They tried to get me to stink bomb the old man's house last year," he mutters to me. "Assholes, all of them. You really weird about the cow?"

Considering a cow to be a dog isn't *weird*, is it? "Only so long as it makes Kami happy." I raise my voice. "Yeah, dude. They make tap-dancing shoes for cows. It's a specialty shop on the internet. You want, I can send you the link."

Cranky Grandpa's watching us. Pretty sure Alex knows it too. He claps me on the shoulder. "Let's keep looking for that switch to stop the poison from the kittens, man."

"Kami, you think we could get Sugarbear on ice skates?" I call.

"It really could be worse," one of the J-men is saying to Cranky Grandpa.

"Nick, sweetie, just keep looking for clues," Kami says.

We share a look, and I am *so* getting laid for this tonight. "Anything for you, hot stuff."

She sucks in another smile, and we all go back to looking for the next clue while the older generations of Wankers and Johnson-Wankers glare at all of us.

I definitely owe Kami a make-up date.

And I can't wait to pay up.

TWENTY-EIGHT

Kami

I DON'T KNOW how I make it back to Nick's Cherokee before I completely and totally lose it. We both hop in the car, look at each other, and start laughing so hard my eyes burn.

"Oh. My. God," I gasp. "That poor couple."

"Did you—hear—bowling—for roosters?" Nick howls.

"The flaming poop bomb!" I cry.

"The hay—in the car!"

Tears are streaming down my aching cheeks, and my stomach is cramping, but I can't stop. Until a sudden thought strikes me.

I bolt upright and point at Nick. "No," I declare so forcefully that he stops wiping his eyes, and his chuckles roll to a stop.

"No?"

Oh, shit. The puppy dog eyes. Not the puppy dog eyes. "No what?"

"No, you are *not* going to use *any* of those pranks on your teammates."

There's a subtle tug of his lips and a barely-noticeable lowering of his lids that very clearly says *challenge accepted*.

"If I get wind of even a *hint* of you pulling anything mentioned *or inspired* by tonight, I'm cutting you off sex."

He tilts his head, all of his cockiness coming out to play in that smile spreading over his face and lighting his green eyes, and god help me, he's so stupidly irresistible. My panties are already wet.

Just from *one* look.

"So you're telling me I get to have sex with you again."

My body cries out an *oh, fuck, yes*. "I d-don't put out on the f-first date," I stammer.

Because I really shouldn't sleep with him tonight.

I should resist.

I should make him *earn* me. I should demand more than one day of him saying what I want him to say.

"It's technically over," he tells me. "So you could put out *after* our first date."

"You haven't taken me home yet."

"What if I want to take you on a second date right now?"

Yes, please. "You have a game tomorrow."

He pulls my hand into his, dwarfing mine. Thick veins run from his knuckles to his wrist, and the heat off his skin is warming my entire body. "Way I've been playing, I don't think anyone would know the difference."

"You're going to play amazing tomorrow night."

"Yeah?"

"Yeah."

"Why's that?"

"Because I'll have sex with you if you have a shutout. But only if you have a shutout."

He groans and squeezes my hand. "Fuck, Kami."

"No pressure or anything," I add, "but I really miss your cock. And I'll be really, really sad if I can't have it tomorrow night."

"Are you coming?" he breathes.

"Um, not at the moment," I breathe back, but holy hell, my body's primed and ready for it.

"To the *game*," he clarifies.

"I—yes," I decide. I've given away every set of tickets so far, but tomorrow, *hell* yes, I'll be at the game.

He's suddenly crushing his mouth to mine, and I fall into his kiss. I *do* miss this.

For all the ways he's dense sometimes, he knows how to kiss me. When to go hard. When to go soft. How to stroke his tongue into my mouth to make my nipples so hard and my clit so achy that I have to straddle him.

My ass hits the horn as I climb into his lap. Neither of us reacts to the noise—he just helps me over, pulling my hips tight against his so I can feel the giant bulge in his jeans.

I rock against him, because *oh*, I've missed him too.

He's kissing me like he's starving, like he hasn't seen me in three years instead of three weeks, like it'll be three more years before he sees me again.

"God, I missed you," he gasps into my mouth, and that heady feeling of being *wanted*, of being *seen*, of being *valued*, not because I take care of his pranks and laugh at his jokes, but because we *fit*—it's all so intensely right that I don't know how I survived three weeks of resisting him either.

I grip his shoulders while he squeezes my breasts, still licking into my mouth, those satisfied groans emanating from the back of his throat while I grind over his hard cock.

My right leg is squished between his steel beam of a thigh and the door. The bottom of the steering wheel digs into my lower back, but Nick's fingers are sneaking under my shirt and stroking my sides, tracing the edges of my bra, and everything fades away except the heady sensations his fingers draw out of my skin.

His touch is feather-light, teetering on the edge of ticklish. He brushes my nipples through the lace of my bra, and pleasure rockets through my core.

"Yes, *more*," I gasp.

He unhooks the damn thing with one hand, and suddenly he's cupping both my breasts, lifting my shirt so he can lick first one nipple, then the other.

"Oh, god, Nick," I moan, offering him more.

"So fucking delicious," he rasps before sucking me all the way into his mouth.

Fireworks are ricocheting through my belly, sending jolts of electrified bliss straight to my pussy. I rock harder against him while he snakes one hand between us and unbuttons my jeans.

And then his fingers are stroking me, and he's still sucking on my nipple, and the entire world is awash in pinks and purples and the silvery shimmer of impending orgasm.

I couldn't stop my body's instinctive rhythm against his fingers if I wanted to, and when he slips two inside me, then presses hard on my clit, I shatter without warning, screaming his name, my head thrown back against the top of the car, pleasure spilling out of me while my walls clamp and spasm around his fingers.

He grazes my nipple with his teeth, and my body spirals even higher and harder as my climax bursts free with enough power to light the night sky.

I bear down on his fingers and ride out the waves while he nestles his head between my breasts and whispers, "That's it, beautiful. That's my girl."

When I finally sag against him, as useful as jellyfish, the only syllable I can force from my sleepy lips is, "*Wow.*"

"You are so fucking hot when you come," he murmurs. He's pulling my shirt down, but he's also sneaking my bra straps down my arms, like he knows a thing or two about taking off a bra under a shirt.

He pulls it out my sleeve and pockets it.

"Did you—" I start, struggling to find where the marshmallow fluff under my skin ends and my bones and muscles begin.

"Gonna need a good luck charm for that shutout tomorrow night."

I'm still enjoying the lingering fireworks show behind my eyelids, but I can hear the smile in his voice.

"You don't—"

"Shh." He puts a finger to my lips. "Nothing else has worked. Let a man have a little motivation. And you are *definitely* motivation."

"You're still *very* hard," I point out.

"If you had the view I just had, you would be too."

My right leg is going numb, and I'm becoming aware of that steering wheel in my back again.

He strokes my back and kisses my temple. "Kami?"

"Hmm?"

"I think I'm gonna like dating you."

I snuggle closer to him, because yeah, I think I'm gonna like dating him too.

TWENTY-NINE

Nick

I GET to the arena early Wednesday so I can tape Kami's bra into the back of my chest protector without the Bergers noticing.

Not because I'm embarrassed to be playing with a pink lacy bra, which still smells like her pussy since I fingered it the entire ride home last night—the bra, not Kami's pussy, though I would've done both if it was safe to stroke and drive—but because if one of them knows, Felicity will know, and we can't have that, now can we?

I might also get to the arena early because it's been long enough, and I've been happy enough about Sugarbear, that now is mathematically the ideal moment for revenge against Zeus Berger.

Part one of my revenge plan, anyway.

It's dumb. He'll think I'm a total idiot.

And he'll never see part two coming.

After everything's set up, I head upstairs to wait for Felicity to get into the office. And because she's Felicity, and she basically has thicker hockey blood than I do, which is fucking impressive, I don't have to wait long.

"What did you do?" she asks as soon as she walks into her office, which is a hidey-hole between the marketing and accounting departments, since she works in both.

They don't like her to get bored.

She sometimes works with the trainers in the massage and PT

room too, when she's not using Thrusty to make promo videos with all of my teammates.

"I came to say hi to my sister," I reply innocently.

I smirk on the inside when she whips her phone out, knowing she's texting Ares a warning that I did something, and he and Zeus better be on the lookout.

Too fucking easy.

"What else did you do?" she asks, rightfully so. "Swear to god, Nick, if you ordered more dick cookies for someone…"

"I took Kami out last night," I tell her.

Because yeah, actually, I *do* want to talk to Felicity about me dating Kami. I don't want it to be a secret.

I want my sister to know I'm trying.

She doesn't have to know about my good luck charm, and she doesn't have to know that my dick's still aching from not getting any relief last night, but she can know I'm trying.

"How was it?" she asks cautiously, and I get the feeling she's more Team Kami than Team Nick, which is probably a good thing.

Kami has a much better reputation than I do.

"The part where I was with her? Awesome. The part where we accidentally ended up doing an escape room with a bunch of warring farmers? That's more…memorable."

"Only you," she says on a laugh, shaking her head. "Warring farmers?"

I fill her in on the Wankers, and next thing I know, the room's full of curious onlookers, including Ares and Lavoie, and I better text Kami to give her a heads-up that basically the entire planet has heard about our date now.

Or maybe I'll call her.

Considering the gift that's supposed to be delivered to her office today, I probably definitely want to call.

"You're taking her out again?" Felicity asks.

I nod. Not because we firmed up any plans, but because if we win, I'm heading over to her house as soon as I can get out of here tonight.

Fuck, if we lose, I'll probably head over there too. She gives good scalp rubs and makes all the right sympathetic noises.

"Well, don't fuck it up, Murphy," she says in her cat puppet voice. "We like Kami!"

"Speak for yourself, pussy happy pants," she replies in her grouchy grumpapotamus voice. "She's too fucking nice all the time."

"Aww, don't be jealous. You never had a shot with her anyway, Harold," I tell the puppet, even though he's probably locked in a chest in her bedroom a few blocks away, but if Felicity can talk like the puppet, I can answer the puppet.

"You're an ass, Murphy," Harold the Grumpapotamus replies.

"But a loveable ass!" Felicity vents in her happy cat puppet voice.

Ares grunts.

"Yeah, I wouldn't go that far either," Lavoie adds with a nod. "C'mon, Murphy. Skate time."

"Practice good, boys," Felicity calls.

We hop the elevator and get back to the dressing room right behind Zeus, who's hanging up his phone with a goofball smile on his face as he walks in.

"Joey?" Ares asks.

"She's coming in tonight for the game." He's grinning so big, he looks like a monument to happiness. "Staying until we leave for Nashville Friday."

"She must be excited to see her sister," Lavoie says. "Too bad she has to see you too."

Frey chokes on air and goes back to pulling his pads on for practice. Probably because he's married to Zeus's wife's sister, and knows too much about the formidable Joey. And also because that was a hell of a zinger.

"Don't be jealous," Zeus tells Lavoie with a grin. "Someday a woman's gonna want to blow you again too. You too, Murphy. Hang in there, fuckers."

That would be a lot funnier if my dick wasn't still a little cramped.

But Kami's worth earning.

I don't think I'm ready for all this marriage-and-kid stuff, but I can't stand the idea of Kami marrying someone else.

So I'll give her everything else I can.

Even if I'm not always sure it's exactly the right thing. I'm trying.

Zeus turns to his locker, pulls down his jersey, and jumps, but quickly covers it with a snort. "What the fuck? Somebody thinks *this* is supposed to scare me?"

"Your cubbie has the spots, Berger," Frey says cheerfully.

"Fuck, those are eyeballs." Jaeger shakes his head. "You got a thousand googly eyeballs watching you."

Zeus bends over and peers at them closer while more of the guys filter in and check it out too. "They're not even glued on straight. Whoever did this is an amateur."

"Fucking creepy amateur," Klein mutters.

"That's seriously lame," Lavoie says to me.

"Shut the fuck up. It is not." Gluing googly eyes inside Berger's locker?

Yeah. That's lame.

But the dumber I look now, the more surprised he'll be next week.

Lavoie's shaking his head. "Losing your touch. Hope that date last night helped your game. Didn't help your pranks."

I keep my poker face while I grab my own pads and start suiting up. "Feeling good today. Think I'm getting sorted out."

Thank fuck.

Because that game against Indianapolis is creeping closer and closer, and I. Cannot. Lose. To. Them.

It would be like admitting defeat in the playoffs a month into the season.

Practice feels good. Despite the occasional twitch in my still disappointed cock, I feel more grounded today.

Like I can see the ice better today, spot the pucks faster, move quicker.

Like I'm five years younger.

After practice and lunch with the team, I head back to my parents' place for a few hours. Last I heard from my real estate agent, I needed to lie low and be a fucking choir boy for a few weeks, and then she was pretty sure she could get me hooked up with a place downtown again.

But downtown doesn't have room for Sugarbear.

It's weird how attached I'm getting to my cow-dog. Instead of conking out on the couch with my DVR'd copy of the Master's—seriously, you want to nap, put on some golf—I head out back and toss the ball around with my cow.

And then I call Kami.

"Hey, you," she says brightly after the first ring. "How'd you know it was my lunch break?"

I might've called her office earlier. "Lucky guess."

"How was morning skate?"

"Good."

Sugarbear charges me as I lounge in one of the pool chairs, but I dodge and toss the ball back out under the oak trees, and she snorts and changes course.

"Are you playing fetch with the cow?" Kami asks.

I laugh. "You could tell?"

"Lucky guess," she quotes back to me. "I've been laughing to myself all morning over you asking the head Wanker if he'd sell you a couple more cows so you could get some cow hockey going."

"That's all you're thinking about?"

"If I want to function today, yes."

Huh.

My gift must not have arrived yet.

"And as much as I appreciate your generosity, would you *please* stop sending apology gifts?" she adds.

The woman can read my mind. It should be terrifying, but I'm so distracted by the total awe of someone else riding my wavelength that I almost miss the calf charging me again. I sidestep at the last minute with a small *oof*, and manage to snag the yoga ball and fling it deep into the yard again. I wince when it comes close to Mom's garden shed, but Sugarbear avoids it like a pro.

"Nick?"

"They're not apology gifts anymore. Now they're just fun."

"You had thirty drawstring bags *with my picture on it* delivered to my office."

"I thought about sending them with my picture, but I didn't want to be presumptuous."

She snorts out a delicate little snort-laugh, and I rub that soft spot in my chest.

"You know there are only seven people who work here, right? That's like four bags *each*."

"Or it's a lifetime supply. You could switch them out once every two years, and they'd last until you're ninety."

"No one will recognize me as the woman on that bag when I'm ninety."

"You're going to be gorgeous when you're ninety."

"I'll be a plump wrinkled prune with white curls and a cane yelling at all the kids to get off my lawn."

"You'll be a beautiful raisin," I assure her. "And you'll be the old lady everyone's afraid of because you'll try to give candy to all the kids, and all the moms will be yelling, *don't take candy from strangers who keep cows for pets!*"

She laughs, and yeah, I'm feeling like I just had my tenth shutout in a row, just from making Kami happy.

"You're still coming to the game tonight?" I ask her.

"I was thinking of skipping it. I mean, you guys play Minnesota a few times a year, and I could just watch it on TV."

"Probably a good idea," I agree. "Then you can't distract me."

"Oh, please. You don't get distracted on the ice."

Not usually. "Great. So you'll be there."

She laughs. "Yes. I'll be there."

I offer Sugarbear a high five. She snorts at me and paws the ground, waiting for me to toss the ball again. "Good. Because I'm wearing your bra."

She makes a strangled choking noise, and I grin. "I mean it's tucked into my uniform. For good luck," I clarify.

"I think my mother would actually be proud," she murmurs.

"So that's where you get your good taste in sports teams."

"Oh, most definitely. Dad wasn't a fan until she basically told him she wouldn't marry him unless he learned to love the Thrusters."

"You bringing her tonight?"

"No, she and Dad are hosting friends in their box. I'm bringing Muffy and Aunt Hilda and Alina."

I wait for her to laugh and tell me she's kidding, but she doesn't.

"Wait, seriously?"

"Why wouldn't I? Muffy and Aunt Hilda are on a tighter budget and don't get opportunities like this very often. And Alina's missed a lot of games because of her weird travel schedule. They'll have fun."

It never occurred to me that there were people who'd want to go to a game but couldn't afford it. And here she is, offering to share tickets with annoying family. "Fuck, I really don't deserve you."

"Oh, stop. Who else would've played a total dodohead to make another guy look better to his completely irrational future grandpa-in-law? And I *know* you made it well worth Elmer's time to get him to serve us dinner last night."

"You make me sound nicer than I am."

"You're not *mean*. Not unprovoked, I mean. Even if sometimes you're not *directly* provoked. You're just not always…"

"Nice?" I supply dryly.

"Acutely aware of other people's feelings and wishes," she finishes diplomatically.

"Huh."

"But you've never really made it a secret that hockey's your life, so it's not like you're lying about wanting to be something you're not."

Sugarbear gallops over again, tongue lolling like a dog, her tail swishing. I rub her head before I toss the ball again.

"Kami?"

"Hm?"

"Thanks for giving me another chance."

"You earned it."

There's a smile in her voice that makes me smile too. "I'm coming over after the game."

"I'll consider answering if you get a shutout."

"Tiger will let me in."

She sighs dramatically. "She's so easy. I need to get back to work. I think my next patient just showed up. Play good tonight. Muffy and Aunt Hilda deserve a good show. And Alina will give you shit for weeks if you don't."

"You sweet talker, you."

"And no more presents," she warns.

We'll see about that.

"Oh, dammit, I have to go. My battery's dying."

I smile. "Better get that thing charged, because you're gonna be snapping pictures of me all through the game."

The last thing I hear before I hang up is her laughter. I toss the ball around with Sugarbear a while longer before heading inside to start my normal pre-game power nap routine.

Kami's coming tonight.

And I'm going to play the best fucking game of my life.

On the ice.

And then off the ice too.

THIRTY

Nick

MY FAVORITE THING about Mink Arena is that you can hear the crowd from the dressing room.

You know the fans are out there, waiting, hopeful, excited, ready to scream their fucking lungs out to cheer us on to victory.

I was four the first time I had a hockey stick in my hand. Five the first time I stood in the crease. I didn't even know what the crease *was*, but I knew if I could play goaltender in hockey, I could be tougher than any shitheads who wanted to shove me around on the playground and tell me my mom slept with the mailman.

Fuck, I didn't know what *your mom slept with the mailman* meant then either, but I got the feeling it was something worse than everyone having happy nap time like we had after lunch every day in kindergarten.

But tonight?

Tonight, there are seventeen thousand people up there, waiting for us to take the ice and kick some Minnesota ass.

Ares is getting his ankles taped.

Sokolov and Jaeger are trading Pokémon cards.

Don't mock it.

Habits are habits and superstitions are superstitions, and they're both on fucking fire this year.

"You shaved again," Lavoie says, sitting down and pulling on his skates—right skate first. He'll put the left on before he ties the laces on either, because it's what he does.

"The beard wasn't cutting it this year."

He eyeballs me between tying his laces. "Looks like you found your game brain."

Coach said the same earlier today.

I'm trying to not let it go to my head, but I *feel* different tonight. Like I could fly if I wanted to.

Coach comes in for our final pep talk before the game, then we all pull on our jerseys and line up to hit the ice.

Our entrance song starts when we enter the tunnel. The spotlight's spinning over the doorway, lights flashing, announcers booming.

Felicity's out there somewhere. Heard she was pulling a stint in the announcer's booth with Thrusty tonight.

And Kami should be sitting right next to the home bench.

I knew she was pissed at me when the seats I bought her for our previous games were empty. She and Felicity and Maren and Alina don't pass up good seats for *anything*.

Never have.

I lead the pack and stop so everyone can rub my helmet on the way out onto the ice. They file past, and I hit each of my guys with their normal complicated handshake if we have one, which is fucking ridiculous with all our gloves on, but it works. The crowd roars louder with every one of my teammates that skates out onto the ice, and when I join them, it's pandemonium.

Don't feel like I deserve their loyalty this year, but I'm fucking grateful for it.

I circle our half of the ice, stick gripped tight, one arm lifted in a wave to the crowd, and then I find what I'm looking for.

There's Kami, front row, right next to the bench, hollering and cheering with Alina, Muffy, and her aunt.

She's here.

I'm going to fucking kick *ass* tonight.

I flip my helmet down and head to my spot at the net, digging in good to get ready for that biscuit to drop. "Hey, Jaeger!" I call.

The second-line forward skates over and flips his helmet up. "Yeah?"

"Your girlfriend's over there with her mom. You should toss her a puck."

I nod toward Kami, and swear on my left skate, the dude goes pink in the cheeks. "You're such a fucker," he mutters, but he bends over, grabs a puck that Zeus just sent flying my way, and carries it over to toss it over the boards.

Muffy's eyes go huge, and she catches it, clasps it to her heart, and sinks into her chair.

Thank you, Kami mouths to me.

I wink at her, then reach out to grab one of the pucks flying at me from Ares, Lavoie, and Frey, who are lined up and taking practice shots.

"Head in the game, eh, Murphy?" Frey says with a grin.

The crowd fades away as we count down the final seconds to game time, and there's just the ice left.

Just the ice, the enemy, and me standing between them and the goal.

Lavoie, Frey, and Ares head to the center line.

Zeus and Sokolov skate over to me, and we trade fist bumps.

"Got your back, Murphy," Zeus says.

Sokolov nods.

"Your wife here?" I ask Zeus.

He grins and points behind the bench, where Joey, Gracie, and the baby all wave.

"Don't embarrass her, okay?" I tell him.

Sokolov laughs. Zeus punches me in the arm, but he pulls it so I don't even waver from where I've dug in at the crease.

"Let's play hockey, bitches," Zeus says.

And that's exactly what we do.

THIRTY-ONE

Kami

THESE. Seats. Are. Amazing.

I've been to dozens—hundreds?—of Thrusters games over the years, but I've never sat right here. At the edge of the rink.

Watching *my boyfriend* play.

Oh, I've watched Nick play plenty, *wishing* he was my boyfriend, but tonight—I think he really is.

"Ohmygod!" Muffy flings herself back in her seat as Zeus shoves a Minnesota player into the boards right in front of us, pivots, and takes off again like a demon on blades, chasing the puck before Nick has to stop it.

"Shew, those boys are hot." Aunt Hilda fans herself.

Alina's dark brown eyes meet mine, and her lips twitch in an amused smile. "How many more sets of tickets do you have?" she asks me.

"Twenty-seven. I think only six of them are front row, but the others are really good too. None more than third—*Oh!* BLOCK IT! GET IT—*phew*."

I sink back into my own seat next to Muffy.

That was close.

I thought Minnesota was going to score.

But Ares and Manning are driving the puck toward Minnesota's goal now, and Nick's still holding steady.

He hasn't looked this way since the game started. Not even when they left the ice between the first and second periods. He was downing water and talking to the goaltender coach, brows drawn together, sweat dripping off him.

And there I go getting all warm and excited between my thighs.

My phone dings. It's Mom—she's watching the game from the box she and Dad get every year, and she wants to know how my view is.

I'm not sure what I text her back, because I drop my phone when Minnesota goes on a breakaway, heading straight for Nick, unopposed because Zeus and Sokolov are caught off-guard, which means it's just the big bad Minnesota guy and Nick, and—

And *oh my god*, how does he stretch his body that fast? He's like a freaking panther on the ice, dodging and lunging and dropping and deflecting the puck so fast, it takes me a minute to find it again.

"This is so fucking awesome," Muffy breathes.

She's clutching her puck to her heart, and I don't know if it's intentional or not. I'm too busy watching the game to see if she's watching Jaeger flying over the ice, or if she's watching all of it.

"Kami, you know I love you," Alina starts, and I tear my gaze off the action on the ice to glance at her cautiously as she continues, "but I'm starting to wonder if you might need to take one for the team and just sleep with Nick until he retires, because he's fucking *hot* tonight."

"That…wouldn't exactly be a hardship," I tell her.

"Does he want kids?"

I sigh. "He knows I do, but we haven't really talked about it."

"If you want kids and he doesn't, you have two options," Muffy informs us. "One, get yourself accidentally knocked up, which I don't recommend, because hello, problems. Or, two, discuss with him if he's willing to get you pregnant and you promise to do all the heavy lifting if he really doesn't want to be a dad. Also not really a great option, but you have all of us to help you out, so there's that."

I don't really like either option, but seeing as even when I was hanging out with Maren at Chester Green's and wasn't really feeling anything beyond amusement at the men hitting on us, I don't know that my body would even *let* me be attracted to anyone else.

So I need to decide.

Do I want to be with Nick, even if he never wants to get married and have kids, or do I need to press the issue and find out if he's willing to consider permanence? Since we've barely started dating publicly, it seems like a question that can wait a week or two.

I'm spared from continuing the conversation because Duncan Lavoie is sent to the penalty box for elbowing, which is such a bullshit call, because that other player was ten times worse. "Open your eyes!" I yell as Alina and Aunt Hilda boo. "He almost had his head taken off!"

Duncan's pissed. He throws his stick on the ground and stares sullenly at the game, muttering what appear to be several words I try not to use in front of my dogs.

Also?

My heart's in overdrive, because *this* is when Nick's most vulnerable.

When the other team's on a power play.

I grab Muffy's hand without realizing I've done it and watch Minnesota charge toward Nick.

"He's got it. He's got it," I mutter to myself.

But this is when he's been scored on most this season.

We're up three-nothing. We're in a good spot, but I want *so badly* for Nick to get a shutout.

And not just because I teased him about sleeping with him if he does, but because I think he needs it for his confidence.

I hold my breath. Everyone's charging the crease. Nick's there, squatting low, thighs and knees moving, ready to drop or dive, one man against seven.

Holding his ground.

Minnesota shoots.

Nick deflects it with his stick.

They go for the puck again, but Zeus digs it out and sends it up to Manning Frey, who takes off, and all of my breath whooshes out.

And we're only fifteen seconds into the penalty.

"He's got this, Kami," Alina tells me. "*This* is championship Nick Murphy."

She's right, of course.

He's a pro.

He had a rocky start to the season, but he's sharp tonight. It's like he's more aware of the game. More determined. More driven.

I suppress a smile while my nipples tighten under my fleece vest.

Or maybe, he's just a little more motivated.

I'm motivated to want him to win. Because if last night was a preview of his idea of makeup sex...

"I don't know what you're thinking," Aunt Hilda says, "but if I were dating a hot young thing like that goaltender, you bet your britches I'd be thinking it too."

"Don't ever say that in front of Felicity," I say, eyes glued to the hockey players zipping by on the ice. Someone takes a long shot, but Nick easily catches it in his glove and tosses it to Sokolov.

"Honey, given who *she* sleeps with, I don't think it would bother her to know you're settling for second best."

"She's *related* to him."

"That's why he's *seventh* best."

I don't bother arguing, either about her changing the number or any other part of her wrongness, because I suspect she's just trying to see if she can get my goat.

Duncan's finally sprang from the sin bin, and Nick's still holding Minnesota off.

And now I can take a full breath again.

"Does Felicity get this exhausted every game?" I ask Alina. "It doesn't seem like she does."

"She's been doing this a lot more years than we have." She nods to Nick, who's so into the game, tracking the play at the other goal, he might as well be in a different building. "She worries about him too, but she's never known any different. And Ares—"

The rest of her words are drowned out by the entire arena collectively shoving to their feet and screaming as Ares knocks in another goal seconds before the buzzer sounds to end the second period.

Muffy and Aunt Hilda are hugging and jumping up and down, making Muffy's braids whip all about. The Thrusters head off the ice for the break between periods, but this time, I get a sly grin from Mr. Goaltender himself.

And yes, my heart flutters, my breasts tingle, and everything below my belly button tightens up in a thick, delicious coil of anticipation that makes my panties wet.

"Oh, honey," Alina murmurs. "You have got it *bad*."

I do.

And I don't think I mind one bit.

THIRTY-TWO

Nick

I AM FUCKING *BACK*.

Five-nothing, baby. We shut those fuckers out, I got a win, and I'm on my way to see Kami to celebrate.

I've been through the showers, tossed out a few morsels to the sharks—I mean reporters—lurking outside the dressing room, and now I'm finally heading to the garage. She texted me just after the game, and sadly, it wasn't a boob shot, but it was a note that she was going out for a drink with the ladies while I changed, and if she doesn't answer, it's because her phone battery died.

I'm supposed to text her—or Alina—when I'm leaving, but instead, I head the four blocks to Chester Green's with Lavoie, Sokolov, Klein, Jaeger, and The Bear.

It's packed tonight, and we don't get three feet inside the sports bar before cheers go up around us.

Feels like we won the cup all over again.

"Hey, Nicki-poo," the two bunnies who offered me medical and financial advice call from the bar. Three more zoom in on the guys around me. Drinks are offered. Nachos. Firstborns. Whatever we want.

I want to find Kami.

And there she is, at a table for six with the usual suspects, minus Felicity but plus her cousin, aunt, and mom.

I step around fans and the four people in the entire bar who have no idea what the big deal is—obviously not hockey fans—until I'm bending over and planting a kiss on this beautiful brunette with the bright smile and the sparkling eyes.

"Hi," she whispers.

I just grin, because who the fuck needs words.

"So this is the gentleman who's been flooding my clinic with an excessive number of gifts," Kami's mom says.

Pointedly.

"Somebody's in trouble," Maren sing-songs. "And I don't think it's Kami…"

I take a chair somebody offers and pull it up to the table, realize Kami's giving me the mother of all *don't be a dick* looks, and turn to thank the guy.

Lady.

Using a cane.

Shit.

"Uh, how about I get another chair," I say, shoving it back at the lady.

"You gave me hot flashes watching you block that last shot. Keep it. I gotta get me some fresh air." She fans her face while she navigates away through the crowd.

"I'm going to enjoy watching you *not* be a star someday," Alina says thoughtfully. "When you're just some nobody that old ladies whack with their canes when you pull dick moves."

"Oh, stop. Both of you." Kami points at Maren too, who looks like she also has something to say about elderly people offering me the shirts off their backs.

Metaphysically speaking.

Or is that metaphorically?

Zeus Berger took me down a rabbit hole the other day about those words, and now I'm backward. The fucker.

"Mom, you've met Nick, haven't you? Maybe at the Murphys' Christmas party?" Kami says.

Her mother, who has the same thick hair—though streaked with gray—brown eyes, and round cheeks, shakes her head. "I'm pretty sure I'd remember meeting *any* of the Thrusters. *Especially* if he's kissing my daughter."

"She and the mister got distracted by your dad's trophy room and made out there all party," Muffy whispers to me. "I had to hear the details from *my* mom, who was super jealous that they got to touch a real Chester Green trophy."

Kami's mom's face goes pink. "Or maybe we did," she says quickly. "Nice to see you again, Nick. Be good to my daughter. I have scalpels and know how to use them. And I'd like to be able to find my break room again."

"But I haven't met you yet," Kami's aunt says, holding out a hand and wiggling her eyebrows. "I'm Hilda. You can call me Hil. Or Da. Or Aunt Spanky-spanky."

"Please don't call her Aunt Spanky-spanky," Muffy says. "Or else *I'll* have to learn how to use a scalpel, and that didn't go so well the first time."

"And you see why I feel like the boring one in the family," Kami murmurs to me.

"Wanna throw down?" I murmur back. "We can do that. Try being related to Felicity *and* Ares Berger."

She cracks up. Maren and Alina both lift their glasses. "Love 'em both, but the man has a point," Maren says.

"Yo, Murphy, nice harem." Zeus elbows through, which is a surprise, because usually when Joey's in town, the two of them disappear and only emerge three days later smelling like a squirrel orgy. Joey's throwing a few elbows of her own, probably to make a wider path for Gracie and the baby, but I swear she's leaving Frey to fight his own battles.

With the bodyguard.

Felicity and Ares are bringing up the rear.

"You using this table?" Zeus asks the six people at the next table.

"Not if we can get autographs," one guy stutters.

Zeus pulls a sharpie out of his back pocket and scrawls his signature on the guy's forehead. Frey shrugs, takes the marker and signs too, then passes it to Ares.

"Murphy?" Ares growls.

I add my signature to the guy's chin, because it's the only space that's left. Sticks in his scraggly beard, but we all have our crosses to bear.

Zeus and Ares take a few selfies for everyone else at the table, and then we're all squishing in together.

"You want your froofy drinks?" Zeus hollers after them as they join the ranks of the standing-room-only crowd at the bar.

"Oh. My. God." Aunt Hilda's fanning herself, muttering the words over and over.

"You want—" I start, but Muffy practically leaps on me, shouting, "*No!*"

But it's too late.

Aunt Hilda's whipping out her knockers and offering them to Zeus. "Give an old lady a thrill, you big glorious lumberjack."

Zeus looks at Joey, a dark-haired, librarian-faced, wiry woman half his size, who shrugs. "Go for it. Might as well practice for retirement in a few months when that's all you get offered."

"*Joey*," Gracie hisses, but everyone else is cracking up.

Joey lets a rare full smile blossom, and okay, yeah, I guess I get what Berger sees in her.

"You ready to go?" I ask Kami.

"Nuh-uh, Murphy," Zeus says as he signs Aunt Spanky-spanky's hooters. "We have to do body shots to celebrate you getting your mojo back."

Felicity sneaks behind everyone else to give me a hug. "Proud of you, you obnoxious pain in the ass," she says. "*That's* the Nick I expect to see when Indianapolis gets here. Kami, whatever you did to him last night, keep doing it. And do *not* give me details."

"You can give me the details," Aunt Spanky-spanky offers.

"Stop it," Kami hisses to me.

I lift a brow, because she looks pissed. "What?"

"I know what you're calling her in your head, and I do *not* want that mental image."

I swipe away a smile. Felicity slips an ice cube down my back, and I yelp, because *fuck*, where did she get that from?

"I don't know what you're thinking, thank god, but I agree with Kami. Stop it."

I slide an arm around Kami, because *dammit*, she feels good. "What happened to *awesome game, Nick*?" I ask them both with a cheeky grin.

"Some of us have to keep you humble," Felicity replies.

She keeps circling the table, hugging Kami's mom—I should probably learn her name at some point—and then squatting between Maren and Alina to whisper with them about the game. Muffy asks if it's true that I only shave one armpit because it makes for a better hold on my stick, and suddenly all the guys and I are one-upping each other with utter nonsense about our favorite superstitions.

"Berger's game day socks are rainbow toe socks," Frey offers.

No one asks which Berger, because Zeus jumps in immediately. "Prince Happypants here has to turn in a circle three times, click his heels together, and say *there's no kingdom like mine* until we all carry him into the shower."

"I only eat the left half of apples on game days," I confess, which makes Kami snort her beer.

"How do you know which half is the left half?" Muffy demands. "Can't you just turn it around?"

"Fuck, no. That ruins the magic. You see that shot I caught in the second period? If I'd turned my apple around, I would've missed."

"You are utterly ridiculous," Felicity tells me with a grin.

"I want to watch him eat only the left half of an apple," Alina says.

"I want to record him only eating the left side of an apple, and then play it back to him, and watch his brain explode," Muffy says.

"Oh, no, honey, you can't do that," Aunt Spanky-spanky says. "We need his brain intact for the wedding."

"What wedding?" Alina asks.

Muffy's giving her mother the *shut the fuck up or I'll cut you* sign. Kami's suddenly pushing her chair back.

"Restroom?" Maren asks her.

"Kami's wedding to Nick," Aunt Spanky-spanky announces, and my entire body freezes like I've been Zambonied into a rink. "She told us last year at Thanksgiving that she'd have a ring by—*erp!*"

"Oh my god, Mom, don't swallow such a big bite of pretzel next time!" Muffy yells, grabbing her mother from behind and doing a terrible Heimlich.

"I haven't seen Sugarbear yet today," Kami suddenly shrieks. She backs up and collides with a server, who looks at our table, does a double-take, and apologizes to Kami. "And work! I have to be at work in the morning."

"Hilda," her mother says to Aunt Bomb-Dropper, "*shut up.*"

"Great game," Kami says weakly. "Gotta run."

"Go after her," Felicity hisses at me while Maren kicks my shin under the table.

I scoot my chair back, and the same server is there, but this time, she doesn't save the drinks.

Nope, this time, they rain down on my neck and shoulders, ice and liquor and beer coating my jacket.

"Sorry," I stutter while she does the same.

A phone camera flashes. "Nice pose, Murphy," Zeus says. "Got it. And that picture's going up everywhere. I'm even gonna make a new

Instagram account. *Nick Murphy Wearing Food And Drinks.* Ma'am, you put those drinks on my bill. Pay you triple if you can get him again."

I flip him off, but I owe him a beer or twelve:

Because I'm suddenly in motion, chasing Kami out of the bar.

I burst out of the bar just after her, and I realize she's stuck downtown when she stops abruptly and looks up and down the street, like she's trying to remember where she put her car.

"Hey."

Her shoulders go tense under that cute ivory vest thing she's wearing, and the long sleeves of her maroon shirt under it seem to tense too.

"I completely forgot to check and make sure Sugarbear has enough grain to get her through the weekend," she babbles.

"So let's go check. Your car here?"

She finally looks at me, but she's way more shy and hesitant than I've ever seen her. "No."

"Mine's around the corner."

I offer her a hand, and relief shudders through me when she finally takes it. "It was the eggnog," she says quietly. "It was spiked, and I apparently have a low tolerance for bourbon. I didn't actually —I mean I might, but I—we don't have to talk about—never mind."

"Hey, we all have our weaknesses. Yours just happens to be bad taste in men."

She doesn't smile. "I *don't* have bad taste in men. But I *was* stupid to think I knew you better than anyone else. I *still* don't know if I know the *real* you, but I can't stop—you're always—it's just *you*. I can't resist *you*."

"Kami—" I try, because there's this desperate, sad loneliness creeping into her voice that's making everything about me just *hurt*, like my body's being twisted and crushed in some kind of vise.

I don't want her to hurt.

And I especially don't want her to hurt because of me.

"I just had this romanticized version of you that you're something more than hockey, whisky, sex, pranks, and hockey. That I could see something nobody else could. That I was…*ugh*. I'm not making this any better."

And now I'm feeling pretty fucking naked.

But I'm also feeling something akin to relief.

Because I don't really know who I am past hockey, whisky, sex, pranks, and hockey either, but I know I'm *something*. And she believes in me too.

I take her face in my hands and block her from the street with my body. "You always make everything better."

Her eyes widen slightly, but there's still that crease in her brow putting a charley horse in my chest.

"It's what best friends do," I add in a rough whisper, because I've never had a best friend before. A month ago, I would've told you a hockey stick was my best friend. A month ago, I was a moron. "And you're the best fucking friend I've ever had."

Her eyes shimmer in the darkness. "Do you mean like the best friend you've ever fucked, or the best damn friend, but even better because *fuck* is a degree above *damn*?"

"Yes." Fuck, this is hard. Felicity's right. I've always been a selfish ass. And she always adds *with good intentions*, because she's my sister so she *has* to think I'm more than just hockey, whisky, sex, pranks, and hockey too, but am I?

I want to be.

For Kami.

"I've got some pretty stiff competition to be yours," I add, "but I'm doing my best."

"Why?"

Because she's sweet. Because she makes me laugh. Because she's my good luck charm on the ice.

Because I don't deserve her, but I'm a selfish bastard who wants her anyway.

"Nobody else has ever believed in me like you do."

"The entire city believes in you."

"*Not* for hockey." Fuck, who *am* I? I shake my head. "And a month ago, that was okay. But I—Christ, Kami, I don't know why you'd even want me. You're right. I'm a selfish bastard who only cares about hockey."

That finally earns me a smile.

Fuck, that smile. What is it about her smile?

"That's not true," she tells me. "You care about your cow too."

And now I'm cracking up even though I feel like a total shit and smell even worse. "C'mon," I tell her. "Let's go see *our* cow. And get me a shower."

"Is that an—*ohmygod*. Nick. I didn't—you're—what happened?" She touches my jacket, then yanks her hand back and tries to shake it off.

"Wake-up call," I tell her with a grin. "You coming or not?"

It's late.

She has to work tomorrow.

But she still smiles at me and nods. "Yeah. I'm coming."

THIRTY-THREE

Kami

I'VE NEVER FELT like more of a total disaster than I do on the ride out to Nick's parents' place.

We were supposed to go to *my* place and have crazy monkey sex to celebrate his shutout, but because I flipped out when Aunt Hilda mentioned my stupid drunken ramblings about how I was finally going to go for it with Nick and marry him by this Christmas, I feel like some manipulative puck-chaser.

And then when I tell myself it was never about wanting him just because he's a really hot hockey player, I start to feel all stalkerish and weird like I might be one of those people who sees a celebrity on TV and thinks that they're *actually* talking to me when they smile and make their secret gestures to their family, because I can see past their celebrity-ness to the person inside, and I just *know* we're meant for each other.

Except it's not like that.

I don't think.

Oh my god. I'm crazy and I just don't know it.

"Did I tell you what I did to Berger to pay him back for Sugarbear?" Nick asks as he steers us out of downtown, completely oblivious to the *second* mental breakdown I'm having.

I tell myself I'm a normal, healthy adult who's had a crush on *her best friend's brother* for years, because I *did* actually know him—kind of—all the way back in high school even though he was a year ahead of me and didn't know I existed because I was not a hockey puck, stick, jersey, skate, or rink, and I concentrate on the fact that Nick's back to playing pranks, because of course he is.

This is normal.

"Please tell me it didn't involve anything live," I say, because this is *also* normal.

He laughs. "Nah, after your stunt with the penguins, not even the Berger twins and Frey together are willing to risk it."

"I don't know what you're talking about."

"Coach knows it was you, doesn't he? You called him and worked it all out before those birds ever hit the ice."

He's damn right I did, but admitting that would be akin to giving him power, and no matter how much I like him—rightfully or crazily or whatever—I can't.

Also, I still felt like a horrible human being, because the penguins could've been legitimately traumatized, and I've never been one to go running to the teacher just because I didn't like what someone else was doing. "I used to sneak out of my parents' house and go over to Muffy's house so we could write anonymous love emails to our secret high school crushes."

"What? No, you didn't."

"I did. *And* we'd sometimes sneak a beer because we needed liquid courage on occasion."

"No, you were—fuck. We went to high school together. Why do I always forget we went to high school together?"

He doesn't seem to be asking for an answer.

Not with that face. He's scowling. At himself.

"You were on your way to a hockey scholarship." I shrug and squeeze his thigh. "You had other things on your mind."

"I'm a real dickweed."

"Stop," I say on a laugh. "You're trying. That's the important part. And you always have, in your own special way."

He cuts a *you're not helping* look at me in the dark, and I start to relax for the first time since we left Chester Green's.

"I'm not saying that shipping a thousand dick cookies to Felicity's ex was the *right* way to make your point about him being an ass who needed to leave her alone, but your heart was in the right place."

He shakes his head like he's seeing *himself* for the first time, which is also crazy, but he just looks so…astonished.

Like he's having one of those life epiphanies where you've sort of known that Earth rotates around the sun, but you didn't actually realize until *right this minute* that that makes Earth secondary in the solar system, because the sun actually can survive without Earth.

"Do you know how rare it is for someone to be able to focus as hard on one thing as you do?" I say softly. "And not just focus on it, but *succeed* at it? You have dedication at a level most people will never be able to understand, much less apply."

He's still frowning. "You save animals' lives every day."

"Trust me, it's definitely *not* every day."

"Maren's saving the environment."

I hide my surprise that he knows what Maren does for a job, because that's not going to help here. "She has a passion. Everyone has a passion. I like to think they do, anyway."

"I just stop a puck from going in the net."

"There's value in entertainment, Nick. You give people an escape. And something to cheer for. And you give kids a role model."

He cuts another look at me.

"Most kids don't know about the dick cookies. Or that book you wrote."

He cracks a grin at that one. "Those royalty checks all go to charity," he says.

"I know."

Crazy man wrote a book mocking another one of Felicity's ex-boyfriends, and even though he published it under a pseudonym, people know it was him.

Hopefully not people under the age of twenty-five, or better yet, forty-seven, because it's really terrible in both the plot and the writing, and I'm pretty certain he meant it to be, but it sells, and he writes a check every month to a local organization that provides supplies for women's shelters.

Because he's *not* a bad guy.

He's just a little blind sometimes.

"And *no one* gives gifts like you do," I add.

He doesn't even smile at that. "I'm trying, Kami," he says instead.

"It doesn't take much," I whisper. "I'm pretty easy when it comes to you."

He pulls my hand to his lips and kisses my knuckles.

And it's the most perfect thing he could do.

THIRTY-FOUR

Nick

I PARK down the drive so my headlights won't wake my parents, and we tiptoe back to Mom's garden shed, where Sugarbear's sleeping for the night, because Mom couldn't stand the idea of the cow sleeping outside in the elements and getting cold. She lifts her head when we sneak inside, and she moos.

"Aww, you sweet girl." Kami leans over and kisses her head.

Doesn't have to lean far. The cow's growing.

"Who's a good puppy?" she whispers, and I crack up.

"If the team docs knew I was calling this cow a puppy, they'd have me talking to shrinks."

"They have no imagination at all."

Sugarbear moos again and nuzzles Kami's stomach.

"I still need to find her a forever home," she says on a sigh.

"Fuck that. I'm buying a farm."

I'm not, but when Kami turns to me with all that wide-eyed hope, shit.

Maybe I *am* buying a farm.

"You can't get a farm," she says on a laugh. "You're gone half the year. And you spend at least a solid month playing pranks."

"So I'll hire a caretaker. And we'll get a big farmhouse where you can spend the night if you don't want to drive back to the city after playing fetch with the cow all night, and Tiger and Dixie and Pancake can get a doggie playground."

And the idea's growing on me faster than I can keep up.

"Quit teasing me, Murphy. It's like you're trying to talk your way into my pants."

"Always. Do you know anything about growing avocados? Felicity would shit if we had an avocado tree."

"I'm pretty sure we're too far north to grow avocados."

"Then we'll build a greenhouse and grow avocados inside and we can make them all organic and tell her she has to say three nice things about you every time she wants one."

Kami's shaking her head at me. "It's like you don't even want to make her work for it."

Sugarbear moos in agreement. Stinks like wet cow in here, and my jacket isn't helping, so I shrug out of it and toss it outside before pulling the door shut on the shed again. My parents moved all the garden supplies and the riding lawnmower to the garage, so the shelves are bare and Sugarbear's tied to a hook at the far end.

But just for sleeping overnight.

She'll get free rein of the yard again in the morning.

"You really want to live on a farm someday?" I ask Kami, because I do pay attention from time to time.

"Sometimes," she says slowly. "I love the open space, and the lack of traffic, and it just feels so…romantic, I guess. I'd probably actually hate it if I lived there. Plus, all my family's here. All my friends are here. If I moved out to the country—they'd be so far away."

"I could get you a helicopter. Cuts down on commute times."

She tips her head back and laughs, and I can't help myself.

I grab her at the waist and lean down to kiss those smiling lips.

"Ohmygod, you stink," she says on another laugh.

"I really do," I agree.

"Maybe you should lose the shirt too," she whispers against my mouth.

"Done."

I whip off the polo and toss it somewhere behind me, backing her against the wall between the door and the window and sliding my hands down her hips. "I missed your lips," I tell her before I rub mine against hers.

"You do that so well," she whispers.

"I want to do it all the time."

I graze her bottom lip with my teeth, and her moan makes me hard in an instant. Painfully, instantly, insistently hard.

"Again," she gasps.

I bite harder, just to the point that she's panting, and scrape her lip again. She grips my hair and pulls me tight, wrapping one leg around my hip while she dives into kissing me like we might never see each other again.

Fuck that.

I'm gonna kiss her so good, she can't imagine life without me.

And I know what she likes.

I know she likes when I go exploring under her shirt, but her vest is tight, so I have to get it off. Except I'm fumbling with the zipper like a toddler, because I want her naked so bad, right now, that I can't function.

All I can do is kiss her and fumble and *oh, fuck me*, she's pinching my nipples, and every last inch of my skin is so fucking turned on now, I swear I'm vibrating. My dick's straining, and who the fuck thought tight jeans were a good idea?

Her hands are everywhere, and I still can't get the damn zipper down. My tongue's halfway down her throat, and she's both whimpering and giggling as she takes pity on me and helps me get the fucking vest off.

"Never wear that again," I order as I yank her shirt up and cup those beautiful round orbs in my palms. "Or this," I say as I slide one hand around her back and manage to actually unhook her bra in one try. "I'm taking it too."

She laughs while she bites my shoulder. "You cannot have all of my bras."

"I'll buy you more. I'll buy you a hundred. But I get them after you wear them."

That giggle—I want to bottle it and play it on repeat every hour of the day.

Forget the roar of a crowd.

This is what I've been chasing my whole life.

Kami.

I drop to my knees, push her shirt up, pull her bra down, and lick her breasts until she's panting and gasping and digging her fingers into my shoulders and sliding down the wall, legs parting, that delicious scent of aroused Kami tickling my nose.

And I'm not about to let my nose have all the fun.

So I trail my fingers down her sides and dip them under the waistband of her jeans until she's panting my name.

"I'm going to take these off you, and I'm going to devour your pussy," I tell her.

"*Yes*," she gasps.

Her knees are wobbling on either side of my shoulders while I kiss and lick and suck my way down below her belly button, pulling her jeans and panties down inch by inch until I can bury my face in that sweet little triangle of perfection between her thighs.

"Ohmygod—cow—watching—*yes*!"

I get one of her legs free, and I hook it over my shoulder to open her for me.

And there it is.

That beautiful pussy glistening and ready for me.

Touching it last night wasn't enough.

I lick her seam, and she shudders and moans and tilts her hips into my mouth. "Oh, god, Nick," she moans.

I treat her clit to the same grazing her lips got moments ago, and she bucks against me. "More," she gasps.

"Oh, I think I'm gonna take my time and enjoy this," I tell her slick folds. I part her with my thumbs and lick her all the way up again, and yeah, I could totally do this every day.

For the rest of my life.

And it's not scary. The idea of being with Kami—*just* Kami—forever doesn't make me feel trapped.

No, I feel *free*. Like I'm soaring.

And I'm gonna eat Kami like she's never been eaten before, because I don't have a lot to offer, but I'm a fucking god when it comes to—

"*I told you kids to leave my cow alone!*" my mother suddenly screams, and then it's wet.

Everything's wet.

Kami's shrieking and leaping away from me and trying to cover her cooch and lunging behind the cow, who decides to charge and moo and *holy fuck*, I have to throw myself against the wall to avoid taking a hoof to the leg.

Mom's firing a super soaker, and it's fucking *cold*, and I'm not in a shirt, and my dick's throbbing, and she's still yelling too.

"*She's an animal with feelings and rights and*—ohmygod, NICHOLAS?"

I swipe the water off my face and I'm trying really hard not to glare at my mother for cock-blocking me, but it's fucking hard when my jeans are soaked and weighing down a two-ton erection that's not getting any relief now because Kami just snatched her own wet jeans from under Sugarbear, and she can't quite crouch low enough to not be recognized.

"KAMI?" my mother screeches. "Nicholas Archibald Murphy, *why are you go—lick—aaaaahh*. You leave Felicity's friends alone, do you hear me? AND QUIT MAKING OUT IN MY COW SHED."

She leaves as fast as she came, slamming the door behind her.

Sugarbear's mooing so hard and fast she's gonna give herself a stroke.

I can't tell if Kami's laughing or crying.

Or both.

"Oh my god, your mother saw my vagina," she moans

"Probably not," I say. "I mean, my head was in the way."

"*That's not any better*. Oh my god, I can't get my pants on. They're soaked. *Dripping*. Sugarbear, I am so sorry. I promise I'm going to find you a home where people like me don't try to have sex in your bedroom."

"Kami—"

"I can never look your mother in the eye again." She pops just the top half of her head over the top of Sugarbear's back, and her brown eyes are huge and horrified and she's blinking really fast, like she's definitely trying not to cry.

"You know, odds are pretty good that my dad has—"

"*Do not finish that sentence if you want to live*," she screeches.

"You are *so* grounded, young man!" my mother hollers outside the shed. She's still muttering, and it's probably something about either telling my father, or being really fucking grateful that she's *not* telling my father.

"I *told* you she was my girlfriend," I yell back.

"*No one believed you!*" she shrieks. "*We thought you were pranking us because this is too good to be true!*"

"I'm buying that farm tomorrow," I tell Kami. "We can do it with cows and chickens and—"

And *there's* the laugh I've been looking for.

It's a little high and tight and unhinged, but it's a laugh. "You are so very, very wrong," she huffs out.

"I'm not afraid to get hay stuck in my butt cheeks if that's what you're into."

"Where's my vest? And my purse? I need to call a Lyft."

"We could take this back to your place," I offer. "I probably shouldn't sleep here tonight either. Bad vibes. Might fuck with my game brain."

Also, I'm pretty sure I can't whack off in my parents' basement shower without knowing that my mother will realize that's exactly what I'm doing, so even if Kami's not planning on letting me anywhere near her pussy again tonight, I still can't sleep here.

I am definitely buying a farm first thing in the morning.

"I need to get some sleep. I'm neutering three dogs tomorrow, including putting neuticles implants on one, and I need to not be that vet who screws the pooch. As they say."

I wince. "Okay, that's helping the boner situation."

She glances down at my crotch, and one of her *sorry* smiles wrinkles her face. "I'd offer to work that out for you quick, but your mother would probably come back with the whole hose, and poor Sugarbear's already traumatized."

The cow's huddling against Kami, trapping her between the back wall and the shelves. And she's still snorting out moos while Kami rubs her back.

I'm jealous of a fucking cow right now.

I grab my shirt—which is relatively dry, though it still smells like liquor and beer—and check out the door. "She's gone. C'mon. I'll drive you home."

Kami lifts a brow.

I grin.

What can I say? I'm ever the optimist.

THIRTY-FIVE

Kami

AFTER GUILTING Muffy into checking on my dogs for me, I spend the night at my parents' place, because there's no reason for Nick to spend another hour on the road when he can drop me five minutes away.

And spending the night at *his* parents' place is *not* an option.

For every reason under the sun.

I roll out of my parents' guest bed—they've converted my brother's bedroom to an office for Dad, my sister's bedroom to a photography room for Mom, and my bedroom to an adorable guest bedroom decorated with Dalmatians—and stumble downstairs with every intention of raiding the fridge.

I don't care if I'm thirty or seventy-three, it will *always* be appropriate to raid my parents' fridge. It's a life rule.

However, when I walk into the kitchen, I realize I'm not the only one with designs on my parents' food.

Muffy's there. With Aunt Hilda. And Maren.

This is…unexpected.

Muffy's in crazy curly bedhead and red footie pajamas, her feet stuffed into Ugg boots, and she's scowling over a cup of coffee at the kitchen table. Aunt Hilda's in a pink boa, sunglasses with flamingoes at the edges and pink lenses, pink leather knee boots, black leggings decorated with ghosts and pumpkins, and an oversize Christmas sweatshirt with Buddy the Elf.

Maren's in work clothes.

She looks oddly out of place. Not that Aunt Hilda and Muffy look *in* place, but the three of them are a weird combination.

"Um…" I start, because I'm hungry, tired, and borderline mad at myself for not just saying fuck it and sneaking into Nick's bedroom for some hanky-panky last night.

Aunt Hilda leaps up, knocking the table and making Muffy's second mug of coffee slosh over the edge. "Kami! Oh, my sweet niece. I am *so sorry* for my big mouth."

"It's okay," I start, but she grabs me in a huge hug.

"Muffy yelled at me the whole ride home. I forget this is like that time she got kicked out of med school for sleeping with her professor."

"Mother," Muffy grits out. She's always been cagey about the reason she left med school. I've always assumed she'd tell me if she wanted me to know.

"Or so the story goes," Aunt Hilda adds hastily. "I don't actually believe that bullhonky, do you?"

"What happened with Nick?" Maren asks. "You okay?"

"We're fine," I tell her.

One corner of her mouth twitches, and I realize she knows.

She knows his mother caught him going down on me.

Which, strangely, actually explains why she's here. Felicity's probably at Nick's, which means Maren got the *check on Kami* task.

"Oh, good, you're up." Mom bustles into the kitchen in her usual khaki pants and simple blouse. She stifles a yawn and heads to the empty coffee pot, then gives a side eye to Muffy, who doesn't notice, because she's now double-fisting her coffee and alternating sips out of each mug like that'll wake her up faster. "And you're getting a ride home to change from your dear cousin, I see?"

"I'll call you a Lyft," Muffy mutters.

"We were just about to ask Kami about how Nick proposed," Aunt Hilda declares.

"He didn't propose," I say over the rattle and thumps of coffee cans and mugs dropping all over the kitchen. "Go easy on him. He's never had a real relationship before."

My mom frowns. "He's thirty years old."

"He's been in a relationship with himself for all of those years," Maren offers helpfully. "He has *some* experience."

"Not helping," I tell her.

She wrinkles her nose. "It's hard to help. I've known him too long."

"People change."

"Yeah, but…how much? Sure, he's probably beginning to realize he can't play hockey forever, but do you want to be the thing he stumbles into doing instead, because it's easy, or do you want to be the one thing he'd actually give up hockey for?"

Considering how our whole relationship started—way back in February—the only honest answer is, "Both."

I'm probably a complete and total idiot.

"Why didn't you stay with him last night?" Aunt Hilda demands. "Oh, Sally, don't make that face. Our girls are old enough to have responsible, protected sex. I know Muffy does it at least twice a month."

Maren's eyes bulge, but Muffy just sighs and goes back to sipping off both her coffees.

"Hilda," my mom says pleasantly, "shut up."

I have a sneaking suspicion Aunt Hilda is living vicariously through Muffy's fantasies, but considering I ran away from a bar last night because the man I've secretly been in love with for years found out that I'd planned our Christmas wedding a year ago, I don't have much room to talk.

Or to spill her secrets.

My dad walks in, phone in hand, earbuds tucked into his ears. "I don't care what your book says, black holes will always be more interesting than quarks, and string theory is hypothetical."

"Morning, Dad," I say. "Tell Atticus hi for me."

He waves, stops dead at the sight of the empty coffee pot, and shoots a scowl at Aunt Hilda and Muffy. "But the greatest curiosity in the cosmos," he says, "is if we can send a person *into* a black hole."

Maren rises from the table. "I need to get to work. Kami, you want a ride home?"

Muffy pops up like her body just got a jump from cables attached to her coffee mugs. "Yes. Yes, she does. And we need to talk about your profile."

Your profile? I mouth to Maren.

"Bet your dogs need to go out," she reminds me.

Oh, shit. She's right.

I hug Mom around the shoulders and wave to Aunt Hilda and Dad, who's arguing with Atticus now about astroparticles. My dad and my brother both love a good intellectual conversation to get themselves ready for their days.

"Your family is so weird," Muffy mutters to me while we troop to Maren's car.

"Says she whose mother has no filter," Maren points out.

"It's part of her way of getting attention since her divorce."

"Wait. Aunt Hilda got married again?" I ask.

"What? No."

"But—we weren't even in high school yet when she divorced your dad."

"Uh, yeah. You haven't noticed she's been like this for years?"

"She seems…worse."

"Nope. Just branching out to let you share in the misery now. Or maybe it's menopause making her realize she really isn't going to have any more children."

We all climb into the car, buckle up, and Maren points it toward my house. "What really happened to you in med school?" she asks Muffy.

"I got a tapeworm that made me hallucinate," she answers promptly, which is definitely *not* the truth.

"Better than getting caught by your boyfriend's mother while he's going down on you in a garden shed, I guess," Maren says.

"Oh my god," I mutter. "I thought that was why you were here. Who told you?"

"Felicity. Apparently Nick's no longer the favorite child."

"*What?*"

"Yeah. I mean, you can't get pregnant by oral sex, so…"

"*What?*" I gasp again.

"Kidding," Maren assures me with a grin. "I just think that having Nick move back home with a cow might've finally opened Mrs. Murphy's eyes to the fact that he's not perfect."

"That's not—" I start, but I stop myself.

Because I don't think Mrs. Murphy thinks Nick's perfect.

Since he told me about being so small and picked on when he was little, certain things have started to click.

Like, I've never heard his mother say he's perfect. But I've heard her say the announcers are way too hard on him for how much he tries. Or that Felicity shouldn't mess with him before a game, because he needed all his concentration. Or that all those people on social media are judgmental assholes for saying he shouldn't have gotten that endorsement deal from some sports clothing company because he didn't have the right reputation.

I took Tiger home not just because she was adorable, but also because I heard three people laughing at her weird little howl. And if I'm that overprotective of a four-pound dog, I can't imagine what it must've been like for her to see her five-year-old son being bullied.

"I don't think Mrs. Murphy intentionally plays favorites," I say slowly. "But she has two uber-talented kids, and Nick's spent a lot of his life defending and protecting Felicity for everything under the sun. Even when Felicity sometimes hates him, she still loves him, you know? His mother probably just feels it even bigger, because she's his mom."

"Do you really think he can learn to be a good boyfriend?" Maren asks.

"Have you ever seen him fail at anything he put his mind to?"

"I've only seen him put his mind to hockey, pranks, and defending Felicity."

"God help whoever tries to insult *you*," Muffy says on a yawn from the back seat. "The way he ran out of the bar after you last night—I got chills. Like *holy shit he's going to marry her at Christmas* chills."

And now *I* have chills. "We're not getting married," I tell her. "I mean, we're not *not* getting married—we haven't discussed it one way or another. We're just…exploring doing this in a *real* relationship kind of way."

"It was nice to see him win a game," Maren says, "but if all you are to him is a lucky charm, I'm going to dismember him, starting with his favorite member. Just so you know."

"I'm sure he knows there'll be a line."

She nods thoughtfully. "He'd have to truly be an idiot to not see that coming. And he's definitely not an idiot. Not a total idiot, anyway."

My phone dings, and I pull it out of my pocket to see a text from Nick.

"Aww, what did he send you?" Muffy's angling over the back seat, looking at my phone. "It's from him, right? I never see you smile like that for anyone else. Ever."

"Man and cow," I say.

"Is that code for a dick pic?" Maren asks.

"*No*. It's Nick and Sugarbear. Having coffee."

"Here. Let me selfie him back." Muffy grabs my phone before I realize she's serious, and when she hands it back, there's a picture of her in my text message box with Nick.

She's making duck lips and pushing her already curly, wild brown hair even higher. The top of her red footie pajamas are showing all the way to where *Muffy* is embroidered over her boob.

A new picture pops up from Nick.

It's Felicity, Ares, Loki, and Duncan Lavoie all glaring at him on the Murphys' patio.

Knowing Nick, he probably asked them all to turn around and moon him so he could send me a picture of the night sky.

A new text pops up from Felicity.

I don't know what you see in him. He wanted us all to moon you.

I spend the rest of the ride to my house doubled over laughing. And when we pull up to my curb, I realize today's present has arrived.

Muffy and Maren both climb out of the car, because whatever it is, it's big enough that the pile of boxes is as big as two refrigerator boxes put together.

It's entirely possible I don't have a big enough house to date Nick.

"Is he *still* apologizing for missing your birthday?" Maren asks.

"Yep."

"I might have underestimated him."

"I thought you'd have known better by now."

They help me carry the boxes in, and I hustle my puppies to the backyard. When they've all done their business and gotten fed, I return to the living room, where Maren and Muffy are still waiting.

"Are you sure you want to see this?" I ask them. "It could be naked miniature Nick dolls."

"Anatomically correct, yes, we know," Maren says. "Though the boxes aren't big enough to be Nick dolls, because he wouldn't do himself in miniature."

"We definitely want to see," Muffy confirms. "You owe me. I mean, you hired me to match you, and now look at you all smiling and happy."

"You didn't hook her up with Nick," Maren points out.

"I helped her see what she was missing in breaking up with him," Muffy replies triumphantly.

I don't know if she's serious, or if that's her new tagline, until she adds, "And you wouldn't have hired me if you didn't believe I could do the same magic for you."

Maren goes a rare raspberry color in the cheeks, and I put her out of her misery by tearing into the first box.

"Awwww!"

"Oh my god, he did *not*."

"*So CUUUUUUTE!* Can I have one? I want one. Please? Please, Kami?"

I pull out the pillow, stamped with Sugarbear's face, and find another pillow with a different picture of Sugarbear underneath. "They're all different!"

We tear through the boxes, and sure enough, Nick's delivered an entire cow photoshoot on throw pillows. Thirty different Sugarbear photos.

Some are just her face. Some are whole body shots. Some have her in costumes, wearing a mustache or a bonnet.

"He is *not* doing this all himself," Maren says.

"I think he is." I can't stop smiling, because this is so ridiculous it's awesome. "The dick cookies? The book? The billboard? That's evil Nick. This is sort of also evil Nick, but with purer intentions."

Maren blinks at me, and then we're both cracking up.

"Okay, fine," she says, throwing her hands in the air. "A life with Nick Murphy would *not* be boring. I'll give you that. But I'm still not convinced he deserves you."

I'm convinced.

And not because of the cow pillows, but because of everything else.

The date.

Him talking me down last night over my embarrassment over Aunt Hilda leaking my secret obsession.

The way he hugged me before we got into his car for him to take me to my parents' place. Nick doesn't do anything half-assed, and hugging is no exception. He had me wrapped in his body, in his scent, in his heat, and it was only the porch light flickering on and Mrs. Murphy sticking her head out the door that had kept my hands from going wandering into his jeans.

"I'm moving out first thing tomorrow," he'd said, "and when I get back from Texas, you and me and Sugarbear are going on another date."

I know he likes my body.

But there's something magical about realizing he likes *me* also.

"She has it bad," Muffy whispers to Maren.

"He damn well better too," Maren replies.

Dixie, Pancake, and Tiger all claim Sugarbear pillows.

My phone dings, and I pull it out again, ready to reply to whatever Nick's sent this time.

Except it's not Nick.

It's a contact I made at the Heartwood Manor Farm Park a couple weeks ago.

Kami – you still looking for a home for a calf? We might have space. Call me later this morning when you get a chance.

My heart sinks.

This should be good news, but...how am I going to break it to Nick?

THIRTY-SIX

Nick

THE AMBUSH DOESN'T SURPRISE me.

I knew Felicity knew Kami had a crush on me while I was oblivious—and a dick—but I don't know if Felicity knew Kami had said she was going to marry me.

So when she, Ares, Loki, and Lavoie come trooping into the kitchen while I'm on the phone with my real estate agent, I grab a plate of bacon, hit the coffee maker button to start a new pot, and head to the back porch so they can chew me out without Mom overhearing.

But they're not chewing me out.

They're asking what they can do to help me get moved out of here.

"You cannot date my best friend when you can't have her sleep over at your place," Felicity declares.

"Or if you're crashing with friends," Lavoie adds.

I just stare at my sister. "You're not here to chew me out?"

"You sent Kami dog treats."

"Ah…"

"That takes *thought*, Nick. That takes noticing someone other than yourself. And you not only did it, but you also adopted a cow."

"She's more Mom's than mine," I say quickly, even though I'd arm wrestle my own mother if she tries to keep me from taking Sugarbear when I finally get a new place.

"*Mom* doesn't play fetch with her and take thirty million pictures of her a day."

Fuck, I think I'm blushing. "Big dudes need big pets."

Ares hands Loki a bag of dried fruit and smirks at me, because he's a big guy with a little pet.

"Pets with big personalities count," I tell him.

"The whole team's signing an agreement to not engage in purchasing or taking possession of animals for the purposes of pranks," Lavoie tells me. "Ares, Frey, and I are going to talk to the manager in their building with it. We can get you hooked up with a new place before we hit the airport this afternoon."

While they detail all their plans to help get me moved out of my parents' basement, I text back and forth with Kami—and her weird but growing on me cousin—because I already have plans. "Thanks, but not necessary," I tell them. "I can't get rid of Sugarbear. She's my good luck charm. You guys want to turn around, drop your pants, and bend over? Kami missed seeing the moon last night."

They all glare at me, I get the picture, and I shoot it to Kami.

Then I pop the last piece of bacon in my mouth and head back inside. "Appreciate the help, but I've got it under control."

"The last time you said that, penguins invaded the arena," Lavoie points out.

I just smile.

It makes them nervous.

But thirty minutes later, when Lavoie leaves to go get packed for our road game, and Felicity gets sucked into a conversation with Mom about which bedroom upstairs would be best for the nursery Mom wants to put in the house for when she babysits the baby, I join Ares in the living room and prop myself up in the recliner.

He's watching last night's game coverage from all the teams in the league. I should be too—always good to know what new tricks the enemies are trying—but I don't want to watch more hockey.

I need advice.

I hit the mute button, and he looks at me like he's just waiting for the inevitable. Like he knows what I'm going to ask, but he's going to wait for me to ask it, because he's not going to do me any favors.

"Good game last night," I tell him.

I get the dry Ares look of *you're being a dumbass and wasting my time.*

Damn good thing I've never seen him give my sister that look.

I drop the footrest and lean forward, elbows on my knees, and I drop my voice. "How do you do it? How do you balance hockey and being a good boyfriend?"

"Don't fuck her in the shed," he says.

For fuck's sake. "Yeah. Figured that out. Thanks."

He smirks.

"I'm serious, jackass. Kami's—she's—if any other woman in the world was plotting to marry me in two months, I'd be freaking the fuck out. But I'm not. Because she's *Kami*. She's—she gets me. And she still likes me. And that's…"

"Weird?" he offers.

Except I'm pretty sure he's not making fun of me, because it wasn't that long ago that Ares didn't date either.

Because he was *weird* too.

I nod.

He takes a deep breath. "When you know, you know. Just don't fuck it up again. She comes first, always."

"Tried that last night," I mutter.

"With your clothes on too. Make sure she knows she's special. Only one for you."

He makes it sound so simple.

Maybe it is.

She's not hard to please, which makes me feel like an even bigger asshole for never trying harder before. But I'm trying now.

"I feel like I'm getting more out of this than she is," I confess to my brother-in-law, which is also a weird feeling.

Loki chirps and throws a pen at me, as though he agrees with my assessment and also loves Kami.

He probably does. She's his vet, and sometimes she monkeysits him.

"Do you see her?" Ares asks me.

"As often as possible."

And now I'm getting the *don't be a dumbass* look again. "Not happy Kami. What she wants and who she is. The parts that she hides."

"Oh."

He just went over my head.

That's not good.

Because Kami doesn't hide stuff.

She hid how much she liked you, dumbass, a snide voice that sounds like Zeus reminds me.

And does her family know she wants to live in the country?

What other secrets could Kami possibly be hiding? She's *Kami.* She likes dogs. She's followed the Thrusters her whole life. She was a cheerleader in high school. She feels like the *dumb one* in her family.

Fuck, I'm totally lame. If I'm supposed to be reading between the lines here, I didn't even know I'd opened a book.

"I don't think I deserve her," I tell Ares.

He nods. "Step one. Good job, Nick."

"Step one is realizing I don't deserve her?"

He nods again. Loki shrieks with laughter, the obnoxious little fucker.

"What's step two?"

He grins, and I realize the bastard isn't going to tell me. Felicity pops her head into the living room, glancing suspiciously between us. "Were you two…talking?"

It's a legit reason to be suspicious. That's more words than I've gotten out of Ares total since he started dating her almost a year ago. I know he talks to her more—I've walked in on the two of them whispering before—but he doesn't use words with the rest of us unless he has to.

"Hockey strategy," I tell her.

She frowns. "Ares's hockey strategy is *win*."

"He was giving me more complex advice."

He nods, clearly sucking in a grin. "Win *big*."

Felicity smiles at him, and *that*. That smile. That *you're my world* smile. The *I love you* smile. That *I know your secrets* smile.

Do I even have it in me to give all of that to Kami?

Dad stops behind Felicity, larger than life even in his late sixties, his hair grayer than brown, the lines in his face getting deeper every day. He gives me a strangled sort of look. "I'm supposed to talk to you about where babies come from. Your mother says you were doing it wrong."

Felicity has a sudden coughing fit that has Ares off his feet and across the room making sure the baby's okay before I can finish thinking *fuck*.

"I told her she should've given you a few more minutes," Dad adds. He clears his throat. "So the shed should be free tonight."

Felicity's leaning against the wall, laughing so hard she's crying.

Loki's gripping her around the head and patting her hair, his eyes huge and terrified, like female tears scare the shit out of him.

Ares's whole body is vibrating with silent laughter.

Dad clears his throat again and nods to me. "So, practice good. You're welcome to stay here as long as you want."

I grab my phone and text my real estate agent.

Because I am moving out *today*.

And I'm taking my fucking cow with me.

THIRTY-SEVEN

Kami

IT'S BEEN four days since I've seen Nick. When my dogs explode in barks of joy just after lunch Sunday, I dash past the boxes still littering lower level to squeeze around and open the door.

He grins at me, and every question I've had the last four days about if I'm crazy for wanting to be with him or if he'll be mad about the arrangements I'm making for Sugarbear fades away. I don't know if he's serious that we're going to a Halloween party later, or if he actually has secret plans to whisk me away somewhere so we can just enjoy each other's bodies, but I don't care.

So long as whatever we do, we're together, I'm in.

"I missed that smile," he says, and then he's stepping into my house, wrapping his arms around me, and kissing me like I'm his missing piece.

I barely notice Dixie jumping on us or Tiger howling. Nick lifts my ass, I wrap my legs around him, settling my center over that thick bulge in his jeans, and it's not until he turns and six boxes tumble onto us that I remember what I meant to tell him as soon as he got here.

He steadies us both before we fall, which is good, because I'm too intent on trying to get his attention to realize he's still holding me up, and I grip him by the cheeks.

"No more presents," I say sternly.

Or try to.

My gaze collides with those heated, amused green eyes, and I've barely made it into the second syllable of chastising him before I'm smiling back.

"Fuck, I missed you," he says.

I'm stroking his lips with my thumbs because I have to. "No more presents," I whisper again.

"You didn't like the Nick dolls? Oh, shit. Wait. Sorry. That's tomorrow."

My eyes are so wide my vision is rattling and going out of focus. "You. Did. Not."

He finds the wall and gently cradles me against it, a laugh rumbling out of him while he buries his head in the crook of my neck. "I love the way you smell," he murmurs, his breath teasing my skin.

"Nick. Tell me you didn't—*oh, god, yes, there.*"

I don't know if he always knows just how to nibble on my neck right, or if he could touch, stroke, lick, or bite me anywhere on my body and make me instantly hot and wet because it's *Nick*, but his lips and teeth and tongue are working down to the low collar on my light sweater, and thinking is suddenly completely unnecessary.

"I love the way you taste." His words vibrate against my skin, and I clamp my legs harder around him.

I can't help myself.

He's holding me against the wall with his body, and his fingers trail under the curve of my ass, sending waves of delicious goose-bumps over my skin. My breath catches, and I tilt my hips while he strokes my thighs, still suckling on my neck.

"You like?" he asks.

"Always."

"Here?" He teases my ass again, sparks race from my cheeks to my heels, my clit throbs, and I rub my core against his hard cock to relieve some of the pressure.

Except all that rubbing Nick's cock ever does is make me want him more.

"Upstairs," I gasp.

"Now," he agrees. He palms my ass again, turns, and three more boxes topple over.

"Fuck," he mutters, but I lean in to bite *his* neck, and before he can stop to think about the boxes, he's carrying me up the stairs two at a time.

I land in the center of my bed, and he stops just long enough to strip out of his Thrusters hoodie, toss his wallet on the simple oak nightstand, and shuck his jeans before he's crawling up the bed to join me.

"You're overdressed," he informs me as I reach for the thick length dangling between his legs.

"I am, aren't I?"

It's been almost a month since I've had any playtime with naked Nick, and I was starting to worry my memories were a little inflated, but if anything, he's even thicker and longer than I remember. I squeeze and stroke, and his eyes pinch shut.

"Slow," he grits out. "Fuck, I missed your touch."

He captures my mouth again, pushing me gently to my back until I have to let go. But then he's pushing my sweater up and stroking my belly, my ribs, my breasts, and I spread my legs until I can wrap them around him again.

The bed sags next to me, and something cold and wet licks my temple.

I keep kissing Nick and try to push Pancake away, but then the bed sags on the other side too, and Nick suddenly yelps and pulls away.

"Dixie! Down! Oh my god, did she try to hump you?"

He's rubbing his armpit with a grin. "No. Just wasn't expecting that. Here. Let me help you with that shirt. It's blocking my view."

Tiger howls from the ground. Pancake slinks under me to sprawl across my pillow. Dixie wags her tail and sticks her nose into Nick's side.

"Down," I tell both my dogs on the bed while Nick tugs my sleeve down my arm and deftly blocks Dixie's tongue. "And out. Go on. Go wait for Mommy downstairs."

Pancake pouts.

Dixie ignores me and moves on to sniffing Nick's bare ass. He jumps again.

"New plan," he says, sliding off the bed. "You strip. I lock the door. C'mon, pups. Who wants a treat?"

He races them out the door, and then I hear all four of them elephanting down to the kitchen before I can warn him not to tease my dogs.

A month ago, he would've needed prodding to follow through on giving my dogs treats when he offers, but based on the sounds coming from the kitchen below, he's got this figured out.

And that's putting a warmth in my chest that rivals the heat simmering between my legs.

I strip out of my clothes as fast as I can and push all the covers off the bed. I'm debating if I want to be on my side, looking seductive, or just spread-eagle and ready—Nick's really not all that picky—when I remember there's something even better hiding in my closet.

I dash across the room, snag it off its hanger, and dive back onto the bed just as Nick slides back into the room and slams the door shut. He turns, sees me, drops his gaze to the fabric covering me from shoulders to mid-thigh, and the biggest smile I've ever seen spreads over his face.

"Is that what I think it is?" His steps are slow and deliberate on his way over the carpet to the bed.

"It is if you're thinking it's a Duncan Lavoie jersey," I reply coyly.

His eyes widen for the briefest second before he catches on, and I shriek with laughter as he dives onto the bed and tackles me.

"Somebody's a bad, bad girl," he says, rolling me over so he can see for himself whose name is on the back of my Thrusters jersey. "A-*ha*! You *do* have terrible taste in hockey players. I knew it. Oh, what's this? A bare Kami ass? Hmm…whatever should I do with this?"

Light fingertips graze the curve of my butt, and my eyes drift close while I inch my legs apart. He circles my ass, coming back to the center crack, and traces all the way down, inducing shivers up my spine and along my hamstrings to my calves and out through my toes.

"Love it—touch—my ass," I sputter out as his fingers dip into my pussy.

"I seem to remember something about this very sensitive ass," he murmurs, pulling his fingers back out and stroking up my butt again.

I arch into his touch, lifting my hips, and he shifts so he's behind me, both hands squeezing my cheeks. "Higher, gorgeous," he says, and I lift my hips higher, completely bare to him, completely comfortable with trusting my body to him.

"Wider." His voice is going hoarse, his long fingers and thumbs teasing me until I have my face buried in my pillow, my ass high in the air, legs spread.

"Perfect," he murmurs, and then he's licking my pussy from behind while he kneads my ass, and my entire world erupts in a shower of rainbow glitter while he finishes what he started in his mother's garden shed the other night.

I'm rocking against his face, shamelessly arching my ass into his hands, while he devours every bit of me, licking my seam, sucking my clit, grazing it with his teeth, teasing my entrance until that thick, heavy dam bursts and pleasure soars out of me in a surge of sweet release.

He's still eating me, licking me clean while my orgasm pounds through my core, and just when I think I'm done, he slips two fingers deep inside me, and my inner walls clench all over again.

"*Ohmygod*," I gasp as the second wave overtakes me, my fists clenching my sheets, my voice muffled in my pillow. "*Nick!*"

"That's it, Kami. Come for me. Come harder."

He's pumping his fingers into me, and *ohmygod* doesn't do it justice. He's hitting that sweet spot deep inside me while my body squeezes and clamps around his fingers until I'm completely spent, and I collapse back on the mattress.

He presses a kiss to the bottom of my spine. "You're so fucking gorgeous."

I huff out a laugh. "All you can see is my ass."

"And your jersey. It's the best part."

I can't catch my breath, but I'm still laughing. "You are such an egomaniac."

He rolls me onto my back and grins at me as he slides a hand under my jersey and cups my breast, which sends aftershocks through my core. "If by *egomaniac*, you mean the guy who's going to make you come three or four more times before we head out tonight, then yes, yes, I am."

I trail a lazy finger down his chest. It's so familiar, the chiseled muscle, the light sprinkling of hair, the puckered copper nipples, but his body also seems *new*.

Like maybe this time, it's really mine.

From his long, strong fingers, to his thick biceps, his wide shoulders, his straining cock, his hard thighs, and that beautiful smiling face.

"Three or four?" I ask. Three or four more orgasms might kill me. "You strike me as the type who could go for at least six or seven."

I love when his green eyes dance with laughter. "Six or seven? Is that a challenge?"

My hand reaches his belly button and drifts lower. "Maybe."

"You're on."

THIRTY-EIGHT

Nick

MY DICK HURTS so bad from holding out that I think I pulled something vital, but this isn't about me.

It's about Kami.

I snag her hand before she touches my cock, which would be pretty much all it would take for me to blow my load, and I pull it to my mouth to suck on her fingers, which makes her breath catch and her eyes drift closed. She's so fucking sexy, so fucking responsive to *everything*.

I could probably seduce her by wiggling my brows at her elbow.

Her free hand is gripping my bicep, her short nails digging into my skin while she pants and lifts her breasts under the jersey, and I could stay here all day.

All night.

Kissing her. Stroking her. Making her gasp for breath and lose control.

Loving her.

"More, Nick," she pleads, her knees falling open. "Want you —so bad."

I thread our fingers together and have her help me push up the jersey until I'm sucking on her nipples, making her gasps come faster and her hand grip mine tighter. She's pumping her hips against me, and I fumble for my wallet and the condom inside before I lose my head.

Both of them.

"Let me," Kami says, still breathing hard, her eyes so dark that it's like she's hiding the night sky behind her lowered lids.

She takes the condom, and as she rolls it down my length, I have to think about my grandmother naked to keep from losing it.

"I love touching you," she whispers as she cups my balls, and I can't hold back any longer.

"Kami," I gasp in warning, but she knows.

She's Kami.

She always knows.

She spreads her legs wider and grabs my ass, guiding me to her sweet pussy, and I shudder with relief as her body takes me.

"Missed you so much." I bury myself deep and then stop, dropping my face to her shoulder, because *fuck*, she's so tight, so hot, two strokes is all it's going to take, and I'm going to make her scream my name before I come, I swear I will.

I want to deserve her.

"Nick," she whispers, her hips tilting into me. "*More.*"

I lift my head, watching her while I pull out, grit my teeth, and drive back into her. Her lips are parted, lids lowered, her jersey bunched between us, and she's holding my gaze while I rock into her again.

And again.

I'm so fucking hard I could pound steel, and every brush of her fingertips on my ass, on my back, over my shoulders, sends that deep throbbing in my nuts deeper, more insistent, warning me I physically *cannot* hold myself back much longer.

I roll us so she's on top, straddling me, her breasts bouncing as she rides me, squeezing me. I capture her in my palms and thumb her nipples, making her head arch back. "Oh, god, *yes*," she moans, slamming her body down harder and faster while I pinch and pull and tease, my dick getting heavier and thicker and aching so fucking bad that I—just—can't—

She leans forward, grabs my face, and kisses me, and her pussy suddenly clenches around me so tight that I come with a blinding flash of light behind my eyes. She grinds down hard against me, holding there, her inner walls matching me spasm for spasm as she cries my name in my mouth and comes all over my pulsing cock.

My shoulders are off the bed, my tongue clashing with hers, our bodies synced in wave after wave of release. All my nerve endings are firing, my dick still chasing release even while I'm coming inside her. A shudder passes through her, and she slides out of the kiss and slumps over me, chest heaving, while my cock continues twitching inside her.

"Holy hell," she gasps.

I wrap my arms around her and hold on tight, because *holy hell* doesn't begin to touch it.

She's—that—it—*fuck*.

I have to marry her.

Because I have to have Kami in my life every single fucking day. Her smile. Her laugh. Her sneaky wit. Her dogs. Our cow. Her in nothing but my jersey.

Her coming for me.

Offering me her pussy.

Stroking my cock.

Kissing me.

Rubbing my neck after a tough game.

Letting me rub her feet after a long day.

I want to bake her brownies, and I've never baked a fucking thing in my life past a frozen pizza.

I want to feed her ice cream in bed and torment her by suggesting we call our boys Willoughby and Fitzgerald, just to see her nose wrinkle, and our girls Fairybelle and Kami Junior, spelled with a Q to keep them straight.

I snort softly at my own private joke, and she stirs on top of me, squeezing my dick, still inside her, which lights up my nerve endings again like a Halloween tree made of fireworks.

And now I'm apparently hallucinating, which makes me snort again.

"Do I want to know?" Kami asks sleepily.

Yeah, I'm right there with her. Drifting off into a happy sleep that I haven't had in a month. "Love you," I mumble.

I think.

Everything's hazy now, and she's so warm and perfect, and I'm never, ever letting her go.

Not even while I sleep.

THIRTY-NINE

Kami

I DON'T KNOW how long we sleep, but the light coming in my bedroom window is slanted against the far wall when I drift back to awareness.

I lost my jersey but I'm not cold, because Nick's holding me to his chest. He's not snoring, but he's not sleeping quietly either, muttering to himself about blocking biscuits and *just try me, fucker*.

I smile and kiss his chest, because it's there.

Did he really say he loves me?

And *loves* me-loves me, or friend-loves me?

"Snuffle your own beater," he grunts.

I choke on a giggle, and he bolts straight up in bed. He blinks around the room, and when his gaze lands on me, a sleepy smile spreads over his face. He touches my cheek. "You're wearing my nipple," he announces proudly.

My fingers fly to my face, where I have the smooth indentation of sleeping on something that left a mark.

"As long as your mother doesn't know it's *your* nipple, I think I'll be okay," I tell him.

He stares at me for a beat, and then we both crack up.

"We had a couple awkward texts the last few days," I tell him as he pulls me in for a cuddle, which is new, but utterly perfect. "Your mom and I, I mean."

"She's cool now," he assures me. "Felicity pointed out I could've brought home three bunnies instead, and you're now her favorite person in the entire universe. I think she likes you even more than Ares, and that's hard. She just didn't really believe we were dating."

I poke him in the ribs. "You better not be bringing home three bunnies."

"But you—*oh*. *That* kind of bunnies. No, Felicity meant the furry kind. With big ears."

"Did she?"

"Yep. She knows Mom's not ready for more animals by the pool."

I kiss his chest, because it's there and I can. "You're a really bad liar."

"I'm an exceptional liar. You just happen to see right through me."

"Or you're not trying very hard."

"I can give you hard."

I laugh, because it's a terrible line, but also not ineffective. Especially when the growing evidence that he's not lying about giving me *hard* is right there next to my knee. I give it a little *boop* right on the tip, *boop* noise and all, like a great big dork. "You can, can't you?"

And he does, until my dogs start scratching at the door an hour later.

I brush my hair out of my eyes and wobble on shaky legs to let them in while he steps into the bathroom to discard another condom. Pancake, Dixie, and Tiger all swarm in and overtake the bed, though Tiger needs help, poor thing.

Nick pokes his head out of the bathroom. "Hey, I told you this is a costume party tonight, right?"

"No…"

"Huh. Must've forgot. But I got you a costume, so we're set."

I fold my arms and look at him.

He grins and leans in my doorway.

And I'm pretty sure it's not a *you're adorable when you get all Stern Kami while you're naked* grin.

Nope.

That's a classic Nick Murphy Is Up To Something grin.

"You remember how mad you got when you found Sugarbear at my place?" he asks without an ounce of shame, which sets off even more alarm bells in my head.

"That would be a little difficult to forget. You made me do Mad Kami things."

His grin is getting wider and wider, and he's so freaking *hot* when he's plotting something, especially when he's naked and in my bedroom plotting something, and I am completely and totally not immune.

"Mad Kami things like the penguins?" he asks.

"You're a very deep sleeper, and I'm not nearly as nice as I pretend to be, and I have no idea what you're talking about."

"You're way nicer than any nice that's ever niced in the nice-iverse," he tells me, which makes me crack up, even though I'm trying very hard to not fall for whatever he's up to. "You know Zeus Berger is the one who took Sugarbear from her mama, right?"

"Yes," I say slowly, because I *do* know it, but I *don't* know what Nick's plotting.

"He thinks I tried to get him back last week by gluing googly eyes in his locker."

It takes me a minute to understand what he means. "Wait. Googly eyes, like the kind you get at craft stores for putting eyes on pompom animals and paper people?"

"Yeah. Those." He's grinning big again. "Lamest prank I've ever pulled, and now he thinks I'm losing my touch, which means he's not going to be expecting true justice."

"I don't want to know, do I?"

"Please, Kami? Please wear the costume I found you?" Now he's crossing the room at a slow pace, somehow managing to draw my attention to all that bare skin and the extra broadness of his shoulders and the solid muscle he hides under all those goaltender pads.

And those eyes.

Those mischievous, sexy leprechaun eyes are promising me very promising things, and now my brain and my vocabulary are all back-firing because he's doing the Nick Murphy Smolder on me.

"I promise if you hate it we'll just show up and leave and come right back here and I'll be your sex slave for the rest of the night."

Dammit, I can barely walk as it is, but I'm getting all hot and bothered again. It takes effort to keep a stern face. "What, exactly, is this costume?" I ask, as if I'm not going to completely cave just because he asked me to participate, which I am, because I'm physically incapable of telling Nick *no*.

And that's how I end up downtown in a surprisingly comfortable costume with more legs than I've ever had, riding a private elevator to Manning Frey's penthouse apartment less than two hours later.

I texted Felicity, who wouldn't lie to me and who confirmed that she and Ares are going to the party in costume too. She also told me not to worry about the whole prince thing, because Manning's just one of the guys here, despite being the third son of a real king of an actual kingdom in the north Atlantic.

Nick's giddy.

And when I say *giddy*, I mean his cheeks probably hurt from grinning so big and he keeps quietly cackling to himself.

It's utterly adorable.

"What?" he asks me when I smile at him.

"What are you going to do if you're wrong about this?" I ask.

"I'm not." He tugs one of my upper legs, and insists again, "I'm not," when I laugh.

"But if I am," he concedes, "there's always tomorrow. Oh, we're slowing down. Awesome."

"He might not be here," I point out.

"He'll be here."

The elevator stops, the doors open, and Nick tries to slip an arm around me, but all of our legs get tangled together, so after a few awkward re-tries that leave me laughing so hard I can't breathe— seriously, I poked him in the eye with one of my legs, and then got him up the nose with another one—he snags my hand and pulls me toward the music.

We step from a marble foyer into a large living room with high ceilings, modern lighting, and Halloween decorations covering the walls. There's enough food on the tables along one wall to feed an entire country, cobwebs strung between the lights, and a smoking punch bowl on the long counter between the living room and the kitchen.

The party's crowded and already in full swing, with some people dancing, some standing in groups eating, and some having an arm-wrestling contest at a far table. Everyone's in costume, and Nick tells me that while half the people are his teammates, Dax Gallagher from Half Cocked Heroes—yes, the rock band—is supposed to be around here somewhere, and there might be a few actors or actresses too. There are two blow-up dinosaurs that Nick tells me are probably Manning and Gracie. Tyler Jaeger's working a blow-up costume of his own that makes him look like he's riding a unicorn.

"Lost a bet," Nick explains, then points to Connor Klein, who's wearing an honest to god suit of armor and is only recognizable because his face shield is up.

I don't see Zeus and Ares right away, which most likely means they're not here yet, because they'd be impossible to miss if they were.

"Kami! Oh my dog, those costumes—Zeus is going to freak," a feminine voice says from inside one of the T-Rex costumes.

Nick gives the dinosaur a hug. "Hey, Gracie. You lose some weight?"

The other T-Rex punches him in the arm. "You'll kindly quit discussing my wife's waistline," a posh European accent informs him before turning to shake one of my legs. "And lovely of you to join us, Kami. Delighted to have you and all your spare appendages. If Murphy doesn't watch it on the ice, he might need an extra appendage or three permanently attached to help him stop the puck."

"He played fantastic last night," I say, because even though they were in Colorado, of course I stayed up to watch.

With Felicity and Maren and Muffy.

Alina's in California for one of the last few cities on her tour, because she has an even cooler job than Felicity and gets to travel for performances.

"He doesn't need an extra appendage," Felicity says behind us. "He needs an extra brain."

She tries to fling an arm around me for a hug and ends up getting a leg in the eye too. She gives up and punches Nick lightly, because it's apparently the thing to do. "I cannot believe you talked Kami into doing your dirty work for you."

"It's for Sugarbear," I say.

Ares, playing a scantily-dressed and very chiseled Cupid with Loki on his shoulder to Felicity's red-haired princess, is giving Nick a look like he'd better sleep with one eye open next road trip.

I start to say hi to him, but that's when the screaming starts.

First, it's a high-pitched scream from the doorway.

We all whip around and spot a 7-foot-tall clown screaming and pointing at me and Nick.

With at least seven clowns behind him.

All in full make-up.

Striped clown jumpsuits.

Big red noses.

Bigger red shoes.

Clowns.

The clowns are attacking. They're invading and they'll be pulling out their flower water squirters and their horns and *they're fucking attacking*!

I scream.

Nick screams.

Three of the clowns point at us and scream.

"CLOWNS!" someone shrieks, and at least a dozen other people start screaming.

Security rushes the room.

"SPIDERS!" the clowns scream back.

Felicity shoves between Nick and me. She grabs me by the shoulders and forces me to the ground, and I realize Ares is doing the same to Nick.

"Clowns," I whimper to her. I point, but all I can see are legs and blow-up costume legs, and I can't see the clowns, and I don't know where they are.

"It's Zeus." She pats my cheeks like she's trying to wake me up. "Kami, *it's Zeus,* and he's not going to quit screaming until the spiders are gone. He's terrified of spiders. *Stay down.* He can't see you here."

The screaming stops, and I stay there, huddled near the ground in a sea of people.

I fucking hate clowns.

"I fucking hate clowns," Nick sputters.

Ares is gone, and Nick creeps closer to me, his face white as a ghost. "You okay?"

Felicity's coughing like she's trying not to laugh as she stands and backs away, because of course *she's* not afraid of clowns. She's a fucking ventriloquist. She probably has parties with clowns all the time.

"Fucking clowns," I mutter.

He reaches around to hug me and gets a spider leg in his ear, then up his nose again, and we both end up on our backs, right there in the middle of the party, catching our breath and staring at the fake spiders in the webs hung from the ceiling.

"So, great plan," I say.

"Fucking clowns." Duncan squats to the ground next to us in a Ghostbusters costume and shoves his dark, curly head between his knees. "Berger's going down."

"I know a guy who can get a horse tranquilizer," I hear myself say.

Both men look at me. Then at each other. Color's coming back to

Nick's face, which is a huge relief, because until this very minute I would've sworn there wasn't anything in the world that scared him.

I like my world better where Nick's not afraid of anything.

"She's on my team," Nick tells Duncan. "So don't even think of crossing to the Berger side."

"I hear you, man, but spiders are all we've got on him. Dude has no shame."

"He still deserves a dick in a box," I mutter.

They look at me again.

Nick starts grinning.

Lavoie looks around like he's making sure nobody walking around us is listening. "A dick in a box? Like...some dude's actual dick?"

"Lavoie. Seriously?" Nick shakes his head. "Your prank game is weak, man. Weak. But *you*—" He points at me. *"You* are fucking *awesome*."

"Aren't you supposed to be Felicity's sweet friend?" Duncan says to me.

"Not when clowns attack."

"How about when spiders attack?" Nick asks.

"When—what?"

He grins.

And then he grabs me, pulls me to him, and kisses me.

Right there in the middle of the party.

With everyone watching.

Like I'm his entire universe.

I smile into kissing him back.

Clowns be damned. I'm pretty sure this man right here loves me.

Not friend-loves me. *Loves me* loves me.

Which is amazing.

Because I'm also pretty sure I'm going to love him forever.

Just like I always have.

But better, because *this* Nick truly is everything and more that I always hoped he could be.

FORTY

Nick

THE PARTY PICKS up after Zeus and his posse leave and return without costumes, giving us a wide berth, but Kami and I still don't stay late. Mostly because I can't stop touching her, and there aren't enough hours before she has to go to work and I have to go to practice tomorrow and Manning's spare bedrooms are already occupied.

We climb into my Cherokee in the parking garage after shedding our spider costumes, and she settles a hand on my thigh while I drive us out of downtown and toward her house.

"I didn't know you don't like clowns," she says while we wind through the streets lit with solar-powered streetlamps.

I suppress a shudder. "Gammy went through a clown doll phase when Felicity was just starting all the ventriloquist stuff when we were little. You?"

"I got lost at the arena when we went to see the circus when I was about ten. My mom let me go to the bathroom by myself, and I accidentally found my way into the room where all the clowns were getting into the car. Three of them yelled at me, because I wasn't supposed to be there, and then two more with the angry faces painted on had to escort me to security, and it was basically the most terrifying fifteen minutes of my life."

She shivers, and I squeeze her hand.

Ares is right.

I don't know enough about Kami. "What else?" I ask.

"What else did the clowns do?"

"No, what else scares you? So I know when I have to man up and take care of it."

That laugh. Fuck, that sweet laugh gets me every time. And she's so fucking generous with it, like she doesn't know she could keep it to herself.

"You know those dreams where you're back in high school and you missed your finals and you can't remember your locker combination?"

I frown. "No."

"No? Seriously?"

"I haven't dreamed about high school since I was in grade school, plotting how to get all the girls in high school."

She rolls her eyes out loud—swear she does—and I crack a grin in the darkness.

"I sometimes dream I'm driving to the arena for a game, but I keep taking wrong turns," I confess.

"Close enough." There's a smile in her voice, and I'd confess to shitting my pants in a haunted house if it would make her happy.

Even though I never have.

And you can't prove otherwise.

"Corn scares me too," she says.

"*Corn*?"

"I snuck out of bed while my parents were watching…you know, I actually don't know what they were watching. But I know this freaky half-eaten ghost-zombie thing kept whispering, *The corn has ears. It can hear your screams, and it likes it*, and we went on a field trip to a farm the next week for school, and I had to be carried out sobbing. I still can't eat it without feeling like someone just walked over my grave."

"Christ," I mutter.

"I also used to sneak out of my parents' house to go see Muffy all the time," she says.

"What? No. You were—"

"Head cheerleader, prom queen, and *not* as sweet and innocent as everyone thought I was. Smiles lie, Murphy. If anyone should know that…"

Her hand glides over my thigh, and my cock twitches, because it always springs to life at the slightest hint of interest from her.

"Does Felicity know?" I ask. Because I want to know Kami better than Felicity does. Better than *anyone*.

"I don't know. I didn't really know her in high school, and didn't she graduate my freshman year?"

I frown and try to do the math on how fast Felicity went through high school, then give up with a shrug, because I don't even remember what year I was in when Felicity graduated. I just know she was gone before me. And if my birthday wasn't six months before Kami's, we probably would've been in the same grade. "Probably."

"Anyway, it wasn't like I went *every* weekend. And she and I didn't get close until after college. College for me, I mean."

"Do you need to go home right now?" I ask.

"Why? You have another party to take me to?"

She's smiling now. I love that I can hear it when she smiles. "No, something else. A surprise."

"Tell me it's not thirty of something."

I bark out a laugh, remember all the boxes on her main floor, and instantly sober. "Ah, no. Not thirty of something."

"I still can't believe you had a Sugarbear bobblehead made. Do you have any idea what some of your fans would bid for a collection of thirty insane gifts from you? Not that I don't appreciate them, I just…don't have room."

"And I still have ten more days of presents," I add. Ten more days of presents…and fourteen days until we play Indianapolis.

She sucks in a breath, and now I can hear her cringing, which instantly soothes any panic that might be rising at the idea of facing the Indies.

She'll be cheering for me.

We're going to kick some Indie ass.

"I know," she sighs.

"The Nick Murphy dolls are super tasteful," I tease her. "And clothed so the average person doesn't know they're anatomically correct."

"Oh my god," she mutters.

I rub her hand. "It'll be okay. We'll auction them off for charity. Just a little detour. You up for it?"

"Sure." She leans her head on my shoulder, the sweet scent of her simple shampoo filling my nose, her hair tickling my neck, and why the fuck haven't we been doing this for years? "But can I tell you something and you can't be mad at me?" she asks softly.

"I could never get mad at you, but if I pretend to be, will you rub my cock?"

She laughs. "It would be my pleasure."

"Then I can handle anything you need to tell me."

"I found Sugarbear a home."

I slam on the brakes, my heart suddenly in my throat. "The fuck you did."

"Nick—"

"Maybe *I* found her a home." A car veers around us and lays on the horn, but I don't move. "She's my cow-dog. She was delivered to my condo. She's at my parents' house. You can't have her."

"Nick—"

"I'm not a total useless dickhead all the time. And I like my cow-dog. I feed her. I clean up her shit. *I'm* giving her a fucking home." I suck in a breath and go on before Kami can say a damn word. "I've never had a pet. Not a pet that was *mine*. And I've never wanted one, but I'm tired of hockey being my life. There's so fucking much *more*. You can't give me more and then take it away. I'll get a fucking permit to raise her at the stadium if I have to. I'm keeping my cow-dog. And you're either with me, or you can walk your pretty ass home."

My heart's pounding in my ears, because *fuck*, I am *not* giving up on Kami, but she can't take my damn cow away.

I love my cow.

"A man has to have a line, and that's mine," I tell her.

Silence rings through the car, and fucking shitbombs, I just yelled at Kami.

I just yelled *at Kami*.

My hands tremble on the wheel, so I grip it tighter. My lungs are shrinking like they did when I was a kid, heading out for recess when I knew that fucking Jeremy Winters would be waiting with his fucking gang of first-graders to shove me around and tell me my parents didn't love me.

"Are you done?" she asks quietly, and there's something in her voice that soothes my panic even though I know she's going to give me hell right back, because I deserve it.

I'm throwing a fit over a *cow*.

A fucking *cow*.

A cow I love, but still—when did I start loving a *cow*?

And why am I being the idiot giving up on *Kami* over a cow?

Fuck.

"Yes," I say tightly.

I'm staring straight ahead at the streetlights, at the cleaners and the dentist office and the barbecue joint just ahead at the T in the road, my jaw clenched, nose flaring as I try to get myself under control, when a soft hand cups my cheek.

"I love how much you love Sugarbear," she whispers. Her lips follow where her hand was, and she strokes down my arm to rub the back of my hand over the wheel. "You're a much better man than the world will ever know, Nick Murphy."

I blink three times against an unexpected sting in my eyes while my breath whooshes out of me.

"She gets me," I say gruffly.

"Every boy needs a dog," she agrees, and there's nothing mocking or teasing in her voice at all.

I risk a glance at her, and Christ, what the hell did I ever do to deserve that simple, unquestioning trust shimmering in her eyes?

I was fucking *yelling* at her, and she just sits there and takes it.

Because she's Kami.

"I don't deserve you." The raw truth of it makes the words burn my throat.

"Nick," she says softly, "there's no one I'd rather be with than someone who gets upset over an innocent animal."

"I've been a shithead to lots of innocent animals."

"And you knew exactly where to go to make sure those animals were taken care of."

"I took advantage of you."

"Would you do it again?"

"Jesus, no. I'd leave the animals out of it and stick to cookies and books and newspaper ads."

She doesn't say anything, and I drop my head to stare at my crotch. "I know. I'm still a total dick."

"You're very dedicated to your causes."

I'm a shithead. I pick causes like delivering dick cookies to my sister's ex-boyfriends and donkeys to her husband's pet monkey. I'm already plotting a new prank to pull on Zeus because of the whole fucking clown thing.

"I don't like to lose," I tell her.

She's quiet again for a long minute while my heart pounds in my ears, and when I glance at her again, worry lines are marring her forehead.

"Is that why you fought so hard to get a second chance with me?"

she asks so quietly, so haltingly, that my chest almost cracks in two. "So you wouldn't *lose*?"

"*No.* Kami, I—fuck, I'm going to say this all wrong."

"Well, you don't have any better audience willing to give you five chances to get it right than the one sitting right here."

There's a note of self-deprecation in her voice that makes me want to hit something. Probably myself, because see again, *I don't deserve her*.

But I still reach across the car to grab both her hands. "I've been an idiot for a long, long time. When you told me to go jump off a bridge, I was too stupid to realize the reason everything felt wrong was because you were gone and I hadn't realized what I had. I knew I fucked up, but I'd never—I've lost friends before. I've never missed them. But you—I couldn't stop thinking about you. About everything you always did for me that I never said *thank you* for. You remember at Felicity's wedding, when Lavoie kicked my ass on that damn unicorn bull ride, and I was going to get back on that thing until I broke his record?"

"I'm pretty sure everyone even three islands over will remember that," she says mildly.

I squeeze her hands. "Exactly. You talked me off the ledge without making me feel like a spoiled dumbass when we all know that's *exactly* what I am."

"You aren't a spoiled dumbass. You're just...a little blind sometimes."

"You left, and I finally opened my eyes. And it shouldn't have taken you leaving. I should've asked you out for real months ago, but I liked living in my little world where I got to have it all without dealing with Felicity being pissed at me and my mother getting ideas about grandkids and the fear that I'd fuck up and let you down and lose a friend and be the worthless baby shit those fuckhead first-graders told me I was twenty-something years ago. Not if I kept you as just a friend. I don't want to just have it all now, Kami. I want to earn you. I want to deserve you. And instead I'm sitting here yelling about a cow."

She's quiet again.

Probably because she could do so much better than a spoiled hockey player who lives for pranking his teammates and yells about cows.

"But why *me*?" she asks so softly I have to strain to hear her.

"Because you're *you*." It's lame, and I know it's lame.

I should be able to tell her it's because we have the same favorite color. Or because she understands all my secrets and my dreams. Or because we've been through so much together.

But all I really have is this gut-level feeling that her soul and my soul fit like two puzzle pieces, and I've just been facing the wrong direction my entire life.

"My life's brighter with you in it," I add, and I don't think I'm making it better. "Fuck, Kami, this is hard. You know people think Ares is dumb because he doesn't talk? When he does, he's fucking brilliant. I talk all the time, and all that comes out of my mouth is total shit. You just—you're my pumpkin pie after a turkey dinner, and here I am, a spoiled asshole, getting seconds and thirds on his turkey dinner and still wanting the whole damn pumpkin pie too. With whipped cream. And cinnamon ice cream. Because if you're gonna do pumpkin pie, do it fucking right. And you're the best damn pumpkin pie in the world. With all the toppings. And sprinkles."

And I need to shut the hell up, because *she's pumpkin pie with sprinkles?* Maybe I should get out and walk home and just give her my car instead.

She blinks twice, and *damn it*, her eyes are going shiny in the darkness. "The pumpkin pie's the best part," she whispers.

I slump in my seat, relief flooding my bones. "Exactly," I whisper back.

Another car honks and whizzes past us. Kami kisses my cheek again. "I'm really your pumpkin pie?"

"With cinnamon ice cream and whipped cream and sprinkles *and* a cherry."

Her laugh sounds watery and weak. "I'm honored to be your pumpkin pie."

"I'd skip the turkey dinner," I add.

"We need to move," she whispers as yet another car zooms past us.

I sit back up, the words *I love you* sitting on the tip of my tongue, but I don't want her to think I'd say it right now. It feels like a cop-out. Like telling a woman what she wants to hear just to get what I want.

So instead, I'm going to show her.

I've always been better with actions than words, even if I might've gone overboard with making up for missing her birthday.

"You can't be mad at me for this," I tell her as I push on the gas again. My equilibrium is coming back, and with it, my ego. "It might be a little shocking at first, but you're going to realize I'm right, so just go with it."

"Do you know what I love about you?" she says quietly.

"Everything?"

"You're never boring."

Well, shit.

And here all I was going to do was take her for ice cream, because it sounded good, but now I've built it up beyond realistic expectations because I can't help myself.

Guess she's getting the triple brownie fudge sundae with extra caramel sauce.

And then we can take it back to her place.

And I'll lick it off her.

All night long if she'll let me.

I feel like I've finally found her. And now I'm going to do my damnedest to keep her.

No matter what it takes.

"Nick?" she says softly.

"Yeah?"

"Sugarbear really should have other cow friends," she whispers softly. "And you'll be able to—"

"One more week," I grit out. I squeeze her hand, realize I'm probably about to crush her bones, and I let up. "Please? Just give me one more week. I want to fix this on my own."

We pass under a green stoplight and go another half block before she answers.

"Okay," she says.

Because she's Kami.

And she never tells me no.

And fuck if I'm not going to do everything in my power to make sure she never regrets that.

Ever.

FORTY-ONE

Kami

IT'S DAY THIRTY, I'm still pushing off the people from the Heartwood Farm Park who now have room for Sugarbear, because Nick swears all he needs is three more days, and I've spent the entire day jumping every time the clinic doorbells jingle.

He's in Seattle for a game against the Badgers, so I doubt he's sending another coupon book good for thirty orgasms. That would be cruel to both of us.

Also, I'm highly impressed at his creativity since he realized just how much room his gifts were taking. This past week, I've gotten several coupon books. One for thirty awesomely outrageous dates. Another for thirty homemade dinners, with the caveat that he'll order pizza *without mushrooms* if his homemade dinners taste like shit. Another for thirty midnight ice cream runs. The big mama gift certificate book worth thirty spa days.

Thirty breakfasts in bed.

Thirty back rubs *without* the expectation that he'll be rewarded with sex, though he agrees to be my love slave if I so desire after having his oiled hands all over me.

A month ago, I never would've believed he could've been so thoughtful.

And even when he was sending physical gifts, they got more and more personal every time.

And *that's* the Nick I always thought was hiding under the pranks and the ego and the ass.

Not that I need presents. Just hanging out with him—naked, clothed, at home, in a bar, wherever—is everything I've ever truly wanted.

"You're so smiley today, Dr. Oakley," my last patient of the day—or rather, her owner—says as I finish listening to the dachshund's lungs. "I saw you in the paper the other day with the Thrusters' goalie. Are you really dating him?"

I pull back Bruiser's lips to inspect his gums and teeth. "Nick and I have been friends for a long time," I answer diplomatically, because I've seen enough of what Felicity gets asked for just because she's related to him to know not to commit to anything.

"Such a handsome devil. And those are all his real teeth, aren't they? Did he really pull that Jell-O prank on the team management last year?"

I suck in a smile, because *that* story might've gotten a little inflated when it hit the press. "His sister works in the front office, and yes, she found her stapler and computer mouse inside a Jell-O mold one morning over the summer, but the Thrusters have never formally commented on who they think was behind it."

"What about all the computer screens and keyboards in Jell-O?"

"That was exaggerated."

"It was him, wasn't it? I heard about those cookies." She lowers her voice. "You know the ones. On his grandmother's lawn."

There's a knock, and my mom sticks her head in the room, sweeping a glance at the dog to make sure he's not about to take off. "Kami, you have a phone call. And a delivery."

My heart leaps. "Five minutes," I tell her.

She slips into the room. "Oh, you go on. I'll finish up here. How's Bruiser this afternoon?"

Normally I'd argue—I don't like my patients to feel like they're getting passed around—but I'm more than happy to escape gossiping about my private life.

Especially when I get to the phone and see a number that I think I know lighting the display.

There's a package the size of a shoebox sitting on the front counter.

I transfer the call to the phone in the break room and carry the box down the hall, then shut myself inside before I grab the receiver. "Hey," I say more breathlessly than I mean to. "How's Seattle?"

"Lonely and dreary. Did you get your last present?"

"I'm opening it now. If it's a glitter bomb, I'm going to strangle you."

He laughs, and *god*, I miss him. He just left yesterday, but I *miss* him. Not in a *maybe someday he'll see me* kind of way like I used to dream about him, but in an *I miss my best friend* kind of way.

He fixed us tacos two nights ago, and we ate them over a romantic comedy that he didn't once complain about watching, and then he sat there astonished that he liked it, arguing over which character should've realized they were in love faster, and how much less shit the heroine should've put up with.

And then he'd blinked at me like he'd realized what he just said, and then he gave my dogs treats and carried me upstairs like a caveman and made me come three times.

But my favorite part is waking up with him still in my bed.

And only partially because he talks in his sleep in the early morning.

The other part is that sleepy grin and the, "Hey, gorgeous," that happens as soon as he cracks open his eyes.

"I should keep sending you presents every day," he tells me now. "It's a good use of my time and energy."

"I don't need anything else," I tell him while I carefully unwrap the brown paper around the box.

"But you might *like* it."

"The law of diminishing returns says I'll appreciate each gift less and less."

"Not when they're coming from the genius of my brain," he counters.

I'm laughing as I peel away the paper and find a simple white box inside. I lift the lid, and— "Oh my god, you didn't. No, you *did*. Please tell me this isn't—never mind. I'll look later."

His rich laughter rumbles over the connection. "You should look now."

"*I am not taking this doll's clothes off to see if it has a penis,*" I hiss. "I haven't done that since I was nine."

"Handsome, isn't it?"

"He's freaking adorable." My own little brown-haired Nick doll, complete with bright green eyes and that grin that sits right on the border between charming and cocky. It's in a Thrusters uniform, from the jersey to the pads to the shorts to the skates. There's a helmet and a stick in the box with him, and this doll has more muscles than any doll has a right to have.

"Adorable? You mean studly and hot."

"*So* cute. Like a teddy bear in a pink tutu."

"Check out what he's packing in his pants and see if you still want to call him a teddy bear. More like a lion. Or an elephant."

I glance at the door to make sure it's closed, and I carefully peel back the doll's pants, feeling like a total peeping tom the whole time.

And then I burst out laughing again. "Oh my god, there is something wrong with you," I gasp.

The doll has no genitalia, but there's a bow printed where a penis would go.

As though he's hiding a present.

"You'd think dollmakers wouldn't be so picky about giving customers what they want," he says like he's cross, though we both know he's not. He probably already has a video waiting to go up on in Instagram page of the doll reading his fan mail.

"I'm disappointed," I tease him. "I thought for sure you'd glue on some acorns."

"*Fuck.* I'm losing my touch."

I suddenly freeze. "Oh, no. Tell me there aren't twenty-nine more of these waiting in crates at my house. Nick…tell me this is the only one."

"Are you kidding? I ordered three *hundred* of these puppies."

I wince so hard my eyes cross. "Nick—"

"And two hundred ninety-eight of them are being delivered to the children's hospital," he finishes with undisguised glee.

And there goes my heart getting all melty. "Oh my god," I say suddenly again, stopping all melty soft happy feelings in my chest. "Tell me they don't have bows. *Tell me they don't all have bows.*"

"You know you're adorable when your voice gets all high-pitched like that? Makes me want to kiss you until you're getting squeaky because you're turned on and desperate for my tongue between your legs."

If I wasn't already sitting down, I'd have to sit down now, because his words send a jolt of undiluted lust straight to my pussy. "When did you say you're getting home?"

"Friday," he grumbles.

I glance at the clock. "Are you alone?" I whisper.

"Lavoie. Get out."

"*Oh my god, Duncan heard you talking about going down on me?*"

There's another low rumble of laughter. "No, just teasing. I'm alone."

"You are in *so* much trouble."

"I don't have any problem with anyone knowing I like to eat you though," he says. "Their loss that they don't get to. Hey, pull the string on the back of the doll."

"The—oh! There's a string. That's—"

I pull it, and Nick's voice comes out. "Hey, gorgeous. I miss you."

I pull it again. "You are so fucking sexy."

Once more. "I want to eat your pussy until you go blind."

"I'm getting turned on by a doll," I whisper.

"Just don't try to have sex with it, because that would be weird, and if you knew half the things I've fantasized about doing to you, you wouldn't think I had the right to call anything weird."

"What have you fantasized about?" I ask, glancing at the door again, because I *am* still at work.

"Butter," he says.

"Butter? Like me rubbing butter all over your cock before I eat it?"

"Fuck, Kami. I was kidding, but now…"

"Are you as hard as a stick of frozen butter?" My clit's tingling and my nipples are aching, and my mother or any one of our vet techs could walk in here any minute.

"Harder," Nick grits out.

"If I was there, I'd suck on you until you felt better," I whisper.

"Jesus…"

"And then I'd strip for you and I'd lick you from your belly button to your chin, and I'd rub my breasts all over your body, and I'd touch my pussy while you watched."

I'm squirming in my chair, and Nick's breathing is going ragged. Phone sex is new. We haven't done this before, but I think I like it.

"Kami," he groans.

"Are you touching yourself?" I ask.

"Yes."

"Squeeze a little harder for me."

"*Christ.*"

"Stroke yourself up and down and imagine it's my mouth."

"Oh, fuck, Kami, your mouth…"

He's losing control. I can hear it in the rawness of his voice. I glance at the door again, try to picture Mrs. Murphy bursting in on us, because I *cannot* get caught playing with myself at work, but I want to touch my own nipples and squeeze my clit and thrust my fingers into my own pussy until I'm panting as hard as Nick is.

"Imagine I'm sucking you so hard you're seeing stars." My voice is breathy and low and desperate, because every ragged breath in my ear is making me ache deep inside my core. I rub at my breast, and my nipple pebbles harder, while I glance back at the door again. "You taste so good on my tongue," I breathe.

"Oh, fuck, Kami, I'm gonna—*fuck!* BERGER! What the *fuck*!?"

There's a commotion on the other end of the phone the same minute Muffy shoves open the break room door and careens in.

I jump, drop my phone, where there's squawking of male voices and I can only imagine what's going on in Seattle.

"Did it come?" Muffy shrieks. "Did it come? Did it—oh my god, are you sick? Your face is all red, and—*oh*."

She ends on a squeak as I grab my phone and hang up on Nick. I text him quick—*call you later from home*—and lunge for the doll. "He finally did it. He got me a Nick doll," I babble.

"Were you having *phone sex*?" she whispers.

"*No*," I whisper-shriek back.

"I hear that's really fun. I mean, not as fun as doing it together in person or anything, but better than nothing."

"Muffy, *I'm at work*."

She blinks twice and looks around the break room, at the posters for flea and tick treatments and heartworm pills and at the puppy pictures. "Oh. Right." Then she grins. "So, who are you taking to the game Saturday night again?"

"You," I grumble.

"Aww, you really are my favorite cousin." She frowns. "Is that doll anatomically correct?"

"*You are not looking at my doll's penis!*"

Mom pokes her head into the break room. "Did you just—never mind. Just tell me when we need to start planning the wedding. That's all I want to know. Except—is he done sending presents now? That has to be the longest apology I've ever seen in my life. God help you both if he fucks up during pregnancy or labor and delivery."

"Your mom just said *fuck*," Muffy whispers reverently.

"She's spent the last twenty years listening to most of the rest of the family argue over whether string theory or molecular bondage is more interesting. She says *fuck* a lot more than you might think."

"Definitely molecular bondage," Muffy declares.

Mom's left eye twitches.

"You want to go to the game Saturday night?" I ask her. "I have *really* good seats. And we can set Muffy up on a date."

Mom tilts her head like she's considering it.

"*And* I can get the popcorn and a Thrusters jersey for you," I say. "I know you've been crushing on Jaeger."

Her cheeks go pink.

So do Muffy's.

"He'd be first line material on any other team," Muffy declares

"Fucking right," my mom agrees.

"Saturday it is. And just wait until you meet the guy I'm gonna set Muffy up with."

Mom grins.

Muffy groans.

And I wonder if Felicity will let me borrow Loki for the night.

"Oh my god," I suddenly gasp. "I'm starting to think like Nick."

Mom and Muffy both stare at me for a minute.

Then Muffy shrugs, and Mom says, "At least he's not an astro-physicist," and we all crack up.

Because she has a point.

But I should still probably find Muffy a better date than a monkey.

Probably.

FORTY-TWO

Nick

SINCE THE GREAT wanker yanker incident—yes, that's *exactly* what Zeus Berger is calling it—our truce is off. We both agreed to cool it after Halloween, but he's going *down*.

I'm on edge the rest of the road trip.

I still kill it on the ice, and we win both our away games, including a second shutout for me, but by the time we get home well past midnight Friday night, I'm ready for some downtime.

I swing by my folks' place to check on Sugarbear—fucking plan is taking longer than it should—then head over to Kami's. I should go to bed—we have morning skate and a home game tomorrow—but I'm desperate to see her.

There's a light on in the living room when I pull up. I knock softly, because if she's sleeping, I don't want to disturb her, but the door swings open almost immediately. "Sshh," she whispers as she opens the screen door for me too. "The dogs are asleep."

I'm good with that. I don't need to talk.

I just need to kiss her.

She's reaching for me the same time I'm reaching for her, and soon we're shoving the front door shut with our bodies.

She squirms out of her Thrusters jersey while I shake off my coat and tackle the buttons on my shirt, kissing her the whole time.

My pants hit the floor by the time I finally get all the fucking buttons on my shirt undone, because Kami's quick, and she's managed to de-pants both of us in the time it's taking me to get out of this fucking shirt.

But once my skin is free, her hands are roaming my chest, her lips are locked on mine, her bare leg is rubbing my thigh, and *Christ*, she's just everything.

"Thought—you—asleep—" I gasp between kisses.

"Missed you," she replies, pulling me closer and going up on her tiptoes to grind her hips against mine.

Fuck, she feels so good.

I lift her against the door, her legs go around my hips, and she centers herself over my cock. I thrust into her hot, slick channel in one smooth motion, and we both shudder in relief.

And now that I'm inside her, everything slows. Her milk chocolate eyes lock with mine, our breaths sync, and I kiss her again, slow and leisurely, while I take my time thrusting in and out slowly.

"Remember—first time—wall," she whispers against my lips.

"Made it to the finals." That night, back in the spring—we'd been out at the bar celebrating. I made eye contact with Kami, and ten minutes later, she slipped out of the bar. I followed her after five more and caught up with her in the lobby of my building. We made out all the way up the elevator and barely made it inside my condo before our clothes went flying. "I should've known that night," I tell her while I stroke into her again.

There was no one else I'd wanted to celebrate with.

She flexes her hips to take me deeper. "I'd never come so hard," she whispers breathlessly, tilting again as I pull back and then fill her once more.

"Your pussy is so soaked for me."

"I was watching you play and touching myself."

My nuts tighten more and my next thrust is harder. Her breasts are pressed between us, and I want to lick them. "Did you have your fingers in your pussy?" I ask.

"So deep inside," she whispers.

"This deep?" I slam into her.

"Deeper."

My dick's turning to iron at the image of her masturbating. "Fuck, Kami."

"When you blocked that last shot—*oh, god, yes*." Her head drops back as I drive deeper and deeper into her, faster and faster, and one eyeball drifts toward her nose. "Your face—so hot—wanted—jump you—kiss you—fuck you—*yes, Nick, YES!*"

Her pussy clamps hot and hard around me, and I roar her name as I come with her, falling over the edge into the perfect heaven of her body, everything fading to blackness except her eyes glittering as she watches me watching her come. Her lips are parted and quivering, her breath ragged and uneven, her eyes barely focused while her pussy squeezes and squeezes and squeezes me, making me come so hard even my toes are shaking.

Kami drops her head to my shoulder. "I missed you," she whispers again.

I pull her close to carry her to the couch when I realize what I did, and my entire body clenches.

"Nick?"

"Oh, fuck, Kami—I forgot—I didn't—"

Her eyes widen as she seems to understand what I'm trying to say. "You—oh." She goes pale. "I should've—"

But she breaks off, and I realize she's not saying what she's supposed to say.

That it's okay.

That she's on the pill or something.

She was always on the pill. She told me so.

"I—quit—when I—we—broke up."

She's so pale, but a warm fuzziness starts in my chest, and as she blinks quickly against the sheen coming to her eyes, I wrap her in a tight hug, because it's okay. *It's okay.* "It's okay," I tell her.

"I didn't—" she starts again, but I squeeze her tighter, because *fuck.*

Kami, carrying my baby?

That's not a terrifying thought at all.

Not to me.

I don't know how she'd feel about raising two kids—both a baby *and* me—but there's a goofy grin spreading over my face, and fucking hell, why did this scare the shit out of me for so long?

"I—*so* sorry." Her voice cracks, and if I thought I could hug her harder without cracking a rib, I would.

"Shh," I murmur into her hair. "Everything's okay."

I carry her upstairs and tuck us both into her bed, pulling her close while she burrows into me.

"I know this isn't what you wanted," she whispers in the darkness.

"You're what I want. Every day. All day. No matter what."

"Nick," she whispers.

Like *I'm* the one who's special. Like *I'm* the one who brightens *her* world. Like *I* matter.

Doesn't she know I'll never be half the person she is?

Or has she started figuring it out, and now *she's* having second thoughts about wanting a future with me?

No, she missed me.

She said so. And Kami doesn't lie.

Not well, anyway.

But she's still trembling as her breath evens out, and I can't help but wonder—has she finally realized just how much trouble I am?

Does she even *want* to carry my baby?

That's it.

No more fucking around for me.

I'm getting my life in order, and I'm going to prove to the entire world that I can be everything she always wanted me to be.

FORTY-THREE

Kami

NICK'S GONE when my dogs wake me up, but he left a note.

Kami –

Had to go take care of Sugarbear. Finalizing plans for her new home THIS WEEK. Promise. Fucking complicated. Don't know why you did this for us for so long.

Miss you already. See you tonight.

XO,

That sexy stranger you banged behind the shed last night

I'm smiling and shaking my head at his signature line when I realize the note isn't all he left.

There are certificates for popcorn, hot dogs, and drinks at the arena tonight, because of course there are.

Nick's not nearly as oblivious to the little things as people think he is.

I'm still smiling over breakfast and contemplating who I should ask to be Muffy's date while my dogs tumble together in the living room when my phone dings with three incoming text messages.

Felicity: Kami, are all four of your tickets claimed tonight? Mom's making "I want to get to know Kami better" noises. Like she doesn't already love you. I think she wants to suck up for ruining…that thing I'm not thinking about.

Muffy: She's bringing me and her mom and a date.

Maren: If I were you, I'd take Felicity's mom.

Muffy: Wait, if you were me, or if you were Kami?

Maren: Both. Kami needs to suck up to her potential future mother-in-law, and you need to not let Kami set you up on dates.

Alina: Isn't it a little soon to be talking about potential future mothers-in-law?

Maren: No

Felicity: No

Muffy: Can I be your maid of honor? I've never been anyone's maid of honor, and since Mom's clearly never getting married again…

Kami: There's no wedding. IF we get married, we're eloping where no family can tell embarrassing stories about either of us.

Felicity: Considering the rumor going around the locker room that Nick gave you a blow-up sex toy as his final apology gift, that's probably really smart.

Maren: WHAT?

Alina: Why didn't I hear about this?

Muffy: Whoa, if that doll I saw was supposed to be a sex toy, was it actually a big dildo, or was there something else?

Kami: THERE. IS. NO. BLOW-UP. SEX. TOY. And for the love of pucks, DO NOT SUGGEST ONE TO NICK.

Maren: Oh no, trouble in paradise? And I was just warming up to the idea of Nick maybe being good enough for you.

Felicity: Please tell me you didn't dump my brother. He would be HEARTBROKEN. And none of us know what that might mean, but it's terrifying.

Alina: Whoa, wait, Nick has a heart?

Muffy: He does really seem to like you, Kami. Don't do it. Don't break his heart.

Kami: Yes, Felicity, I have a spare ticket for your mom for the game. But she can't mention the garden shed or I'll accidentally on purpose spill my soda all over myself and then I'll have to go change, and I'd really like to see the game.

Alina: Fuck that. Spill the soda on her. Nick needs you. He's on fire since you started banging him.

Maren: #truth

Muffy: Called it.

Felicity: Thanks, Kami. I'll tell Mom. And I'm muting you all now.

I absently glance at the front door, remember Nick taking me against it last night, remember that he forgot to use a condom, and everything inside me temporarily freezes.

He gives really good wall sex.

But I don't want him to think I'm trying to trap him into having a baby.

Except…he wouldn't have stayed if he thought I was trying to trick him into something he didn't want. And—I shiver—if there are any lasting repercussions to us forgetting protection last night, I have this feeling he'll be an amazing dad.

He was so—so—*perfect* about it all. *Responsible* has never been a word I'd associate with Nick, but after his initial apology, he didn't freak out.

He took it all on his shoulders and told *me* everything was okay.

He's just *everything*. Everything I always wanted to believe he could be.

And—my heart skips a beat—if I *am* pregnant, I don't think he'd marry me just to give our baby the traditional married parent home.

No, I think he might do that because he loves me.

Pancake skids to a stop in front of me and drops a pull toy on the ground, then goes down on her front paws and lifts her haunches, wagging her tail. "Okay, we'll play," I tell her.

Dixie and Tiger race over to us too, and I spend the rest of the day hanging out with my dogs and cleaning my house and smiling.

About everything.

And texting Nick.

Who also gives good text.

I head over to my parents' place just before dinner. Muffy meets us there, and we all pile into my car to go pick up Mrs. Murphy.

There's a knot in my stomach that I can't quite shake as we pull down the drive. Sugarbear's grazing in the front yard, and she trots over to beg for love when we all step out of the car.

"Oh, she's so cute!" Muffy squeals.

"Very social for a cow," Mom says.

"She's such a good girl." I rub her head, talking doggy talk to her, and I half expect her to flop onto the ground and show me her belly, but she just stands there soaking up the attention and trying to lick us all.

"You should find her a home with other cows," Mom reminds me gently.

I hold up my hands. "Nick says he's working on it."

"Who wouldn't want to keep such a cutie-patootie around?" Muffy croons to her.

She looks like she's gained another twenty-five or fifty pounds this week, and Mrs. Murphy looks mildly flustered when she steps onto her front porch and catches sight of the three of us loving all over the calf.

"We offered to get him a real dog instead, but he says he likes *this* one. Like she's a dog. And she's adorable, but there's nothing cute about stepping in a cow patty at five in the morning. And if you tell his coaches he thinks this cow is a dog, and he gets grounded for mental issues, I'm disowning all of you."

"She is a dog," I reply, which earns me another sloppy, grainy kiss from the calf.

"And he's so good with her," Mrs. Murphy sighs happily. "He's doing right by her too. Even if it's getting mildly inconvenient waiting for everything to fall into place."

I glance at her.

She smiles serenely, and I realize she has a secret.

And she's Nick's mother.

And he *has* to get his skills from *somewhere*, which means…

No, I tell myself. I have to trust him.

He would *not* harm a cow. And neither would his mother.

But they are *definitely* up to something.

"You're sure there aren't any more farm animal pranks being planned in that locker room?" Mom asks as we all troop back to my car.

"Positive."

Except I'm actually cringing at the thought of what else might be going on in the locker room. Because a little birdy told me things are heating up again between Nick and Zeus after our phone-sex-gone-wrong incident.

And by *little birdy*, I mean all of my friends, because it hit the underground hockey blog network, and of course Felicity heard from Ares, though she's kindly refrained from mentioning it.

"Nick learned *his* lesson," Mrs. Murphy tells my mom. "The real question will be if that Zeus Berger has learned his." She sniffs. "Just because he's seven feet tall doesn't mean he gets to be a bully. I sometimes can't believe he and Ares are identical twins. Such very different boys."

"Nick can handle Zeus," I tell Mrs. Murphy quietly.

Because he can.

But after hearing a few more stories about the bullies in his childhood, I can see why she's testy. Nick's a big guy—well over six feet and built—but the Bergers both dwarf him.

"And he's hardly innocent," I add with a head nod toward Sugarbear.

She looks at the calf like she's going to blame Zeus for taking the prank too far, but even she seems to realize it would be pointless.

Nick doesn't do *anything* small.

That is, after all, why the four of us are headed to the arena with front row seats tonight.

"Think he can get another shutout?" Muffy asks when I put the car in gear.

"I think he plays his best games on home ice," I say.

"With his favorite cheerleaders in the front row," his mom agrees.

I should probably worry about when she's going to start asking if I've had my period lately. The thought makes me both smile and worry, because while I know she'd be over the moon at the idea of two grandbabies within a year, I don't want to do babies unintentionally. Especially because Nick and I still haven't talked about our future. But I decide that for now, I'm just going to enjoy that we're all ignoring the shed incident and heading into the arena.

Plus, who wants to worry when we're on our way to a hockey game?

It's going to be an awesome night.

FORTY-FOUR

Nick

I'M PULLING on my pads when my phone buzzes at the top of my locker.

Kami's texting.

It's a selfie of her, both our mothers, and Muffy in front of the new Thrusty statue outside the arena. All four of them are in Thrusters jerseys.

Our mothers are arguing over which one of us is more perfect. I think they're trying to sell each other, she adds to the picture.

I'm so distracted, smiling at the photo of them all happy and bunched together around the giant metal Thrusty for a picture, imagining my mother telling Kami's mom that I potty trained myself at two and a half and that I always give the best Christmas presents, that I almost miss Zeus walking in.

"Ready to kick some ass?" he asks the room at large.

Grunts and *Fuck yeah*s fill the room.

He saunters to his locker and stops with a smirk at the box sitting on the bench in front of it.

"Funny, Murphy. I'm not falling for your shit," he tells me. "You open it."

"It's from your mom," I reply.

He's still smirking when he reaches around it and grabs his jersey.

Like I'm going to put the good stuff in a clearly labeled, very suspicious box.

There's a *pop*!, and everyone around Zeus scatters while a puff of glitter and confetti explodes in the air.

"Fucking *damn* it!" he barks before he rounds on me, glitter and confetti sparkling all over his face. In his eyebrows. Up his nose. Square on the neck. Sticking to his stubble. It's sprinkled all over his Thrusters T-shirt and down the front of his sweatpants, and he hasn't yet realized what's special about the confetti. "Did you talk to my sister, you fucker?"

I scratch my chin. "You got a little dick there on your face."

Snickers and outright belly laughs are going through the room, because the entire team's in here.

Berger scratches his face too, pulls the confetti away, studies it for a minute, and his face breaks into a big-ass grin. "You sneaky moth-erfucker," he says. "Come give us a hug."

Fuck.

Can't help but like a guy who takes a glitter bomb well.

Especially a dick glitter bomb.

So I let him hug me and smear glitter all the fuck over my pads.

He gets me with a hand to the face, and I shove a second glitter bomb down his pants.

"Not the first time," Ares mutters with a head shake when confetti explodes out of Zeus's ass.

"That was you who sat on that fucking bomb the first time," Zeus replies to his brother, rubbing confetti all over his twin too. "Who's next? Come get your game makeup, fuckers!"

He snaps a selfie, and I can't help but stare at the grin.

He got *owned*, and he's standing there taking it like a champ.

Knew I liked him for some reason.

"What in the *hell* are you doing now?" Coach asks from the doorway.

There's two massive piles of glitter and dick confetti all over the Thrusters logo in the carpet, plus trails of it everywhere. None of us are dressed. And everyone's looking at me.

"Team building exercise," I say.

"Fuck, yeah," Zeus agrees.

He plops his three-hundred-fifty-pound ass right on top of the white box on the bench in front of his locker, and my voice—though higher and a little distorted—comes from the general area of Zeus's asshole.

"That'll teach you to fuck with me, jackass! You've got a face only a mother could love! Did your wife have to tie your skates for you this morning?"

It's possible I'm the real asshole here.

Zeus snorts with laughter and rubs his ass harder over the box with the one remaining Nick Murphy doll while it squeaks out slower and more vulgar insults as he destroys the one-of-a-kind voice box inside, which is nothing like the *You're a winner!* messages that went to the 298 other dolls at the children's hospital. "Nice try, Murphy. I'm still gonna keep your ass outta trouble on the ice tonight, because I got a lot of respect for second-rate pranksters."

"You can't beat us," Ares tells me.

"*Years* of experience," Zeus agrees. "Ask my sister sometime."

"Scarred for life," Ares chimes in.

"And she married the fucker who instigated most of it. He's got a billion-trillion bucks now, and me and Ares, we know when to bow to a master."

Ares nods in agreement. "When to ask him for favors too."

Coach rubs his eyes. "I'm coming back in two minutes, and you all damn well better be ready to win a fucking game tonight."

"You can brag on your family later," Lavoie tells them. "Get dressed."

He looks at me, and his lips twitch.

"There's one more in his car," I mutter.

"Kami know you're *this* kind of an asshole?" he asks.

I grin. "She's got an idea. Hey, Berger. Smile for me, sexy thang."

Zeus strikes a pose. Ares turns on the flashlight on his phone and shines it on Zeus making the glitter dicks shine and sparkle. I snap a pic and text it to Kami.

Somebody won't be interrupting private phone time anymore, I tell her.

She replies with a gif of a woman falling over laughing, and I send her a gif of a kissy-face.

She replies with a gif that's probably illegal and makes me break out in a sweat, because it'll be at least three hours, probably four, before I get to actually *see* her.

Coach strolls back in. "You all got your heads in the game?" he asks.

We all nod, serious as we can be.

And when we take the ice, I'm ready.

No question. No hesitation.

Except that minute I pause to wink at Kami's mom and toss her a puck.

Because if Kami has to sit through the whole game entertaining both our mothers, the least I can do is charm hers from the ice.

And they said charm school wouldn't work on me.

Those fuckers were wrong.

FORTY-FIVE

Kami

BECAUSE MY BODY apparently thinks that being nice and sweet and everyone's favorite boring girl next door means that we can't have the scandal of an unexpected out-of-wedlock pregnancy, even in modern times, I get my period two days later.

I text Nick to let him know there are no lasting repercussions, and he doesn't answer.

But I get a bouquet of flowers and a box of chocolates with demotivational sayings inside the wrappers before I leave work.

Despair: It's a step down from destrike.

Cheer up. You could be a dog, and then you'd be really loved. Maybe next life.

You know what's hard? Getting a splinter under your fingernail. That's hard.

They're so wrong, but I eat the whole box, cracking up harder with every chocolate I unwrap. I lick the last one and use it to smear chocolate all over my face, then send a selfie to Nick.

I've accepted your sacrifice to the hormone gods. It is now safe to enter the building.

He sends me back a picture of him, Lavoie, Ares, and Jaeger playing cards on a plane, because they're off to Florida tonight.

He's smiling, but he looks tired, and I wonder if he had a hard practice today, or if he's been more worried about the possibility of me being pregnant than he let on the other night.

I've started thinking that his *love you* was a total fluke, because he hasn't said it again. And he knows I've been in love with him since before I could even say why, so I don't want to say it first and make him feel like he has to say it back.

Even if I'd said it back that night, he wouldn't have heard me.

He passed out so hard the next instant, I had to shove him to get comfortable, and he barely stirred.

After driving home to take my dogs for a walk, I meet Felicity, Maren, Alina, and Muffy for dinner at Felicity's place, because we haven't had a girls' night in forever, and since I called Muffy for Muff Matchers, it's become pretty obvious she needs friends *other* than her mom, so I'm dragging her along.

"How's young love?" Alina asks me over wine while we munch on cheese and, in Felicity's case, sparkling grape juice and hummus.

"Good," I answer automatically. I've cleaned my face off, but I can still smell chocolate under my nose, and I'd rather be pigging out on toffee and brownies than cheese and vegetables.

All four of my friends gawk at me.

I rub at that spot under my right nostril where I swear the chocolate is hiding. "What? Do I have it on me still?"

Felicity's eyes bulge, Maren doubles over laughing, and Alina and Muffy give each other a high five.

"What in the—*oh*! Oh my gosh, I haven't seen him all day. I was eating—you know what? Never mind. Yes, can someone please check and make sure Nick's semen isn't in my nose?"

"I kinda wish I was still morning sick," Felicity says.

"That's really disgusting," Muffy informs me.

"Trouble in paradise?" Maren wants to know.

"No, it's just—hormones, okay?" It's just that I think he loves me, but I can't go blabbing to his sister that I'm afraid I'm reading the signals wrong because I've always been hopeless when it comes to Nick, and what if I actually scared him off and now he's biding his time until he can break up with me because there was that super slim chance I was pregnant, and now that he knows I'm not, he wouldn't be abandoning both me and his unborn child, whom I would be *more* than happy to carry, but not if I'm going to have to do it on my own?

Or possibly hormones are actually the right reason I'm cranky.

"So…no lasting implications from…you know?" Felicity hedges.

"He told you?" I gasp.

"Nick's like a book when you've known him long enough." She flutters a hand. "And I'm also really good at spying on him when I want information. Don't tell him that. It'll cripple me in the war to know what he's up to. And given that it's *Nick*, it's always a good idea for *someone* to know what he's up to."

I can't exactly argue with that. "He sent me flowers and chocolates today," I tell her.

She frowns.

"The chocolates had terrible, awful, hilarious sayings inside them," I add hastily, because yeah, flowers and chocolates are *not* Nick.

But then, he probably didn't have time to throw together a gift pack of things with his picture on them.

"Oh. That's better," she says, but she's still frowning. "Are you okay?"

"What are you two talking about?" Maren demands.

"Oh my god, Kami's pregnant!" Muffy shrieks.

I lift my wine glass and jiggle it in her direction.

"But you *could've* been," Alina guesses.

"That's totally what I meant," Muffy says quickly.

"He would've been thrilled," Felicity tells me.

"Really?" I wince, because I hate the doubt creeping into my voice.

I know the hockey blogs—except Maren's—are saying that dating me is his good luck charm, which is ridiculous, because Nick's a pro. Even if people don't *think* he works hard, he does. There's just a lot of pressure this year.

But at the same time...I don't know that he's ready for the whole wife-and-kids thing either.

And not knowing how long it might take him to *be* ready sometimes makes my stomach drop to my toes as I realize that choosing to be with Nick might mean it never happens.

Felicity rounds the island to stand next to me and squeeze me in a shoulder hug. "He's different, Kami. He knows what he has now, and he doesn't want to fuck it up again. Just...give him a chance. He won't let you down."

"I know." I do know. I *do*. He *has* been different. And even if he's not saying he loves me, he's doing everything I ever dreamed he would, but more, because he's doing it *his* way. And he's funny and sweet and romantic and obnoxious and imperfect and *Nick*. "No one's more dedicated when he has a goal."

My friends all snicker at that, because we all know it's true.

"Did you know he was going to glitterbomb Zeus?" Maren asks.

I shake my head. "He doesn't consult anyone when he gets a plan."

"Ares said it was worse than when their sister got all of them in her husband's office," Felicity tells me. "And that was apparently pretty epic."

"Did they use dick glitter?"

"I think that was the difference."

"Do you have tickets to Thursday's game?" Maren asks.

"I have tickets for *all* the games," I say. "But yes—want to go?"

"To watch them play Indianapolis? Oh, *hell*, yeah." Last year's expansion team almost kept the Thrusters from reaching the championship finals. It'll be a hot match-up. Nick's already asked four times if I'll be there. "But I have to go check on a project in Colorado this week, so I can't go."

"I'm on the last week of my tour," Alina says, frowning. "That was terrible planning. Think you'll get tired of going to every game?"

I consider it for half a second. "Nope."

"I'll go," Muffy tells me.

"I had no doubt."

We dive back into our food, and Muffy starts telling a story about a new client who asked to be set up with only women who have honey brown hair. Nick texts me when they land in Florida, complete with a much happier selfie—I would be too if I were walking on the beach—and by the end of the night, I'm feeling normal again.

Normal, happy, and optimistic.

Nick loves me.

He does.

He's just not ready for the words yet.

So long as he keeps showing me, everything's going to be fine.

FORTY-SIX

Nick

I WALK into Mink Arena Thursday night with my phone pressed to my ear. "You're coming?" I say for the fifteenth time.

I thought playing New York was tough. I thought the Badgers were tough.

But we're up against the Indies tonight, and those fuckers have only lost three games all season.

They're the team we have to fucking *own* if we have any shot at making it through the playoffs to the championship again this year.

"I *promise*," Kami says, and my lungs once again even out.

Since she took me back, I've been on fire. Haven't let anyone score more than two goals on me in a single game, and that only happened once. Lavoie was right.

Having my personal life squared away makes me play a hell of a lot better.

And it's Kami.

She says she'll be here, she'll be here. "Good," I say, "because I know how much you love watching my sexy body in all those pads."

Her laughter eases more tension. "You are such a goober. Go get ready to kick some Indies ass. I'll wait for you after the game, okay?"

"Deal."

The dressing room is tense.

Yeah, it's a regular season game, but it's *the* regular season game. Our test to see if we have what it takes to be champions again.

There aren't any pranks tonight. No friendly insults flying around the halls. Just focused concentration.

Lavoie redoes his skates three times, like his routine's off. I shaved *right* before getting in my Jeep to come to the arena. Sokolov and Jaeger's Pokémon card trade is silent, and they're both scowling. Even Frey, who's always smiling, is grim.

Zeus is pacing.

Only Ares is his normal zen self.

"Joey's coming," Zeus says to his twin. "I tell you that?"

Ares nods and continues methodically wrapping his ankles.

"She wasn't going to," Zeus adds. "But…"

He doesn't finish, but he doesn't have to.

We all play better when our loved ones are cheering us on.

Even Jaeger, when his parents came in. Frey, too, on the rare occasion his father and the queen make a trip over, and he's *never* off his game, even when we're on the road halfway across the country from Gracie and the baby.

Ares finishes his ankles. Once a trainer checks them, he circles the room.

He's the calming presence we all need. Big, quiet, broadcasting *this is what we train for, fuckers* to all of us without saying a word. A bunch of us weren't sure what management was thinking when they gave up two guys to Chicago for just Ares in return before last season started, but I get it now.

He's steady. He's dedicated. And he's the heart and soul we needed to win the Cup last year.

"You got this, Murphy," he tells me.

"Damn fucking right."

Fuck, I hope he's right. We have the Berger twins, but Indianapolis has the Kingsley twins. Johnson, their goaltender, is a fucking beast. And Cranford, their enforcer, knocked Jaeger out cold to earn himself a month-long suspension after the first playoff game last season.

He's barely back.

This will be ugly.

I check my phone just before we have to put them away. No messages from Kami, so I send her a selfie of me making duck lips. *This is my "I'm going to kick ass for you tonight" face.*

I picture her cracking up when she sees it—I love that she doesn't take my ego seriously—and then I get in my zone.

It's hockey time.

Still, when I reach the ice under the roar of the crowd with the spotlights flashing and the announcer crooning to psych Indianapolis out, I immediately look for Kami. She should be next to the penalty box tonight, second row because none of the resellers had first row tickets for *this* game left by the time I had the genius idea to buy her all the tickets.

But where Kami and some of her friends should be, all I see are four empty seats.

Sweat dribbles down between my shoulder blades.

I'll be there, she said.

Probably stuck in traffic.

The game tonight's a sell-out, because it's Indianapolis, and everyone in the entire state wants to heckle Cranford for that sucker punch to Jaeger last year.

"Watch Jaeger's back," I tell Zeus when he circles the net. "Fuck, watch *all* their backs."

He gives me a two-fingered salute. "Three steps ahead of you, Murphy. You just stop those pucks."

I glance at Kami's empty seats again. *Come on, come on, come on…*

But she doesn't show up in the first period.

The Indies are up one-nothing, because they're all fucking beasts tonight.

We get back on the ice to start the second period, and Kami's seats are *still* empty. She hasn't read my text from before the game. I double-checked, and yeah, those are the seats I bought her. Still, I scan the crowd, wondering if she traded up somehow.

But she's not in the first three rows. I don't know which box is her parents', and even if I did, I don't know that I could spot her clearly this far away.

Lavoie catches me looking. "Head in the game, Murphy," he says. "She's here."

She's not fucking here.

Raw instinct and years of practice take over the minute the horn sounds to start the second period. By the time the horn buzzes again, we're tied two-two.

In the dressing room between periods, I text Felicity.

She doesn't answer, and I realize she's working. Ratings go up every time she and Thrusty help call the game. "Felicity in the announcer's booth?" I ask Ares.

"*Game Center*," he answers.

Fuck, she's on network tv tonight.

I text my mom instead, and of course, Kami's not with her. Before I remember I have Maren and Alina's numbers, intermission's over, and we're heading back onto the ice.

"Murphy?" Coach says, giving me a worried once-over.

"I'm good."

I'm not fucking good.

Kami's *not here*. Her car could've broken down. Maybe she was rear-ended.

Or mugged.

Or kidnapped.

Or she went to the bank and she's being held hostage.

Indianapolis scores on me, and Coach yanks me.

I'm dripping sweat, but it's not the usual game sweat. It's a cold, terrified, *something's wrong with Kami* sweat.

I never told her I loved her. I never asked her to marry me. I never confessed how fucking disappointed I was, how I felt it all the way to the pit of my nut sack, how incompetent and *impotent* and utterly worthless I felt when she told me she wasn't pregnant.

How much I'd wished she was.

The bench erupts around me, and I realize Cranford's going at it with Ares.

And the score's tied.

The refs break it up, but not before Cranford's nose is crooked and Ares's lip's bleeding. Takes a lot to lure Ares into a fight. Fucker must've asked for it.

They're both sent to the sin bin.

And Kami's four empty seats glare at me from right beside where Ares is sitting.

She's not coming.

She's not coming, and I don't know where she is.

The last four minutes of the game take a fucking eternity. We barely scrape out a win at the last minute, with Ares, Frey, and Lavoie pulling off a full-on charge through the Indies' defensive line.

It's ugly.

It's a win.

And I don't fucking care.

I grab my phone as soon as we're back in the locker room.

Still nothing from Kami.

I'm out of my pads and skates and pulling on my shoes in under a minute. Coach doesn't blink when I tell him I have a family emergency and tear out of the locker room, past the reporters shouting questions, and down the stairs to the parking garage.

Kami's missing.

She's fucking *missing*.

And if I don't find her, safe, healthy, and all in one piece, I'm not going to give a shit about anything.

Least of all hockey.

FORTY-SEVEN

Nick

SHE'S NOT AT HOME.

Her car's not at home, and when I use the key she gave me to let myself in, her dogs go fucking nuts. "Whoa, hey, it's okay," I lie to them.

I let them out the back, and all three of them race so fast to do their business that my heart goes into a speedskate that's not going to slow down anytime soon.

She hasn't been home to let them out.

She's *always* home to let her dogs out. She leaves work, she comes home and lets them out, eats dinner, then takes them for a walk.

Always.

It's what she does. Even on weekday game nights.

I'm not often here, but she talks about her routine without even realizing she's doing it.

"Where's your mama?" I ask Tiger.

She makes that weird balloon howl and dances on my feet like I'm supposed to tell her.

Pancake and Dixie trot back in, both of them giving me terrified puppy dog eyes.

Or maybe I'm giving them terrified puppy dog eyes.

Or maybe I fucking stink like ass and I'm polluting their home.

"You know where your mama is?" I ask the other two dogs.

No answer.

Dixie skitters to the dog bowl and flops on her belly.

I don't know how much food to give them, so I fill all the bowls. "I'll be back," I tell them. "I'll bring her back."

I race back to my Jeep and grab my phone.

Alina hasn't answered. She's probably off traveling for a concert again.

Maren's out of town too and doesn't know where she is, but asks if I've checked the clinic.

I'm soaking my leather seats with fear-sweat the entire ten-minute drive to Kami's family clinic.

If she was stuck at the clinic, she would've texted me. She would've called. She would've—oh, *fuck*.

That's her car.

In the parking lot.

Right next to a beater I don't recognize.

Someone's holding her hostage at the clinic.

"The fucking *hell* they are," I snarl.

I don't know if I put my car in park, or if I shut off the engine, or if I shut the door. All I know is that I'm banging on the back door of the clinic, and if that fucker hurts her, I will tear him limb from bloody limb and then I'll use his bloody limbs to beat his face until it's pulp, and then I'll—

The door swings open, and a woman in animal-print scrubs leaps back. "Oh!"

"Kami," I say.

Say. Order.

Bark.

Growl.

She backs up and flicks a finger down the hallway to the left.

So maybe I don't look as terrifying as I do terrified, because if I were facing me invading a building, I'd put up a fucking fight.

I'm charging down the hallway so fast, I go right past her the first time.

It's only as I'm passing the doorway that I process she's sitting at a desk in a cramped office, her head bent over paperwork.

I spin and charge into the room, my lungs heaving, because *fuck*, she's gorgeous. And in one piece. And alone. And safe.

And *safe*.

She blinks up at me with big, disconcerted brown eyes that go slightly wide as her nose quivers.

Fuck, I smell like ass.

"You weren't at the game," I sputter, because my brain's still processing that she's here. And she's safe. And she wasn't at the game.

But she's Kami.

She had a fucking good reason.

She probably has ten million fucking better things to do than *me*.

Her lips draw down like she's drawing the same fucking conclusion. "Muffy's cat swallowed a battery and needed emergency surgery," she says slowly. "Mom's at a conference. If we'd waited, it would've died."

"A…what?"

"Right?" She rubs her eyes. "Most cats won't even take a pill. Muffy's swallows a freaking button battery. A watch battery."

I'm dropping to my knees in front of her desk, because *she's okay*. She's fucking okay.

She's better than okay.

She's a perfect fucking superhero.

"I thought something happened to you." I can't shut up. I tell myself to shut up, but I'm babbling like a lunatic. "A car accident, or a robbery gone wrong, or just…*something*. And I couldn't breathe at the idea of this world without you in it. Of my *life* without you in it."

She blinks at me through heavy pink eyelids. "My phone died," she says. "It's been—Nick, I'm so—"

"Oh, fuck. The cat. Is she okay? What can I do?"

"What can you…do?"

Now she's looking at me like I'm an idiot, because what the fuck can a dumbass jock do to save a cat who needs emergency surgery?

"For…you," I finish lamely.

It's Kami.

She doesn't need me. She's smart and strong and capable, and I'm just the guy who can't let her go.

"Or Muffy," I add. Maybe she needs a comforting pat on the shoulder. I can be the hero who patted a woman who almost lost a cat.

She stares at me a minute longer. "How was the game?" she asks.

"The game? Fuck the game. You were here saving a cat. I was just —just—trying to stop a puck from going in a net and watching a bunch of puckheads fight over a fucking *game*. Christ, Kami, I don't know why *you* don't get arenas full of people screaming your name.

You're the real hero. I was just playing a fucking *game*, and you're here saving people's pets."

She's still staring at me like I've lost my mind.

Maybe I have.

But I don't care, because I've finally found the most important part of life, the one thing that money and fame and fake hero worship can't touch, and I'm done putting the wrong things first and ignoring what matters. "Kami—" I start, because I'm not putting this off one more minute.

But before I can finish, she's holding my cheeks and leaning over her desk and kissing me.

Soft, peppered kisses all over my lips that turn into long, slow, deep kisses, her hands anchoring my head while I grip her arms, because *this*.

This is everything I need.

She's safe.

She's not breaking up with me.

She loves me *despite* me. And I'm the idiot who almost lost her because I took too long to notice.

I pull out of the kiss, because this *cannot* wait another minute. I caress her cheeks and hold her where I can look into those beautiful soft eyes. "I love you," I tell her.

It comes out on a strangled whisper, so I try again. "I love you."

Stronger. "I. Love. You."

Her eyes are crinkling at the corners and getting shiny. "Nick," she whispers, and *fuck*, I love my name on her lips. "I know."

"You—"

"And I love you too."

So maybe life *can* get better, because my entire world just went technicolor in 3D.

"Why?" I ask, and she laughs, that uninhibited smile brightening the room even more.

"I just can't help myself." She giggles and licks her thumb, then rubs something off my face. "Crazy man. You're still wearing dick glitter."

"You like it? I'll wear it every day. Or you can be the glitter on my dick. *Shit*. That wasn't supposed to come out. Not of my mouth. I—"

She silences me with a finger while she laughs so hard her face scrunches up.

There's nothing better in all the world than the sight of Kami laughing. She's cookies and cream ice cream on triple fudge caramel brownies. She's winning the Cup all over again every hour of my life. She's the only person in the world I'd trust with my heart.

"You make me so happy," she says with that huge smile. "Just by being *you*."

"I really am this big of a dumbass," I warn her.

"Everyone has their moments. But not everyone makes up for them the way you do."

I can't stop touching her. Her face. Her hair. Her hands. Her neck. Everywhere. I need to touch her everywhere. "I thought—you were hurt. Somewhere."

Her smile fades. "My phone's battery—I usually charge it here during the day, but Mom took the charger to her conference, and then Muffy showed up, and I got so busy—"

"I'm getting you a new phone."

She looks like she's going to argue, so I pull a *don't even try it* face.

"*One* phone," she says sternly. "Small enough to fit *my* hands. None of this bigger-is-better stuff."

Now I'm grinning, because if she thinks those parameters will stop me from going overboard in other ways, she's clearly forgotten who she's talking to. But she's not arguing over me getting her a new phone, so we're making progress.

"And *one* phone case, and it *cannot* have your picture on it, and I do *not* want anything about my phone plan switched or upgraded, regardless of who you think is paying for it, though I'll take three chargers, fine, if they're different from my current chargers, but no fancy earbuds. I prefer the way the cheap ones fit in my ears, and I've tested them, so don't try me. And no adding any apps to the phone, and I'll consent to a battery pack, but only one, and it can't have your picture on it either."

Huh.

That'll make it a little harder.

And all the more rewarding when I still manage to make it the best fucking phone package ever.

"Dr. Oakley?" a voice says behind me. "We have everything under control here. Why don't you go home?"

She frowns. "But Muffy—"

"I'm off tomorrow. I'll stay with her as long as she wants to stay with Rufus. You go on. We'll call you—ah, if you get your phone plugged in, I mean."

"Call me if you need her," I tell her. I grab a business card off

Kami's desk, scribble my number on the back, and hand it to her assistant person. What's she called?

The tech. Right.

She needs a nametag, because the only name I can remember at the moment is *Kami*. Come to think of it, everyone in the entire universe needs nametags.

I don't know my own fucking name at the moment

The tech stares at me for a minute, then the card, then she glances at Kami, who's rustling behind the desk.

"S-sure. Thanks. Did you—did you kick some Indies ass tonight?"

I stare at her blankly for longer than necessary even to hit the awkward stage, because *fuck*. I forgot I played a hockey game tonight.

"Did you?" Kami echoes.

All of it comes rushing back, but mostly just the four empty seats.

Which were empty because Kami was saving a life.

I give her the ol' Nick Murphy grin. "Yeah."

"Good." She slides a hand under my arm and tugs, because I'm still squatting on the floor. "C'mon, you troublemaker," she teases. "Take me home."

Home?

More of my week comes flooding back, and now I'm grinning even bigger than my normal grin.

She wants to go home.

I'm going to do one better than that.

FORTY-EIGHT

Kami

NICK DOESN'T LET GO of my hand once we're both in the Jeep, and I'm starting to think he forgot where he's going, because he's making every wrong turn known to man on the way to my house.

We're not going to his parents' house either.

But now that the color's coming back to his face, he's quit looking at me like he's making sure I'm still in one piece. I try to ask him questions about the game, but he ignores me to ask about Muffy's cat.

Oddly, answering him is settling my own anxiety levels too.

There's nothing as terrifying as a family member banging on the door with a limp cat shrieking about a button battery.

I didn't think Rufus was going to make it.

But he pulled through surgery, probably because he's just as stubborn as he is stupid, and any cat that *eats a button battery* is stupid, I don't care how cute it is or how relieved I am that he's going to be okay.

He's also damn lucky Muffy realized so quickly what he'd eaten.

Her face—so pale. She was like a ghost.

Almost as pale as Nick was when he crashed through the clinic, actually. The major difference being that he looked like he was going to tear somebody apart.

And as soon as I realized that person wasn't *me* for missing a hockey game, every last doubt and worry I've had the last few weeks evaporated into thin air.

He didn't even stop to think I'd just flaked on the game. He came charging in ready to save me from whatever had kept me away, without regard to danger.

Because that's how Nick operates for people he loves.

Head first. Without thinking of the consequences. Without assuming the worst. Even when he has to deal with the fallout.

I squeeze his hand as we lapse into an easy silence.

He squeezes mine back and I rest my head on his shoulder, suddenly acutely aware of how tired I am—emergency surgery tends to do that—until he turns us into a long driveway in the Heartwood Valley district.

"Nick?"

"I moved Sugarbear to her new home," he tells me.

We follow a bend in the drive, and the headlights illuminate a three-story Victorian mansion with powder blue clapboard siding and the ornate white trim. My heart gives a pull of longing at the sight of the turret, and then happiness for the cow settles into my bones.

Anyone who owns a house this adorably charming will be good for her.

"I always wanted one of those," I say wistfully, pointing up. "I could read in there curled up with my dogs for hours."

"Yeah?"

I link my fingers with his and scoot closer to him. He smells like an overcooked sauna, but he's so solid and warm and *here* and he loves me, and he could smell like fermented moldy bratwurst and I wouldn't care.

Probably.

"*Hours,*" I repeat. "Right in the window, with big fluffy cushions and hot chocolate…"

"Good. Because you're welcome anytime."

My mouth opens, but my tongue won't form words. Did he just—

"It's on ten acres," he says, his voice going husky, like he's not entirely certain of himself. "The neighbors down that way have chickens. Neighbors down the other way have two horses. There's plenty of room for Sugarbear *and* a companion cow-dog. It's thirty minutes from the arena and twenty to your clinic. Even during rush hour. And there's at least an acre fenced in for your dogs to run around in."

I still can't find words, but tears are stinging my eyes. "You—you—"

"You can't be mad. I did it for our cow-dog."

"*You* own this house?"

"Signed the paperwork yesterday."

I goggle at him. "You bought a house."

"People do it all the time," he assures me.

I'm reminded why people like to slug him sometimes.

But more, I'm reminded why I like to kiss him.

"C'mon," he says, tugging my hand and sliding out of the Cherokee before I can get a good angle on attacking him for another full-body kiss in his front seat. "I've been waiting to show you this for two weeks, but I wasn't sure it was going to go through until I got it all finalized yesterday."

I let him pull me over the console, and he lifts me out of the car. His entire mood seems to lift as he walks faster and faster the closer we get to the wood-paneled front door lined with stained glass on either side under the wraparound porch. The house isn't new, but the lock is, and his key easily slides in.

"There's a three-car garage around back," he tells me. "So I can get a tractor for mowing the grass and you can't say anything about it cluttering up the yard."

"It's *your* house," I remind him.

"Only until you take over the closet," he counters. "So, only until tomorrow."

He flips the lights, and a modest chandelier sparkles in the wide foyer. Interior stained-glass windows featuring birds catch the light on both side walls, and while the house smells like fresh paint and the walls all gleam a soft ivory in contrast to the dark wood trim, the oak floor squeaks.

"Want the tour?" he asks.

"No."

Worry lines crease his forehead. "You—"

"Tomorrow," I add quickly, turning to wrap my arms around him. "Right now, all I want to see is the bedroom."

I go up on my tiptoes to kiss him, but instead of meeting me half-way, he pulls back. His arms tighten around me though.

"Marry me," he says.

I suck in a breath. "Nick, you don't have to—"

"I *want* to. I want *you*. Fuck, Kami, I don't deserve you, but I *want* you. Every minute of every hour of every day. I'm done waiting for the right moment to tell you. I love you. I fucking *adore* you. I want to spend my life with you. I want to—Christ, Kami. I wanted you to be pregnant. I want to have babies with you. And dogs and cats and chickens and cows and goats with you. And—"

This time, he's not getting away, because I leap into his arms and silence him with a kiss. My eyes are leaking. My nose is burning. I'm cry-kissing him, and he's cradling me so gently, like I'm a fragile china doll.

"I love you," he says between kisses.

I don't realize he's moving until he turns onto the landing on the second floor.

"Yes," I gasp.

He pauses, our faces nose-to-nose, and his eyes light up. "Yes?" he whispers.

"I want to marry you."

"Christmas," he declares, and we're moving again. "Or Thanksgiving. I can't wait until Christmas. Fuck, let's do it tomorrow."

I'm laughing and peppering his face with kisses and when he turns another corner, I'm expecting to see a bedroom, but instead, we start rising again.

The stairs squeak, and the air is getting cooler. We emerge at the top of the stairwell, Nick turns, and I gasp.

The entire top floor is a bedroom with dormers and vaulted ceilings, except for the turret room in the corner. "Is that a hot tub?" I whisper.

"Oh, fuck yeah, baby," he replies.

"Your bedroom has a hot tub in the turret."

"*Our* bedroom. And we can change anything. I'll paint it. Toss the furniture."

"I love the furniture!" In addition to the four-poster king-size bed topped with a buttery yellow comforter, the solid clawfoot dresser and chest of drawers, and the matching nightstands, two wingback chairs are positioned at the far dormer with an adorable tea table between them and a crystal lamp atop it. "It's all so—so—"

Perfect.

But I can't talk because I'm kissing him again.

He turns another corner, and I realize we're in a bathroom.

With a huge walk-in shower.

Nick sets me down and reaches in to flip the water on.

"Yes, please." I'm already tearing my clothes off before moving to help him with his. And somehow I get tangled up in his body with kissing and stroking and squeezing until the room starts to fog up, and he guides me into the shower.

"I love you," he tells my cheek. My shoulder. My breasts. My belly.

"Nick," I whisper as his kisses dip lower and the hot water streams around us.

"I love you," he says against my pussy, and then he's between my legs, his tongue teasing me *oh* so perfectly while I grip his shoulders and lean against the cool tile wall for support. "Love you so much."

He sucks my clit between his teeth and slips two fingers inside me, and my orgasm bursts out of me without warning.

My thighs tremble, my knees buckle, and he licks his way back up my body while the aftershocks roll through me. "Every day," he murmurs. "I'm going to making you happy every single day."

"You already do." My arms are overcooked spaghetti, but I fling them around his shoulders, and I smile back when his eyes crinkle in that huge smile for me.

"Trouble moving?" he asks.

"I have that problem a lot when you're naked."

He's grinning bigger. "I can make it better," he tells me while he angles between my thighs, which he might be holding, because I'm in serious danger of just sliding right down the wall. "I might make it worse first though."

Considering the hot steel pipe poking my belly, yeah, he definitely might.

In the best way.

"You should definitely make it worse," I tell him. "Way, *way* worse. Until I have to call in to work tomorrow with a terrible case of jelly body."

"Jell-O body sounds like something I'd need to treat with full body massages and warm chocolate chip cookies." He's lifting me, lining us until the ridge of his thick erection is nestled between my legs.

I skim my fingers over the short hairs at the base of his hairline, and he leans in to kiss me.

It's a slow, easy, thorough kiss, accompanied by him reaching for the shower gel and rubbing it all over my thighs, my breasts, my arms, and under my legs, his kiss and his touch leaving me breathless with molten sugar spinning through my veins and a desperate need to have him inside me.

"Want you," I gasp.

"Protection?" he asks.

"No, I want *you*."

"Thank fuck." In one swift motion, he fills me completely, and *oh my god*, I'm home.

Home.

With Nick.

Loved.

Adored.

Worshipped.

I pull his mouth back to mine while he rocks into me, igniting my already overstimulated flesh, drawing me higher and tighter and hotter with every thrust, driving deeper and deeper with the cold wall behind me and the hot water streaming over us, our bodies gliding together with bubbles between us until he's driving me over the edge again, and I'm falling in a waterfall with this god of the rain holding me and crying my name as he releases inside me.

I clench my legs tight around him, because I never want to let go, and I want to hold every bit of him inside me forever.

"I love you," I gasp into his kiss, and I realize my tears are mixing with the mist on my face, because I can't physically contain all of my joy. "I love you."

We stay in the shower, kissing, whispering, making promises, until the water runs cold, and then he wraps me in a thick towel and insists on carrying me to bed.

But the bed's already occupied.

"Oh my god," I whisper.

The little black kitten meows indignantly when Nick sets me beside her—him?—on the velvety soft comforter.

"Kami, meet Jennifur Purrphy. Yes, with a *fur* and a *purr*. Jen, say hi to Kami."

The kitten eyeballs me with milky blue eyes, and if I wasn't already in love, I would be now. "You brought the kitten home."

"Mrrrroow mowww mowww mrrrrrrroooooooooww?" Jen says.

"Oh, you got a talker," I say with a laugh.

He slides onto the bed behind me, still wet and very naked, and presses his lips to my shoulder. "Are you talking to her or me?"

"Both of you. Does she pull pranks too?"

"I'm missing a sock."

Jen bounces down the bed and attacks a speck of dust floating in the air, and Nick pulls the covers down and beckons me into the warm cocoon before sliding in next to me. "I love you," he whispers while he pulls me to his chest.

His heart thumps under my ear, steady and strong. I squeeze him tight. "I love you too."

"I want to marry you."

"No take-backs," I warn him.

He chuckles. "I should be saying that to *you*, because I'm definitely getting the better end of the bargain here."

"I don't know. Considering how much you love to give gifts, and how you're always topping yourself, I'm sure I'll be ahead within a year or two." I stifle a yawn and snuggle closer, wanting to hold his whole heart in my hands while it thumps that steady, comforting rhythm. "There are so many better gifts than marriage and dream houses with room for cow-dogs."

"I want to raise babies with you," he tells me softly.

His pulse stays steady, no terrified leaps, and there I go, getting the sniffles again.

Because I was kidding about topping himself, but *there he goes*.

Of course he does.

It's Nick.

That's what he does.

"Kami?" he murmurs while my eyelids get heavy and that soothing rhythm of his heart pulls me deeper and deeper into bliss. "Thank you for dumping me."

"Thank you for fighting for me," I murmur back.

"Always," he whispers. "Always and forever."

EPILOGUE

Nick

NOT MUCH HAS CHANGED since I got myself domesticated.

There's the kitten.

Sharing a house with Kami, three dogs, and a cow, who's only allowed inside on special occasions, and less and less often as she gets bigger and bigger.

There's Sunday afternoon yard duty, which Kami keeps threatening to take away from me, because she doesn't trust what I'm doing with all the bags of dog shit that I keep gathering.

Oh, and the walks around the neighborhood.

I'm one of those guys who takes walks with his dogs and cow and significant other now.

I've also gotten really good at giving baths.

To everything in the house with a pulse, because apparently I still have a lot to learn about dog- and cat-proofing a home.

But I've pretty much nailed being a good boyfriend.

Or so Kami told me while I was giving her a bath last night.

She needed it.

Not because she stank, but because she was on her feet all day baking brownies and pies and sweet potato casseroles, prepping mashed potatoes and homemade bread and some kind of fancy herb butter rub for the prime rib.

Plus, it's officially Christmas as soon as the sun sets on Christmas

Eve—at least, in my family—and I figured a Christmas orgasm in the bathtub was the best way to help get her in the mood for the holiday.

Especially since our house is being overrun with guests for Christmas dinner.

And for the record—I was in the kitchen with her the whole time.

We've been binge-watching Food Network to learn how to cook together. And I'm only a mild hindrance now, much improved from a major hindrance when we first started.

Her parents, brother, and sister arrive first, and I take them all on the grand tour of the first two levels of the house while Kami shoos us all out of the kitchen. Then my parents arrive, who had the tour three times while I was in the process of buying the house, so they don't need the tour again.

Then Felicity and Ares and Zeus and Joey, along with Mr. and Mrs. Berger, their daughter, Ambrosia, her husband, and his mother.

Lavoie and Jaeger join us too.

So do Muffy and Aunt Spanky-Span—I mean, Aunt Hilda.

Because if we're going to host Christmas, we're apparently going to do it big.

Kami shoots me a look over the rolls she's buttering, fresh out of the oven, like she knows what I was calling her aunt in my mind.

She probably does.

I don't get away with a lot.

But I do get away with grinning at her and stealing a kiss on my way through the kitchen.

"Are you the doofus responsible for the dick glitter?" the Berger twins' sister asks me while I carry a massive bowl of mashed potatoes into the dining room, which is surprisingly too small for our first big family gathering.

It's not often I underestimate what I need. I clearly wasn't thinking about extended family when I decided this house was big enough.

"It was Kami's idea," I say, because once *anyone* meets Kami, she charms the hell out of them, and then the odds that I'll be in trouble with this woman for one-upping her with better glitter bombs will go down.

"Completely my idea," Kami calls from the kitchen. "I was pissed he didn't do it sooner."

I fucking love that woman.

"We need to talk later," Ambrosia tells her.

Our guests fill both the dining room and the living room in the old mansion. I go through the food line first, fill a plate to overflowing, and balance both the plate and Kami as I drag her out of the kitchen and make her sit and eat. "You're working too hard," I tell her.

She smiles and shakes her head at me. "I'm not working any harder than you, and I'm having fun."

"Eat."

She gives me a secret smile and obediently takes her fork.

Everyone moans over how delicious the food is, and not just because I emailed them all beforehand and warned them they'd find dead fish heads in their underwear drawers if they didn't, but because Kami can fucking *cook*.

She says anyone could do it after the number of hours we've put into watching cooking shows this last month, but I think she has hidden talents she's been denying.

And I definitely haven't mastered cooking yet.

We both keep poker faces through the meal despite the glances everyone keeps sending at Kami's bare left hand. I know what they're all thinking.

We got serious really fast.

Kami swore to her family just over a year ago that she was going to marry me this Christmas.

They want to know if I'm making an honest woman of her.

So, after pie, I ask everyone to help us feed Sugarbear her special Christmas oats, then I pull all the dining room chairs into the living room.

"For Christmas carols," I add. "I got Kami this sweet karaoke machine for Christmas."

"Oh, fuck yeah," Ambrosia says. "Chase, go get the boy band CDs out of the car."

But Zeus and Ares are already racing out the front door.

Kami's brother and dad try to sneak off, but I call them both out and tell them they have to sing "Grandma Got Run Over By A Reindeer" to start us off.

Felicity almost falls out of her chair, because asking for that song to be sung is like asking to be haunted special by our Gammy for the rest of eternity.

Even Dad shifts uncomfortably, because I'm pretty sure he believes in his mother's ghost too.

But the twins come back, Kami's dad and brother start to make their way to the front of the room, and that's when Kami makes her move.

"No," she says to them.

Her brother sighs in obvious relief, but her dad looks puzzled. "No?"

"I hate that song. And I'm the bride, so *no*."

"That's our cue, bro," Zeus says to Ares as gasps go through the living room.

Ares pulls two rings out of his pocket. Zeus pulls a folded paper with a script on it out of his.

And while they step around everyone seated in the living room, I slide our marriage license out from between Kami's copies of *Pride and Prejudice* and *The Princess Bride* on the built-in bookshelves around the fireplace.

"Ohmygod," her mom whispers.

Mine bursts into tears.

"Are those the happy tears?" I ask her.

She nods as she sobs into a hanky that Mr. Berger produces for her.

"I set them up," Aunt Hilda tells Jaeger. She slides a hand onto his thigh, and Muffy smacks her hand.

"*Mother*," she hisses.

Kami sucks her cheeks in and smiles as she twines her fingers into mine. Her face is wavering on the pale side, and her eyes are tired, but there's no mistaking that smile, and I'm the luckiest dipshit to ever walk the earth to get the opportunity to put that smile there every day.

"We'll get to karaoke," she says to her brother, "but first, we're gonna get hitched."

Dixie and Tiger chase Jennifur Purrphy into the room, with Pancake on their heels.

I snag the cat.

Kami gets Tiger.

Her mom leaps on Pancake, and Dixie, realizing she's lost all of her playmates, slides to a stop at my feet and goes belly-up, tongue and tail panting and wagging.

"But...don't you need a minister? Or a justice of the peace?" Muffy asks.

"Got it covered," Zeus says with a smirk. "We're both internet official."

"They married each other last summer," I tell her.

Jaeger and Lavoie snort into their after-dinner beers.

My sister and Joey both roll their eyes, even though they were there. Zeus married Ares and Felicity, and Ares married Zeus and Joey.

All four of them are married.

Zeus clears his throat as he turns to face our guests. "Yo, mother-fuckers, we're here to make an honest man out of this clown," he announces.

Kami snort-giggles, but she also elbows him because he said *clown*.

Mrs. Berger—the matriarchal Mrs. Berger, not my sister or Joey—sighs.

Ares gives Zeus a head slap.

Zeus just grins, and then he starts the short ceremony for real.

Just as we finish our vows, Kami goes from pale to green. "Uh-oh," she whispers.

"Oh, fuck," I whisper back.

Dixie leaps to her feet and whimpers. Pancake charges from where Dr. Oakley has loosened her grip. Tiger howls.

Ares shoves the rings at us. "Do it," he says, because man, this guy has *been there*.

Kami whimpers.

"Later," I tell Ares, pocketing the rings. "Treats," I tell the dogs, who all dash for the kitchen. Jennifur dashes after them, and Ares, thank fuck, just knows to go get the dogs treats so they're not being teased.

"Wha—*oh my god*," Dr. Oakley gasps. "Are you—is that —did he—"

"Surprise," Kami says weakly to her mom.

And that's all I let her get out before I dash her to the bathroom.

She's actually laughing while she's tossing her cookies. "Your poor mother," she says, which is hilariously, completely Kami.

Feeling sorry for *my mother* while she's losing her Christmas dinner.

"Felicity at her wedding…me at ours…"

The sounds of my mother's sobs are carrying over the karaoke music that the Bergers apparently set up.

Or maybe that's Kami's mom.

Or both of them.

And I'm almost positive it's happy sobs.

"Trust me," I say, rubbing her back, "she'd rather have the grand-kids than picture perfect weddings for her own kids. Feeling better?"

She slumps back against me and sighs. "I think I need more pumpkin pie."

"You're my pumpkin pie." I reach into my pocket and pull out our wedding rings. Because she's Kami, she asked for a simple plat-inum band.

And because I like to spoil her, I had it intertwined with a band of diamond chips. "May I, Mrs. Murphy?" I murmur, tilting it in front of us to watch the diamonds catch the light.

She wiggles her fingers. "Yes, please."

"I'm going to love you for all eternity," I whisper as I slip her ring onto her finger. I gently touch her belly, and add, "And you too."

Kami takes my ring from me and slides it over my knuckles. "I love you to infinity and back," she tells me, leaning back to press a soft kiss to my cheek.

Out in our living room, someone's starting a Bro Code song.

Probably Ares.

He loves that boy band music.

And we should probably get back to our guests.

But I don't want to.

Not when I can sit here, with my wife, holding her and doing my damnedest to make her early pregnancy as comfortable as it can be.

There's a knock at the door though. "Nick? Kami?" Felicity whis-pers. "I have ginger mints, and I think Zeus brought a stink bomb. Give me four minutes, and we can sneak you upstairs before he sets it off and gets rid of your guests."

Kami laughs softly. "We are going to have the most interesting life," she says happily.

I rise and pull her to her feet, watching her carefully for signs of more trouble. But for the moment, she seems okay.

Still, no reason to take any chances, so I sweep my beautiful wife up into my arms. "Ah, gorgeous, we already do."

ABOUT THE AUTHOR

Pippa Grant is a stay-at-home mom and housewife who loves to escape into sexy, funny stories way more than she likes perpetually cleaning toothpaste out of sinks and off toilet handles. When she's not reading, writing, sleeping, or trying to prepare her adorable demon spawn to be productive members of society, she's fantasizing about chocolate chip cookies.

Find Pippa at…
www.pippagrant.com
pippa@pippagrant.com

OTHER BOOKS BY PIPPA GRANT

Mister McHottie
Stud in the Stacks
The Pilot and the Puck-Up
Royally Pucked
Beauty and the Beefcake
Rockaway Bride
Hot Heir
The Hero and the Hacktivist
Charming as Puck
Exes and Ho Ho Hos
Hosed (co-written with Lili Valente)

For a complete up to date list,
visit www.pippagrant.com/books

COPYRIGHT